Here Today Gone Tomorrow

**Lock Down Publications and Ca$h
Presents**
Here Today Gone Tomorrow
A Novel by *Fly Rock*

Lock Down Publications
Po Box 944
Stockbridge, Ga 30281

Visit our website @
www.lockdownpublications.com

Lock Down Publications
Like our page on Facebook: Lock Down Publications @
www.facebook.com/lockdownpublications.ldp
Book interior design by: **Shawn Walker**
Edited by: **Kiera Northington**

Stay Connected with Us!

Text **LOCKDOWN** to 22828 to stay up-to-date with new releases,
sneak peaks, contests and more…
Thank you.

Submission Guideline.

Submit the first three chapters of your completed manuscript to ldpsubmissions@gmail.com, subject line: Your book's title. The manuscript must be in a .doc file and sent as an attachment. Document should be in Times New Roman, double spaced and in size 12 font. Also, provide your synopsis and full contact information. If sending multiple submissions, they must each be in a separate email.

Have a story but no way to send it electronically? You can still submit to LDP/Ca$h Presents. Send in the first three chapters, written or typed, of your completed manuscript to:

LDP: Submissions Dept
Po Box 944
Stockbridge, Ga 30281

DO NOT send original manuscript. Must be a duplicate.

Provide your synopsis and a cover letter containing your full contact information.

Thanks for considering LDP and Ca$h Presents.

Special Thanks and Acknowledgements

I want to thank God first! Then, I want to give a special thanks to my beautiful mother. She gave birth to one of the most talented individuals on the planet, and for that, she must be praised!

Shout out to the rest of my family and friends and love to all my rockstars! A.T.L. my brothers! Looks like we're creeping on a come up!

-

Peace-

    ~ RIP ~
    Kevious

    ~ RIP~
    Skip

Fly Rock

Prologue

Florida 2020

"To everybody watching this, we are very sorry to interrupt your television programs, but we are currently reporting live from what is being called one of the biggest interstate accidents in U.S. history!" The small, petite news reporter stepped to the side and allowed the camera full access to the scene behind her.

The scene appeared to be a pile of burnt rubble and metal scattered across the large interstate road. Smoke and flames could still be seen rising from some of the debris, while a slew of fire marshals did their best to control and extinguish the horrible scene.

The attractive news broadcaster with the jet-black hair stepped back into the camera and began to explain the scene around her. "After speaking with police officials and gathering information from some of the witnesses, it is being said that apparently, ten large charter buses were passing through Interstate 10, transporting a compound worth of prisoners from a facility in Milton, FL to a more secure facility out of state in Alabama.

"As we all know, Hurricane Rocky is expected to be one of the most dangerous hurricanes to touch land since Hurricane Andrew back in 1992. Rocky has been scheduled to sweep through the Gulf Coast next weekend. Officials say the charter buses were supposed to be transporting the inmates to ensure their safety during the disastrous storm. Now officials are saying that during the transport, a group of inmates created an escape plot. Eyewitnesses on the scene are all confirming that while the ten buses were en route, a swarm of trucks and vans appeared, blocked off the interstate and stopped the travel of all vehicles.

"Once all of the buses came to a halt and were clustered together, a herd of masked men leapt from the trucks and vans equipped with an arsenal of assault rifles and without hesitation, began to open fire on the buses. But before the buses could be taken over by the land pirates, a swarm of police quickly got on the scene and joined the gun battle. It's said one of the buses took a lot of damage to the gas tank and began to smoke and seconds later, the smoke elevated into a full-fledged explosion. Witnesses all agree that one explosion created a chain reaction and caused the whole ten-bus cluster to erupt into what is being called a tragic bonfire!"

The news reporter stopped talking for a moment to catch her breath and let the camera man catch a quick glimpse of the very last fire being extinguished. She looked sad and then took a deep breath for effect before continuing.

"Now that the scene has been properly controlled, we have just been informed that there are no survivors to this horrible tragedy. We are now going to end this breaking news and send you back to your television programs. We will continue to give you live updates and information as it comes. This is all for now."

As the news broadcast ended, Bossman turned off his television and slung his remote across his office. "Bullshit!" he screamed in frustration. "Every time I see this bullshit, it pisses me the fuck off!"

"Listen sir, I know you're upset about this, but I promise you this is just a complete misunderstanding. There has to be some type of mistake," Agent Fisher explained.

Before he could continue, Bossman cut him off, saying, "Motherfucker, I'm tired of your shenanigans! The only mistake made around here was placing you in charge of something so fucking simple!"

Agent Fisher threw his hands up in retreat and tried to continue. "Please sir, let me explain."

Bossman slammed his fist down on his desk and shouted, "An explanation is just a well created excuse and I'm tired of your sorry ass excuses! Matter of fact, you're fucking fired!"

"Fired? Sir, I'm the head agent for the FBI! How can you just fire me?"

"Easy! Give me your gun, give me your badge and get the fuck out my office! I'm the head director of the FBI, but do you think any of my superiors give a shit?"

"Sir, if you could just give me an opportunity to figure this out I—"

"Shut the fuck up and get the fuck out! This conversation is over!" Bossman concluded with a sigh and then leaned back in his chair. He shook his head and pointed towards the door with a look of pure disgust on his face.

Agent Fisher realized his words were useless, so he turned over his weapon and badge and exited the office. As he walked across the room it seemed like all eyes were on him. Everybody stared at him from their cubicles, but nobody attempted to speak. Once he made it to the elevator and stepped on, he was accompanied by a scrawny computer tech.

The computer tech pressed the button that led to the garage and said, "What's up, Fish?"

"Not a whole lot," Fisher replied with his head down.

"Word in the agency is that it sucks to be you right now."

"Shit happens."

Fisher had a lot on his mind, and he didn't feel like engaging in small talk and office rumors. When the elevator opened, he quickly power walked to his older model Jaguar. As he climbed into the 2013 SE, his mind was clouded with thoughts about how he would get his job back.

"I don't know what the fuck happened, but I know for a fact I didn't screw anything up. This shit might be a conspiracy to get me blackballed from the agency. Whatever the fuck it is, I'm going to figure it out. One way or another, I will get my job back!"

Agent Fisher then casually drove out the parking lot and headed home, with hope that one day he might return.

***

The head director of the FBI, that everyone referred to as Bossman, leaned forward on his desk and stared at his phone. He had been staring at the phone for the last ten minutes, trying to decipher what his next move should be.

"How in the fuck could something so simple, get so out of hand?" he spoke to himself. "This was supposed to be an easy experiment, and nothing should have gone wrong. How could the FBI let a couple of shit heads outsmart them? There's no way the count should've came up short, but it did. How that happened I have no idea, but there's no way I can let this slip out. I've got to cover my ass."

With nothing left to consider, he picked up his phone and dialed his companion's number.

"I'm here," a soft male voice answered into the receiver.

"Listen carefully. Do you know what I'm calling for?"

"Yes sir, just let me know what you need done."

"I need all personal files and any information that could possibly be obtained, burned and exterminated. I want everything and everybody to become non-existent, and I want this shit swept under the rug."

"No problem, sir, it's already being handled."

"Good, because if the media gets wind of anything, then your ass is going to end up just like those files! Do I make myself clear?"

"Yes sir, I understand completely. But what about Agent Fisher?"

"Fuck Fisher! His stupid ass will probably lead us right where we need to go."

"Okay, well, what about the two men unaccounted for, sir?"

"Do you believe in ghosts, my friend?"

"Uhhh, no sir, I don't."

"Well, neither do I. So, if we ever find any then guess what? We call in the ghost busters. Until then, fuck them! If they ever resurface, we'll crush 'em!"

"Very well, sir. Is there anything else I can do?"

"That's all for now. I'll call you again if I need you."

Bossman hung up the phone and leaned back in his chair. He exhaled deeply and said to himself, "I pray to fucking Mary this shit doesn't hit the fan."

Chapter 1

Gainesville, FL

Tat-Tat-Tat-Tat-Tat!

"Fuck!" Wizz screamed while jumping out of his sleep. He wiped the sweat from his forehead and peered out of the window of the pickup truck he had been sleeping in. He shook his head and looked to his left at Bo-T.

Bo-T was sitting in the driver's seat looking directly at Wizz with his fists up in a fight position. "Damn, lil nigga, all that screaming and freaking out gone make me swang on yo ass, lil nigga."

"I ain't gone do nothing but freak out forreal and hit yo ass back," Wizz joked.

"Yeah, that's funny. But forreal, lil bra, what's up with you? You straight, my nigga?"

"Yeah, I'm good, bra. I just thought I heard something"

"Yeah, nigga, a pinecone fell on the hood. Yo tough ass scared of pinecones now, nigga?"

"Ha-ha, very funny. But on the real though, bra, I been having nightmares about that shit."

Bo-T looked out his window and proudly stated, "I ain't gone lie, that shit be fucking with me too sometimes, but fuck it . . . We out here, my nigga!"

"Yeah, you right, bra. But what's up though? A nigga hungry as fuck! We need to make a move real quick."

"Yeah, you right about that, a nigga is hungry and that purse you snatched yesterday wasn't hitting on nothing! Nigga, yo dumbass took thirty dollars from that lady," Bo-T laughed and slapped the steering wheel.

Wizz joined the laughter for a moment then replied, "Shit, that's what I call, dollar-menu rich! Them double cheeseburgers was swangin'!"

"I ain't gone lie, them bitches was bustin'. But check it out though, we gone do this shit my way this time. I got a plan."

Bo-T started the ignition and as soon as the truck was alive, he eased away from the tree they were parked under. They had been sleeping and living inside the pickup truck for the last thirty days and were barely getting by day-to-day. They stayed on the move and were in constant fear of the unknown, but survival was a must, so every day they kept pushing forward.

Bo-T pulled the old dusty truck into a Walgreens parking lot and backed into a parking space. Directly across the street from them was a Regions Bank, with a few people inside and a few people outside, lined up in front of the ATM machine.

"Alright peep the play, lil bra, you see that Mexican dude in the back of the ATM line?" Bo-T questioned while pointing.

"You talking about this short motherfucka with the fat ass head and dirty ass boots?"

"Bingo! Listen, when fool gets to the front of the line and makes his withdrawal, we gone beat his ass and take him up through there."

"That's got to be by far the simplest plan I've ever heard."

"Yeah…whatever, nigga. I bet we come out better than you did with that purse," Bo-T stated while hopping out the truck.

Wizz quickly followed suit and together they jogged across the street and got into the back of the line, right behind the short Mexican.

About five minutes later, the line cleared out and the Mexican was hunched over the ATM, pressing buttons. Bo-T stepped to the side to get a view of what the Mexican was doing and as soon as he saw the green pieces of paper begin ruffling out of the machine he pounced on the Mexican and yoked him up from behind.

The Mexican tried to scream, but the pressure being applied to his windpipe wouldn't allow it. Wizz ran up to the ATM and began snatching all of the twenty-dollar bills that were pouring out of the machine.

Bo-T put the Mexican to sleep and laid him on the floor. He searched through his pockets and relieved him of his wallet. He then found his attention on the Rolex dangling from the man's wrist and was about to snatch it off, when someone suddenly screamed.

"Hey! What the hell are y'all doing!" the screamer shouted and then dashed back inside of the bank and tried to alert the security officer.

"Ohh, shit! That hoe telling, lil bra! Let's ride!" Bo-T blurted and broke out into a sprint back across the street. He and Wizz reached the truck at the same time and dove in.

Bo-T swerved out of the Walgreens lot like a madman and headed straight for the interstate. Once they were safely on I-75, Bo-T tossed the wallet over to Wizz and said, "Check it out, lil bra, what we hit for?"

Wizz poked through the wallet and emptied its contents onto his lap. "Looks like we got three hundred and forty dollars and a gift card for Applebee's."

"Applebee's here we come," Bo-T laughed.

"We also got five hundred out the ATM."

"Oh, hell yeah! That's what I'm talking bout!" Bo-T shouted. "I told you, lil nigga! That shit was way better than that white lady!"

"Yeah, yeah, yeah, whatever nigga. Check it out though, bra, we been riding around in this hot ass truck for over a month. Now that we've got a few dollars on us, I say we gas up and finally head home. We done came a long way and we're finally almost there. Let's make the final stretch, my nigga."

"Say no more, lil bra, let's do it."

Chapter 2

Orlando, FL

"Make a left right here," Wizz signaled to Bo-T. They kept straight for a few minutes and then crossed through an intersection. "Turn into that first neighborhood on the right," Wizz stated after they cleared a light.

Less than two minutes later, they were pulling up to a well-kept yellow house that resided on the corner of the road. Bo-T parked by the mailbox on the narrow, two-lane street and killed the engine.

"Looks like yo sister living good, bra. This look like one of them quiet ass cracka neighborhoods," Bo-T commented.

Wizz exited the dusty truck and said, "Yeah, it looks like my twin been moving up in the world."

"You want me to go in with you, my nigga?"

"Naw. I'm good, bra, let me check it out. I ain't never been here before and this might not even be the right house. I remembered the address off some of my old mail and I think this is it, but I could be wrong."

When Wizz approached the house, he rang the doorbell several times and waited patiently for results. Right when he lifted his hand to press the doorbell again, locks began turning and the door swung open, with a skinny black dude standing between the frames.

The man who answered the door was tall, skinny, ashy and had long, nappy dreadlocks. He was wearing tight jeans and a dirty tank top that fit loosely on his frail body. He was barefoot and had a joint tacked behind his ear. He locked eyes with Wizz and appeared to be annoyed. "What's up, jit? Do I know you? You must be lost."

"I might be at the wrong house and if I am, then I apologize, but does Ashley live here?"

"Yeah...she stay here, but what does it matter to you, jit?"

"Aye bra, this my sister house, so watch out." Wizz tried to step around the man, but he stuck his arm out and blocked the doorway.

"Hold up, jit, where you think you goi—" Before he could finish his statement, Wizz grabbed his arm and swung his knee into his stomach and when he hunched over to grab his stomach, Wizz quickly sent an uppercut into his jaw. He crumbled to the ground. Wizz was kicking the man in the face when Bo-T suddenly appeared and joined the foot parade.

When the man stopped moving, Bo-T said, "What's up, lil bra? You brought us way out here just to whoop this nigga ass?"

"Naw bra, this twin's house. When I tried to step in, this dirty ass Mark Anthony tried to put his ashy ass hands on me! You know I had to dust him off."

"Alright, now what you waiting on?"

With no further words, Wizz stepped through the entryway and slowly walked down the colorful hallway. The hallway opened up into a living room, and Wizz noticed a female silhouette sitting on a couch, watching a movie he had never seen. Wizz put his index finger against his lips and signaled for Bo-T to be quiet as he tiptoed up to the couch. He quickly reached over the couch and threw his hands over the woman's face and covered her eyes.

"Stop playing, bae! You're gonna make me miss an important part!" Ashley blurted.

"I'm definitely not your bae, and if that ashy ass *chumpanzee* is your definition of a bae, then you got bad taste," Wizz calmly replied.

Not recognizing the voice at first, Ashley panicked and leapt from the couch. "Who the fu... oh my God! Twin!" she screamed and sprang over the couch in one leap. She landed in Wizz's arms and threw her legs around his waist.

Wizz nearly fell to the floor but quickly caught his balance. Ashley was screaming and crying hysterically as she continued to squeeze her arms around his neck.

"Calm down, twin! I can't breathe," Wizz joked.

She placed her feet back on the floor and looked Wizz in his eyes. Her eyes were filled with so many tears, everything was a blur. "How is this even possible? I thought you were dead," she cried.

"Dead? Hell naw! I did almost get killed, but that's a whole 'nother story."

"But what about the accident? I've got your obituary and everything."

"Accident? What accident and what obituary?"

"Aye, lil bra, here come that punching bag," Bo-T interrupted.

Wizz quickly turned around and prepared for combat.

"Who the fuck these fuck niggas is!" the punching bag shouted at Ashley.

"Who the fuck you calling a fuck nigga?" Bo-T asked him.

"I'm about to show him who the fuck nigga is," Wizz stated and took a step forward.

Ashley quickly jumped in between everybody and tried to calm them down. "Mikey! Oh, my God! What happened to your face!" she shrieked.

"These fuck niggas jumped me!" Mikey shouted. "And who the fuck these niggas is anyway?"

"This is my brother, bae! I told you about him."

"Bitch, you told me your brother was dead!"

"Who you calling a bitch?" Wizz blurted.

"Bae, I know what I told you and I'm still trying to figure it out for myself, but this is my brother. I promise!"

Mikey quickly glanced back and forth between Wizz and Ashley and the resemblance was unmistakable. "Hold up . . . y'all twins?"

"Yes, bae! Don't you remember the pictures I showed you?"

"My mind kind of fucked up right now, but it's coming back to me. Aye, my bad about the misunderstanding," Mikey said to Wizz.

"Nigga, fuck you!" Wizz replied aggressively.

"Calm down, twin! He said he's sorry," Ashley interjected.

"Sorry these nuts! Fuck that nigga!" Wizz stated and stepped over to the couch. "Can I sit down without you tryna sneak me?" he joked to Mikey.

"Everything's cool," Mikey said and plopped down on the other couch. He really wanted to say a few other things, but he didn't want to get jumped again and his body was sore, so he bit his tongue and sat back.

Ashley sat down on the couch with Wizz and turned towards Bo-T. "You can sit down if you want."

"Thank you, but I'm alright. I'd rather stand." Bo-T didn't want to let his guard down and he also wanted to monitor the scene from a standing point.

"Aye twin, this my nigga, Bo-T. We were locked up together and we've been through a lot together. Especially now. I consider him a brother now, so consider him family." Wizz then turned to Bo-T and said, "Aye bra, I done told you plenty of stories over the years about my twin sister, but now you finally get to meet her for yourself. Bo-T, Ashley. Ashley, Bo-T."

"Nice to meet you," Ashley said and gave Bo-T a nod and a wave.

"I've already heard so much about you, it seems like we've already met," Bo-T replied.

Ashley turned back towards Wizz, and her eyes began to water again. "I still can't believe you're here right now. Please tell me I'm not dreaming."

Wizz pinched Ashley on the thigh and she shouted, "Ouch!"

"I know this shit seem crazy, but this definitely ain't no dream," Wizz stated.

"Aye Wizz, I ain't tryna interrupt your reunion, but it's getting dark outside and I still gotta hit the road, lil bra," Bo-T stated.

"Alright bet, let me give you a number real quick to reach me at." Wizz looked at Ashley. "Give Bo-T yo number."

Ashley got up from the couch and walked down a hallway towards her bedroom.

Wizz looked over at Mikey and said, "You look real stupid with all that dirt and dried up blood all over yo black ass face. Maybe you should do something about that. Unless you like looking like a dirty ass, pussy nigga!"

Mikey clenched his teeth and didn't respond. He simply stood up and slowly disappeared the same way Ashley had. As soon as he was out of sight, Ashley reappeared with a small piece of paper in her hand. She handed the paper to Bo-T and reclaimed her spot on the couch.

"Just get at me as soon as you settle in with your people," Wizz spoke.

"Alright, bet." Bo-T placed the number in his pocket. "You gone be straight from here?"

"Yeah, I'm good, my nigga. I'ma just lean back with twin for a little bit and see if I can get my life back in order."

"Alright, say no more. Keep your head up and stay safe, lil bra. Don't be out here doing too much until we figure out what the fuck going on. Real shit! We still don't know what's up, so take it easy and lay low."

Wizz's facial expression became serious as he replied, "Bra, if anybody knows how serious our situation is, it's me! We made it out of there, and we made it here together, my nigga! We in this shit together. I love ya, nigga! Remember that!" He stood from the couch and as he approached Bo-T, they shook each other up and embraced each other in a brotherly hug.

"I love you too, lil nigga. Stay safe," Bo-T stated and turned toward the front door. "And keep your eyes on that ugly ass, mark ass nigga." Before he exited the house, they embraced one last time and then went their separate ways.

When Wizz re-entered the living room, Mikey was back on the other couch, scrolling through his phone. Mikey reached behind his ear and started looking around the couch.

Mikey looked puzzled and said out loud, "Where the fuck my joint at?"

"Probably on the porch where we beat yo ass." Wizz chuckled.

Mikey looked aggravated but got up to search for his blunt.

"So, what happened, twin?" Ashley asked when they were alone.

Wizz stared at the television blankly and said, "To be honest, twin, I don't know what the fuck happened. All I know is I'm one lucky mothafucka, and through the grace of God I'm here."

"So, were you involved in the bus accident?"

"Man, I don't even know what the fuck you talking about. I don't know nothing about no bus, nothing about no accident, so whatever you heard was bullshit."

Mikey came back into the living room with his slim blunt hanging from his lips and dropped back onto the couch. He fished a lighter from his tight pants and placed the fire to the tip of his blunt. He took a short pull and leaned back. "You wanna hit this?" he asked Wizz.

"Naw, I'm straight."

"You can roll your own if you want. I got about a quarter-ounce in the room."

"What you smoking on?"

"I got some good zone. Wanna check it out?"

"Zone? Nigga, I ain't smoked nothing under purple in like ten years."

"It's good shit though."

I'm straight."

"Whatever. Suit yourself."

"Aye twin, you got some lotion?" Wizz asked Ashley.

"Of course. In the room, why?"

"Because this square ass nigga so damn ashy, he could've sparked his joint with his elbows," Wizz joked and burst out laughing.

"I know you ain't tryna ride with that dirty ass white shit! A look like you been hugging trees all day!" Mikey shot back.

"I wasn't gone do it to you, bra, but now I'm bout to really ride yo jeepers creepers looking ass. You look like Marlon Wayans on crack, fuck nigga! You so damn ashy, they need to start calling yo ass Mikey the snowman! Nigga, you—"

"Twin! That's enough!" Ashley blurted through her laughter.

"Naw, fuck that!" Wizz blurted. "This nigga look like a cross between Lil Uzi Vert and 21 Savage! Ugly ass fuck nigga! This nigga lip look like a diving board, and his head look like a knotted up pineapple."

"You lucky I don't know how to tell jokes," Mikey plainly stated.

"Shit, yo soft ass don't know how to fight neither," Wizz quickly replied. "So, what you saying?"

Mikey started getting upset, but he kept his anger under control. After the ass whooping he received not too long ago, he didn't want to chance another one.

"Y'all need to cut it out. It is not that serious," Ashley intervened to try and ease some of the tension.

"Yeah whatever. Aye, is it cool if I stay here with you for a while, while I figure things out? I don't wanna go to Ma Duke's house. That shit probably ain't safe. This shit so crazy her whole neighborhood might be under surveillance."

"Of course, twin! You ain't even have to ask me that! Mi casa es su casa. You can have the guest bedroom, and whatever else you might need just let me know, and I'll get it for you."

Wizz stood up and stretched his arms toward the ceiling. "Show me where my room at and let me holla at you for a minute."

Ashley gracefully rose from the couch and led her brother down a hallway that went towards the back of the house. There were three doors in various places, and she explained to him that one door led to her master bedroom. Another door led to a room she had turned into an office because she worked from home. As soon as they approached the last door, Ashley opened it and stepped to the side.

Wizz entered the moderately spacious room and let his eyes take everything in. there was a queen-sized bed in one corner and a large dresser in the other corner, with a big mirror attached to the top. A forty-six-inch flat screen television sat on top of a table directly in front of the bed, and beside the bed against the wall was a small nightstand with a touch operated lamp on top.

"It's not much but it's all yours," Ashley spoke with pride.

"It's perfect," Wizz said softly. "If you knew what I've been through over the years and all the discomfort I've learned to be comfortable with, you wouldn't dare call this not much."

"I know, twin, I know. You don't understand how happy I am to have you standing here right now. I can't even explain how many nights I've cried and asked God for another opportunity to see you and talk to you. If I ever had any doubt before, I'm now totally convinced there is a God, and God is great! My prayers have been answered and I'll never take this blessing for granted. "

A fountain of tears began to stream down Ashley's face, and she threw her arms around her only brother and held him tightly. "I love you, twin," she sobbed.

Wizz took comfort in her embrace and said, "I love you too."

They spent the next few minutes hugging each other in silence, until Wizz wiggled out of her grasp.

"Listen twin, I been sleeping in a truck for over a month, and I been wearing the same corner store clothes the whole time. I know you smell me. With that being said, I'm in definite need of a shower."

Ashley wiped the last few tears from her face and smiled. "You've got your own bathroom right there." She pointed to a door on the other side of the room. "It's all yours."

"Alright, cool. Now listen, it's a few things I'ma need from you, but nothing major. I need a pair of gym shorts, a clean shirt, some socks and some slides. I need to wear all of that when I get out the shower."

"I'll get that for you right now," she said and rushed out the door.

Wizz stepped into the bathroom and turned on the shower. He checked the temperature of the water streaming from the nozzle, and then stepped back into the room.

On cue, Ashley came back in with all of Wizz's requested items, as well as a brand-new toothbrush, toothpaste, a box of Dove soap, a fluffy green towel and white rag. She also had Suave deodorant, a medium sized bottle of cocoa butter lotion, nail clippers, a comb, some Q-tips, and an extra set of all the clothing items he had requested.

She placed all of the items on the bed and said, "This should get you through the night and make you feel clean and brand new."

Wizz gathered the items he would need for the shower and said, "Alright, listen... there's one more thing I'ma need you to do, but you're going to have to be very, very careful."

"Whatever you need, I'll do it."

Wizz carefully explained what he needed and how he needed it and he finished by saying, "And make sure you don't tell Dukes or even attempt to let her know about any of this. Don't even imply it. I'm serious, twin! It's very important that you don't let her know I'm here. I need to figure out what the fuck is going on, before I do certain shit or interact with certain people."

Ashley tried to protest about not telling their mom, but Wizz refuted everything she said and drilled her with the importance of why their mother should be left in the blind for the time being. She reluctantly nodded her understanding and then left him by himself so he could finally get himself together.

Wizz stripped his filthy clothes off and then stepped into the shower. This was Wizz's first real shower in nine long years and the feeling and the privacy was amazing. He scrubbed his dirty body for twenty straight minutes and then stood there for another ten, just enjoying the way the water felt raining on his body.

Once the water started to wrinkle up his skin, he stepped out of the shower and toweled off. He put on the gym shorts his sister gave him and stood in front of the sink. He opened his new toothbrush and as soon as the toothpaste made contact with his mouth, the tingly sensation he instantly felt let him know he had been seriously neglecting his hygiene.

I been living like a real savage, he thought.

He looked at the mirror but couldn't see anything, since the steam had fogged up the whole bathroom. He wiped the mirror off with his hand and stared at his reflection. He had a nappy, yet slightly curly afro, and a mustache that needed to be groomed.

He had a small amount of chin hair and other than that, he had a baby face. His eyes were hazel and his eyes alone made plenty of women wanted his DNA for their children.

He had grown up a lot and aged over the years, but he still didn't look his age, which was twenty-seven. He had been in prison since he was eighteen, serving a twenty-five-year sentence for robbery and attempted murder. At five-ten with a slim frame, he weighed about a hundred and sixty pounds.

Though he was slim, his body was in great shape and fairly toned from his nine years of workouts in prison. He squeezed a glob of lotion into his palms and soothed his dry skin. He had tattoos from his chin to his toes and no skin between those points had been left unscarred by the needle.

His mother was Puerto Rican, and his daddy was black. The racial combination gave him a light-skinned complexion that could be slightly altered, depending on how much time he spent in the sun.

After spending a generous amount of time in the bathroom, he stepped back into the room and grabbed the remote control to the television off of the nightstand.

As he climbed under the cold covers and made himself comfortable, he thought, *I guess I'll just watch a little TV!*

He never got a chance to turn the TV on and the last thing he remembered thinking before his world went black was, *damn, these the softest pillows I've ever felt in my life!*

Chapter 3

"Ay, Dios mio!" a loud voice shrieked.

Wizz's eyes instantly popped open when the loud shout penetrated his sleep. Everything was black and his mind struggled between "What the fuck was that noise?" and "What the fuck time is it?" He disregarded both thoughts when he realized everything was dark because he was still wrapped under the covers.

"My baby!" the voice shouted again.

Wizz was coherent this time and the shout was so loud it startled him. He tried throwing the covers off his face so he could identify the woman's voice, but he wasn't quick enough and the loud intruder crashed on top of him.

The woman was now screaming in Spanish and Wizz didn't understand anything she was saying. The weight of her body, added with the fact that he was still under the covers, made it very difficult to wrestle his way free.

The cover was yanked from his face and the sudden light from the room caused him to shut his eyes and squint, while adjusting to the quick visual change. He felt a pair of lips smothering his face and as his sight came back clearly, he found himself face-to-face with his mother, Doris.

She was still rambling and shouting in Spanish, with tears soaking her face and dripping on to Wizz. He wiggled his way free, rolled off the bed and landed on the floor. Before he could get up, his mother dove off the bed and tackled him to the ground.

"Come on, Ma, get off me."

"Don't be trying to run from me, boy! Have you lost your damn mind?"

"Come on, Ma! You're crushing my arm!"

"Boy, I don't give a damn about your arm! I'll break both of your arms! How dare you tell Ashley to hide you in this house and not let me know you're here!"

"Alright, Ma, just get off me and let me explain."

His mother slowly rose to her feet and wiped her still flowing tears with her shirt. "You better explain this shit real good, because you about to make me lose my religion, boy!"

Wizz rose from the floor and groaned while rotating his arm to ease the pain in his shoulder. He looked around the room and found Ashley standing in the doorway with an "I'm sorry," look plastered on her face.

"Twin, why the fuck did you bring her here!" he lashed out.

"I'm sorry, twin, but she knew something was up when she caught me going through your old room and when she questioned me, I couldn't lie! I wanted to cover for you, but it would've broke my heart to keep this a secret from her."

"Boy, is you out of your silly ass mind! Don't be getting mad at her for telling me the son I thought was dead, is actually alive and sleeping like a damn baby in her house! Do you know how many nights I've cried over my damn son? I don't even know what to say or think right now, but we can start with you telling me what the hell happened!" their mother demanded.

Wizz quickly rushed over to the window and slightly peeled the blinds back so he could peek outside.

"Boy, what the hell you looking at? Don't you hear me talking to you?"

"Just chill out for a second, Ma, damn! I'm looking for the police! You could've been followed!"

"Ain't nobody following me, boy! This ain't no damn movie! Stop being paranoid."

"Paranoid? I've got every right to be paranoid! This shit is dead ass serious!" Wizz faced his mother. "This ain't no fucking joke!"

"Well, you better explain to me what the hell is so serious and tell me what happened! And if you leave out any little detail, I'll kill you all over again! Don't think because God brought you back to me, I won't send yo ass right back!"

Wizz peeked out of the windows one more time and said, "Alright, let me get my thoughts together, while I figure out how to explain this shit." He looked at Ashley and asked, "Did you at least get what I told you to get?"

Ashley pointed to the dresser, and he noticed two brown paper bags resting on top. He stepped over to the dresser and examined each bag one by one.

One bag had a chrome Jimenez 9mm with an extra clip and a box of bullets. It also had several wads of cash with every bill denomination between one and one hundred. The second bag had two Ziploc bags full of purple marijuana and five large El Producto blunts.

Wizz removed one of the Ziploc bags and pulled out a purple nugget the size of his thumb. The herbal aroma quickly filled the room, while he removed the wrapper from a blunt and split it open down the middle. He broke the nugget down with his fingers and noticed the purple nugget had orange swirls on the inside. "Damn, this shit look exotic!"

"I've got a grinder if you need it," Ashley offered.

Wizz smiled and said, "I'm a classic smoker. I like to caress my weed and get to know her before I smoke her."

"Boy, you need to pull your damn shorts up! Why you walking around here free balling?" his mother questioned.

Wizz pulled his shorts up and tightened the string around his waist. "I just got here yesterday, Ma, and I ain't got no boxers yet except the dirty ones I came in. But now that I've got my money and the rest of my shit I had stashed at the house, I'll be sure to get what I need real soon."

"How much money you got?"

"Damn, Ma, get out my pocket," Wizz joked as he finished rolling his blunt.

"Boy, how much damn money you got?"

Wizz looked over at Ashley and asked her, "How much money did you spend on the weed?"

"Three hundred, and I bought the blunts with my own money. I got ten more of them in my room for you. I didn't want them to break in the bag, so I had them in my purse. I forgot to bring them in here."

Wizz thought about it for a second and told his mother, "I got seventy-six hundred. Matter of fact, I got eight thousand. I forgot, I got four hundred more in my dirty ass pants, that I got yesterday out of an ATM."

"I'll give you five thousand more, so save your money and I'll take you to get the small things you need." She sat down on the edge of the bed. "But we'll worry about that later. Right now, you're about to sit your ass down and tell me what happened."

Ashley left the room and quickly returned with the rest of her brother's blunts and a thin folder that she handed over to Wizz.

"What the fuck is this?" Wizz asked.

"Just look at it," Ashley replied.

He opened up the folder and examined the first page. It appeared to be a news article and the headline read, "Tragedy on I-10! A thousand prisoners obliterated in escape plot gone wrong."

"What the fuck?" Wizz said out loud, but more to himself. He quickly read the article that explained how a group of prisoners attempted to escape during a transport mission. The mission was to ensure the safety of inmates during a hurricane that was now long gone and had never made it on land anyway. Hurricane Rocky had turned at the last minute and disappeared into the Gulf.

He flipped through the next couple of pages and looked at the many different photos of the tragic crime scene. The first thing he noticed, throughout the pictures of all the wreckage, was that not a single picture actually contained a dead body in it.

Wizz's anger began to rise, and he blurted out, "This is bullshit!" The last page was an obituary with a picture of his prison mugshot in the middle. Wizz tossed the folder onto the floor and asked, "Where the fuck did this bullshit come from?"

"The prison sent it to us," Ashley replied.

"And who's at the prison now?"

"Nobody. After this happened, they shut it down."

"And y'all believed this bullshit?"

"Why wouldn't we?"

"Where the fuck the bodies at?"

"It came with a letter too. I forgot that in my room, but it says all the inmates were burned beyond recognition and therefore immediately cremated."

Wizz shook his head in disbelief. "Give me a light," he demanded.

Ashley tossed him a lighter from her pocket and sat on the floor in front of the bed. Wizz lit up the blunt and deeply inhaled the tasty smoke.

Their mother rolled her eyes and shouted, "Well, what the hell happened, boy! I'm getting impatient and I want to hear this shit now."

Wizz blew a stream of smoke into the air towards the ceiling and laid back onto the bed. He stared at the roof and took another drag from the blunt. "Well, I guess I'll start from the morning it happened. I don't know shit about no damn bus ride and all that extra shit, but here's what happened."

Fly Rock

Chapter 4

Milton, FL

Bo-T was laid back on his bottom bunk when he asked, "What time you think it is?"

"To hell if I know," Wizz answered and hopped off of the top bunk. He took three normal steps, and was now looking out of the thin, rectangular-shaped window, on the door of the small cell they had been sharing for the last seven months. He waved his hands back and forth in the window until the Haitian man in the cell across the hall noticed him and threw his head up in a "What's up," gesture.

Wizz tapped on his wrist and the Haitian man held up a finger and vanished from view. He returned with a watch in his hand and used his free hand to throw up the numbers 4-3-8.

Wizz gave him a thumbs up and turned back to Bo-T. "It's 4:38."

Bo-T rubbed his stomach and asked, "What you think we got for dinner tonight?"

"Once again, to hell if I know, whatever it is we need it. I'm about to fish to these niggas next door and send them ten stamps for they tray. We can bust that bitch down."

Wizz reached into the back of his locker that was attached to the bottom of the bottom bunk and pulled out a small toothbrush that had his fishing line wrapped around it. (A fishing line is a sturdy piece of string or any material that can be used to retrieve light items from one cell to another.)

Bo-T sat up on his bunk and reached into his locker for his Bible. He ripped a small strip out of the table of contents and threw the Bible back into his locker. He then reached under his pillow for the small piece of paper containing their last few crumbs of weed and said, "This our last joint, lil bra."

Wizz had his line tied to the back of a paper pole and slid it under his door towards the room to his left. "Roll that shit up. We'll come up on some more."

Bo-T slid his hand under Wizz's pillow and grabbed the two AA batteries he kept underneath. He used the batteries and a pair of staples to light the joint and sat back on his bunk.

Wizz finished fishing right as the joint got lit and kicked back on the bunk next to Bo-T.

They passed the joint back and forth until there was nothing left, and then they both leaned back and stared at the wall.

Wizz and Bo-T had met each other at another prison a few years ago and they immediately became tight. They were always together, until they got tangled up in a riot one day on the rec yard. It was blacks against whites, and they stood back-to-back as they stabbed and beat every white person that crossed their paths.

They were separated after that and transferred to different facilities, but two years later they bumped back into each other at the maximum security, closed management camp they were at now. The CM camp was twenty-four-hour lockdown, seven days a week. Ninety percent of the inmates were being held there as a punishment for either stabbing another inmate or assaulting an officer.

They were originally in different rooms, but eventually they were able to finesse the captain into placing them in the same cell. And now, here they were seven months later, with about five more months to go before they could both be reviewed for possible placement back into general population.

The sound of the front door to the dorm popping open snapped them both out of their thoughts.

Bo-T was the first to break the silence. "That might be them meals on wheels right there, lil bra."

Wizz got up to look out the window and said, "It damn sho need to be."

"I'm higher than a bitch," Bo-T blurted.

"Who you telling? I'm higher than a blimp right now," Wizz agreed.

"What they doing out there?"

"Shit, I don't know, bra. I don't see nobody."

"Them crackas playing with that body fuel and I need to gas up."

34

"I think I see them crackas coming in now, bra. Hold up, damn! Them crackas coming in this bitch deep as fuck! They about ten deep and them ain't no regular officers. They in this bitch looking like a mothafuckin SWAT team!"

"Come on, lil bra, stop playing. You gone fuck around a blow a nigga high."

"Nigga, I'm dead ass serious! And they walking in this bitch with big dumb ass sticks! Bra, these crackas got AR's and all type of shit! Real nigga shit, bra! Get up! They coming through the door right now! You gotta see this shit!"

Bo-T leaped off his bunk and jumped on top of the toilet bowl, so he could look out of the top part of the window while Wizz looked out the bottom.

"Oh shit!" Bo-T blurted. "I thought you was bullshitting!"

The masked officers entered the wing and approached the first room.

"The fuck they doing?" Wizz mumbled.

Normally, the police aren't allowed to open your door or enter your cell on CM, unless they put you in wrist restraints first. That rule went quickly out the window as they watched the door to the first cell roll open. Two masked officers aimed their assault rifles into the small cell and quickly let off a burst of rapid shots.

Tat-Tat-Tat-Tat-Tat-Tat-Tat-Tat!

"Whoa! What the fuck!" Wizz shouted.

The police moved on to the next cell without a care.

Bo-T and Wizz were on the top tier and towards the back of the dorm, so they didn't see the actual slaughter but what's understood doesn't always need to be explained.

Extremely loud shots continued to rule the moment and the only other sounds occasionally audible, were the screams and cries of terrified inmates as their doors rolled open and their executions took place.

Wizz looked around hysterically and shouted, "What the fuck we gone do?"

I don't know, nigga, but we ain't going out like that! Just calm down and listen, we gon—"

"What the fuck you mean, calm down! Do you see what the fuck is going on!"

"Bra! Calm the fuck down and listen!" Bo-T screamed. "The only possible way to survive is to hurry up and gather all of our shit, sling that shit in the corner behind the bunk, make the room look empty, and then we gone have to hide under the bunk behind the lockers."

"Oh, hell naw! Bra, I ain't bout to be no sitting duck hiding behind the damn bed, so these crackas can shoot me straight in the ass!"

"Alright, well run yo tough ass out there when the door rolls open and make that ass shot a face shot!" Bo-T began ripping his sheets off of his thin mat with the speed of light and quickly stuffed his property into the corner behind the bunk and looked at Wizz.

Wizz shook his head and quickly followed suit while using every possible curse word he could think of in the process.

Bo-T gave the room one final look and didn't see anything that would suggest that the room was occupied. He ran to the door and looked out the window one last time and saw another cell door roll open with its occupants in plain view.

Tat-Tat-Tat-Tat-Tat-Tat!

Two inmates in the cell took the bullets head on and flew into the back wall and crumbled to the ground.

"Damn!" Bo-T blurted and looked back at Wizz. "Alright, let's do it!" He took one final look out the window and noticed the two inmates that were just gunned down right before his eyes, were no longer crumbled on the floor. He didn't see them anywhere at all and the police had already moved on to the next room. *What the fuck?* he thought. "Alright, lil bra, it's gone be a tight squeeze, but it's life or death right now."

Bo-T quickly got on the floor and army crawled behind the bunk. Wizz crawled in behind him and was nearly right on top of him.

"Get yo ass out my face," Wizz joked.

"Nigga, shut up and be quiet. This is not the time for yo bull-shit. You can crawl yo ass back out and get shot," Bo-T whispered.

They laid in silence for a few minutes while considering what could possibly happen and how things would play out. The anticipation was mentally killing them. They both said silent prayers and waited for the unthinkable.

Seconds later, their door rolled open.

Tat-Tat-Tat-Tat-Tat-Tat-Tat!

The loud shots in the small cell momentarily stripped away their hearing, but through the silence they managed to hear a ruthless voice firmly state, "This room is empty. On to the next."

More gunshots rapidly erupted and screams continued for what seemed like an eternity. They stayed behind the bunk glued together until the chaotic noises ended and a loud voice boomed with authority, "Alright, everybody, tally up the total and get a final count. Move quickly and call in the cleaning crew. I want this place cleaned up before the morning."

They continued to lay in silence for over an hour and never heard anything else. The once bright room was now filled with darkness as the day turned to night.

Wizz decided to be the first to break the silence and whispered, "I ain't heard nothing in a while, bra. You think it's safe or over with?"

" I don't know bra, but I did hear something about a cleaning crew and I ain't tryna just be laying here when they show up. Slide out."

Wizz slowly crawled backwards and squeezed himself out from under the bunk. Bo-T slowly emerged next and began stretching his legs. Wizz poked his head out of the open door and looked up and down the hall. Everything was quiet and dark, and there didn't seem to be a single dead or alive life form in the entire building.

"What it's looking like?" Bo-T questioned.

Wizz stepped out of the room and said, "The coast looks clear to me."

Bo-T stepped out behind him and looked straight towards the back of the hallway. "Oh shit! The back door open! That might be our way out!"

They ran to the door in unison and stared out into the still darkness. The full moon was the only illumination in the night. They scanned the open fields and didn't see any signs of trouble. The only resistance in their way to freedom appeared to be two rusty, barb wired fences.

Bo-T quickly came up with a game plan and said, "Listen, bra, we gone run back inside real quick and grab two mats and a couple sheets. We gone use the mats to snatch down the barbed wire and we gone take the sheets with us, just in case we have to camp out somewhere."

Wizz nodded his head and they dashed back inside the dorm to gather what they needed from the first cell by the door. In no time they were back outside and approaching the perimeter gate. They crouched down and waited for about ten minutes to make sure a patrol car wouldn't drive by.

"Coast clear, lil bra. Follow my lead," Bo-T instructed. He stood up with a mat in his hands and cocked it back. He slung the mat up over the barbed wire and quickly snatched it back, so that it got caught up in the razors and hung down. He then roughly yanked the mat down towards the floor and the barbed wire leaned slightly over but the mat ripped off. "Damn," he huffed. "I thought the mat would yank the whole wire down."

Wizz stepped forward with his mat and said, "Man, that shit didn't work, watch out . . . let me try something." He repeated the same process Bo-T had done, but once he had the mat hooked on to the wire and hanging down, he tossed it back up and flipped it over the gate. The mat was now hanging on the other side, but still covering the top since it was hooked on. He admired his work and said, "Perfect! Now we can just climb up and slide over the mat without the worry of the wire."

"Good job, lil bra, let's do it!" Bo-T slung his mat completely over the gate and it landed on the other side on the floor. Seconds later, he landed right behind it.

Wizz landed next and used Bo-T's mat to repeat the whole process with the second and last mat. Once they cleared the second gate, they smiled at each other and then stared at the dark woods in front of them.

"Which way do we go?" Wizz questioned.

"Any way, nigga! Fuck it, let's go!" Bo-T replied.

They dashed into the woods and began searching for a path to freedom. The prison was located in one of those middle-of-nowhere type places, surrounded by acres of trees and bullshit.

After walking around for about twenty minutes Wizz spoke up. "I think we're lost, bra."

Bo-T busted through a big spider web with a long stick he was carrying and replied, "Naw, we good. We just gotta keep walking straight."

"Man... bra, we done walked past this same big ass tree like three times," Wizz complained.

"All these trees look the same bra, you trippin."

"Oh shit, look!" Wizz blurted and pointed to a Sprite can stuck under a thick bush.

Bo-T quickly scooped the can up and inspected it.

"Bust that bitch down, nigga, I'm thirsty as fuck," Wizz stated.

"Ain't no soda in here, nigga. I'm bout to bust it open and make a knife though."

"Alright, well make me one too then."

"Come on, lil bra, you know it's only one knife per can."

Wizz looked around and found a Pepsi can close by. "Alright, well here go another can right here. Get me right, bra."

Bo-T chuckled and said, "We ain't got time for all of that."

"What we don't got time for is you playing. Get me right, my nigga." Wizz insisted and tossed Bo-T the can.

"Alright, alright." Bo-T laughed. He took the time to get the knives hooked up and sharp, and then handed one to Wizz.

They tucked the knives into their waistbands and continued marching forward.

"You smell that?" Wizz asked.

"Smells like a cigarette," Bo-T answered.

They passed through a thick group of bushes and saw a trailer. As they crept up to the trailer, the cigarette smoke grew stronger.

They continued to creep along the side of the trailer, until they saw an older-looking redneck man, standing beside an old Chevy truck smoking a cigarette.

Bo-T leaned over to Wizz and whispered, "Listen bra, I'ma creep around the back and sneak up on him from behind the truck. When you see me get into position, jump out and create a diversion. I'ma take him out."

"Say no more," Wizz simply replied.

Bo-T silently trotted off around the other side of the trailer and quietly tiptoed up to the truck. Wizz kept his eyes on the redneck, until he saw Bo-T appear behind the truck. Wizz then walked out into plain view with a sheet wrapped around his body and his soda can knife tightly in his grasp beneath the sheet.

"What in the fuck are you doing on my property!" the red neck blurted in a deep country accent.

"I'm lost."

"You got that right! You need to turn your ass around and get lost somewhere else, boy!"

Bo-T quickly pounced from behind the truck and swung his knife into the back of the white man's neck. When he pulled the knife out, blood squirted from the man's neck like a spray bottle and Bo-T hit him again.

The man grabbed his neck and crumbled to the floor. A nasty, blood-filled groan escaped from his lips as Wizz joined the assault and they stabbed him until he stopped groaning.

Bo-T went through the redneck's pockets and found a keychain with four keys on it and a wallet. He quickly ruffled through the wallet and pulled out the few bills, it contained seventy-three dollars.

"One of these keys got to start this truck," Bo-T stated.

"You wanna search the house?" Wizz asked.

"Fuck no! Fuck that poor ass trailer. We need to get the fuck from round here as fast as possible. Plus, it ain't no telling who else in there and we ain't got time for that."

Bo-T tugged on the truck's door handle, and it slung open. He hopped into the driver's seat and shouted, "Come on, nigga!"

Wizz climbed in next to his companion and blurted, "Man, this truck dirty as fuck . . . And the seat wet."

Bo-T shuffled through the key's and one by one he tried sticking them into the ignition. The third key fit like a missing puzzle piece and the truck came to life.

"So, where we going now?" Wizz asked.

"Away from here and wherever the road takes us. We'll figure out the rest when we're gone." He placed both hands on the steering wheel and stared out of the windshield. He turned on the headlights and brightened up the dark dirt road path ahead.

"What's up, nigga? Pull off!" Wizz blurted.

"I ain't drove a car in thirteen years."

"Nigga, so what! It's just like riding a bike, now take off!"

Bo-T dropped the gear shift into drive and hit the gas. The truck lurched forward, and they disappeared into the night.

***

"And we stayed in that same dirty ass truck for over a month, living day by day, stealing and robbing so we could eat and keep gas in the truck. Eventually we worked our way home and now, here I am," Wizz explained and ended his story.

His mother had her hands over her mouth for the entire story, and his sister just stayed glued to the floor, shaking her head.

"So, the story about the transport accident isn't real at all?" Ashley asked.

"Did you listen to anything I just said, or did I just waste my damn breath!"

"I'm just saying, twin, they had that shit all over the news and all."

"Well, fuck all that! I just told you what happened, so all that other shit must be a cover-up. I still don't know why it happened, but it should be easily understood why I need to be careful and cautious."

Wizz's mother stood up from the bed and pulled Wizz up by his arm. She opened her arms and he fell into her embrace. She held him like a trophy. "There's something strange about all of this that

I want to show you on the computer and after that, I'ma go out and buy you everything you need. Just stay in here until you feel safe," his mother stated. Everybody walked over to Ashley's office and got on the computer.

"This is kind of weird I think, but I think you might be able to make more sense of it. It's just something I noticed a couple weeks ago," his mother spoke, while tapping keys and pulling up different websites.

Wizz leaned over her shoulder and for the next fifteen minutes, he contemplated everything he was seeing. He scratched his nappy afro and thought, *what the fuck?*

Chapter 5

Three weeks later

Tampa, FL

"Come on, youngin, I know damn well you ain't cutting hearts already! This the first time hearts got played!" Della exclaimed.

"Stop it, Unc, you can look at me and tell I ain't never had a heart," Bo-T replied. He scooped up the cards with a smirk on his face. He played the four of spades next and when his partner won the book with the Jack of spades, he blurted out, "Dime on time! Y'all niggas suck!"

"Good hit, youngin," Bo-T's spade partner stated while reaching over the card table to give Bo-T a fist pound.

"Y'all niggas cheating," Della joked.

"That's what you get for going against the grain, Unc. You should've played with me, not against me," Bo-T shot.

"Yeah whatever, run that shit back and put your money where your mouth is," Della shot back.

Bo-T rose up from the card table and said, "Naw, I'm straight. I'm tired of whoopin' you old niggas, I'm about to step outside and get some air." He pounded fists with everyone around the table and then left the room. He made his way down a small hallway and then dipped into a bathroom. As he relieved his bladder, his mind couldn't help but think about the life he was now currently living.

After parting from Wizz a few weeks ago, he made his way to Tampa, FL, and found his uncle Della. Della was his mother's only brother, and he had played a major role in his life from the day he was born. Bo-T's mother died while he was in prison and that made Della the only family he had left. He had no brothers or sisters, and his dad was never around from the beginning, so Della was more of a father figure than an uncle. His only other relative was Della's daughter, his cousin Kat, and as of now they all lived together in Della's small apartment.

Bo-T washed his hands and looked in the mirror. He was a little disappointed in his appearance. He was thirty-three years old but having spent his last thirteen years in the prison system, his youthfulness had been preserved. He was five-eight and weighed a hundred-eighty-five pounds of solid muscle. He was in great shape and his entire body was ripped, so that's not what bothered him. His skin was covered with tattoos, but his extremely dark complexion made them hard to see unless you were up close.

As he dried his hands off, he realized what bothered him was his wardrobe. He was wearing his uncle's clothes since all he owned for himself was underwear and a few t-shirts. He didn't have a penny to his name and felt like a freeloader, and being a freeloader just wasn't his style.

He walked through the house and made his way to the front door that was already open. He stepped out onto the porch and averted his attention to his cousin Kat. Kat was sitting in a chair next to her homegirl with a really silly look on her face.

"Damn, cuzzo, you flaw as fuck!" Bo-T stated.

"Boy whatever, what I did now?" Kat questioned.

"You got high without me! That's what! Yo black ass sitting there higher than a motherfucka, smiling and shit like that shit funny."

"Boy, whatever. Yo stank ass ain't gotta act like that. We can go get some more weed right now if it will make you feel better."

"Well, why you still sitting on yo fat ass booty! Let's go!"

"Aww cuzzo, you think my ass fat forreal," Kat joked while standing up and pulling on her shorts that were deeply wedged between her ass cheeks.

Kat was five-four and had an ass that could be easily compared to Blac Chyna's, Buffie the Body's or even better, that porn star chick, Victoria Cakes.

Bo-T looked at her like she was stupid and didn't respond.

"Come on, girl. Let's go before this nigga have a mental breakdown," Kat giggled to her homegirl.

The three of them strutted over to Kat's all-white 2015 Tesla and in no time, they were pulling away from their home in Robles Park Village.

"I'm saying though, why we ain't just go to the weed man around the corner?" Bo-T asked.

"Because I'm saving money," Kat replied. "I know this thirsty ass nigga in West Tampa that be giving me free weed."

"You tricking for weed?" Bo-T joked.

"Cuzzo, don't play with me! It ain't tricking if you got it, and you better believe I got a whole lot of it."

Bo-T leaned back and decided to enjoy the ride. He glanced in front of him at the occupant in the passenger seat and thought, "Kat friend kind of sexy a little bit. She skinny as fuck, but she got a pretty face and all them freckles make her look kind of unique. Fuck it, I'm about to try this hoe." He leaned back forward and said, "Aye, I'm saying though, what your name is?"

Kat's homegirl looked over her shoulder with an amused facial expression and simply answered, "Monica."

"Yeah, you do kind of look like a slim Monica with freckles. So how old you is?"

"I'm twenty-six."

"Oh okay, well, I just wanted to let you know you looking real sexy right now."

Monica blushed and replied, "Well, thank you."

"No problem. I'm just being honest. I wonder what you would look like while I'm diggin' in that pussy!"

"Oh, hell naw. Cuzzo, you dead ass wrong!" Kat blurted.

"How the fuck?" Bo-T chuckled.

"You just tried my homegirl like a thot!"

"How? All I did was let her know I think she's sexy and I made it clear I'm interested in fucking, without trying to finesse her with a bunch of lies, like the rest of these lame ass niggas. She ain't even say nothing. If she felt tried, she would've said something. All she doing is staring out the window blushing."

"Nigga, you definitely just tried me," Monica stated, but kept staring out the window.

"Shit, you hanging out with Kat freaky ass, you got to be at least a little freaky," Bo-T joked.

"You got me fucked up, cuzzo! I ain't no damn freak . . . Alright, maybe just a little bit," Kat laughed.

Bo-T leaned back in his seat again and thought, *fuck it. It was worth a try.*"

About five minutes later, they pulled up to a home with a yard full of dead grass. Kat eased out of the car and strutted towards the front door. Her ass cheeks were swallowing her shorts with every step. She knocked on the door and seconds later, she disappeared inside.

Monica didn't look back, but she opened her mouth and asked, "How old are you?"

"Thirty-three."

"Kat told me about you. You just out of prison, right?"

"Something like that. What's up, though?"

"Nothing, I'm just making conversation."

"Oh okay, well where you live at?"

"I stay in a house on 43rd."

"Who you stay with? Your boyfriend or something?"

"No, no boyfriend for me. My house only holds me, myself and Irene."

"Oh alright, well who's Irene? Your sister?

Monica smiled and giggled. "Wrong again. *Me, Myself and Irene* is a Jim Carey movie. My sister name is Mya and she lives with her baby daddy. I live by myself."

"Yeah, I knew that. I was just being funny," Bo-T lied.

Kat suddenly strutted back through the front door and there was a slim, brown-skinned dude tailing her. She hopped back inside of the car and then spoke to her follower. "What, Mason?"

"I'm just tryna figure out when you gone give a nigga some play?" Mason asked in a manner he thought was cool.

"Mason, you is not my type. I don't like thirsty niggas that think they have all the game in the world."

"Stop frontin'. I'll text you later tonight and see what's up."

"You're entitled to do whatever you please, but I would advise you to save your breath."

"Damn, I ain't know you had company. Who you got with you?" Mason asked and poked his head through the window to get a better look at Bo-T.

"This is my cousin. He just got out of prison."

"What's up, fam?" Mason greeted.

Bo-T simply nodded his head.

"I know how it is when you're just coming home, so if you need a plug then get my number from Kat. I got loud, Molly and coke. Fuck with me."

"Alright," was all Bo-T offered.

"Can you please get yo big ass head out my window and back the fuck up so I can leave," Kat blurted.

"Alright, alright. Ease up, tiger." As Mason stepped back, Kay quickly reversed out of the driveway and then sped off back towards the projects.

"Roll up, cuzzo," Kat stated and tossed Bo-T one of the sacks she just got, along with a blunt.

Bo-T quickly rolled the blunt, fired it up and put it in rotation. They hot-boxed the car all the way home and by the time they entered the projects, they were all good and high.

"Feel better now?" Kat joked.

"Hell yeah," Bo-T laughed.

Kat parked in her usual spot and killed the engine. "What you about to do, girl?" she asked Monica.

"Probably, hop in my ride and take my ass home," Monica answered.

"Alright, I'll call you and catch up with you tomorrow then."

Monica opened her door, but before exiting she looked back at Bo-T and said, "So, what's up? What you gone do?"

Bo-T looked puzzled and replied, "What you mean?"

"Are you going to keep me company tonight or were you just talking?"

"Bitch! Oh, hell naw!" Kat blurted.

Bo-T didn't respond, but he quickly slid out of the car and smoothly headed towards Monica's car.

"Bitch, you a slut!" Kat joked.

"Whatever, trick! I ain't had no dick in almost eight months, and your cousin looks like he knows exactly how to stroke this kitty with his sexy, dark action-figure-looking ass." Monica exited the car and shut the door.

"Don't call me tomorrow, hoe!" Kat loudly blurted.

"Hopefully I'll be so sore tomorrow, I won't be able to," Monica shouted over her shoulder. She unlocked her car and stepped inside with Bo-T in unison.

No other words were exchanged as Kat watched Monica zoom away.

Chapter 6

Bo-T woke up the next morning to the sound of a phone vibrating on top of a dresser. He sat up in the unfamiliar bed and located the source of the noise. He looked at the digital clock next to the vibrating phone and thought, "Damn, it's still early, but I need to slide. I ain't tryna lay up with this hoe."

Monica was slumped on the bed next to him and it seemed like she didn't hear her phone ringing off the hook. Bo-T nudged her with a little force, and she slowly woke up with an attitude.

"What, nigga? I'm tired."

"Aye get up, I need you to drop me back off at the house."

"What time is it?"

"It's 7:51 a.m."

"Oh, hell naw. Nigga, it's way too early. Let me sleep." She rolled over and instantly dozed back off.

Bo-T shook her shoulder with a little more force than the first time, and damn near knocked her small body off the bed. "Man, get yo ass up! I need to go!"

"Why? Why you can't stay for just a few more hours?"

"Because if I stay any longer, then I might fall in love with yo pretty ass. I ain't woke up in a position like this in a long ass time."

"Okay, so? What's wrong with loving me?"

"Nothing. I might could love you one day, but definitely not today, so get yo ass up and take a nigga home. Now!"

Monica heard the seriousness in his voice and after the way he made her body feel last night, she didn't want to ruin her chances at something more serious in the future. She mumbled her frustration and slowly rose from the bed. She was still naked and although she didn't have any ass or titties, the wide gap between her legs was all she needed to keep a man coming back.

She glided over to one of her dressers and pulled out some sweatpants and a tight-fitting shirt. She slipped her feet into a pair of furry house slippers and said, "Alright nigga, you got me up, why yo ass still in the bed?"

Bo-T shot out of the bed and put on his shorts and socks. He picked up his pants and shirt and slipped into his shoes.

They left Monica's house and drove in silence back to Bo-T's place of residence. When they pulled up to his spot about twenty minutes later, he gave Monica a kiss on the lips and said, "I'll hit you up or I'll just catch up with you when you link up with Kat."

"Alright, I'll see you," Monica replied.

Bo-T stepped out of the car and Monica drove away. When he entered the house, he headed straight for his bedroom, grabbed a change of clothes, and then stepped over to the bathroom in the hallway. He took a quick shower and in ten minutes, he was walking back into his room.

"What's up, Cousin?" Kat blurted from his bed.

Bo-T quickly jerked his head up and said, "I almost drop-kicked yo black ass! What the fuck you doing in my room this early?"

Kat held up the blunt she had just rolled and waved it back and forth. "I come in here to smoke with yo stank ass. I heard you come in the house while I was rolling up, and I know if I would've smoked without you, yo stank ass would've started crying and shit."

"Yeah, you better have a good excuse. Any other reason would've got yo black ass kicked out."

Kat lit up the blunt and passed it to her cousin. Bo-T sat down next to her on his bed and filled his mind with smoke.

"So, did yo nasty ass have fun with my homegirl?" Kat joked.

"Hell, yeah! That girl pussy got more juice than a jug of Hawaiian Punch," Bo-T laughed.

"Eww! Cuzzo that is TMI!" Kat laughed.

Bo-T rubbed his hands along his shorts and felt something ruffle in his pocket. He made a quick inspection and pulled out a small piece of paper with a phone number on it and blurted out, "Oh shit!"

"What's that, cuzzo?"

The ink on the paper had smeared from being washed, but the number was still recognizable.

"I forgot to call my nigga Wizz! Give me yo phone!"

"It's too early to be calling people."

"Fuck all that, it's 8:48 a.m., I bet my nigga answer."

Kat rolled her eyes and skipped to her room. She skipped back in and tossed Bo-T her phone.

The phone smacked Bo-T in the face and he shouted, "What the fuck yo problem?"

"Oh shit, my bad, cuzzo! I thought you was looking."

Bo-T rubbed his forehead and dialed the number on the paper. "Hello?"

"What's up, this must be Ashley?"

"I can't think of anybody else that would answer Ashley's phone."

Bo-T laughed and said, "My bad, this is Bo-T. I was trying to catch up with Wizz."

"Oh hey, Bo-T. I'm not home right now but Wizz has his own number, and I'm sure he wouldn't mind me giving it to you."

"Yeah, what's the number?" He entered the digits that were relayed to him into Kat's phone and saved the number. "Alright, Ashley, I appreciate it. "

"No problem, bye."

Bo-T dialed the new number and thought, *why I ain't got my own number yet?*

"Yooooo!" a muffled voice answered.

"Wizz?"

"Yeah. Yeah, who this is?"

"Nigga, this Bo-T!"

"Oh shit! What's up, my nigga! Damn bra, where the fuck you been at? It done been like three weeks, nigga, what the fuck!"

"That's my bad, lil bra, I got tangled up over here and been trying to adapt. This shit crazy, my nigga. I fucked around and for-got to call though, I thought I had lost the number you gave me."

"Damn, bra, so this yo number right here?"

"Naw, bra, this my lil cousin phone but we stay together so you can reach me on this line anytime."

"Okay, say no more. So, how you living, nigga?"

"Like I said, bra, shit been rough. I been maintaining but I feel like a straight-up mark, lil bra. I ain't got shit!"

"We need to link up, bra. I ain't got much either but I'm straight though, I can't complain."

"True that. What you eating, lil nigga? It sound like your mouth full."

"Oh naw, my jaws still kind of sore. I got my mouth hooked up."

"What you mean, you got yo mouth hooked up?"

"I rocked my shit up!"

"You got golds in yo mouth, nigga?"

"Hell, yeah!"

"Perms?"

"Duhhhh! I got a twenty wall. Ten on ten."

"Damn nigga, you hanging the fuck out! You got a phone, golds... nigga, you got a car?"

"Naw... naw, I ain't whipping yet but I got a couple lil hoes be letting me swang in they shit."

"Damn, you hanging out. I just got my first piece of pussy last night."

"You paid for it?"

"You got me fucked up!"

"Nigga, don't act like yo tank head ass won't buy no pussy."

"Yo lil sea-turtle-head ass the one be paying to play. And I couldn't buy no pussy if I wanted to, I'm broke as fuck!" Bo-T joked.

"Damn a nigga miss you, bra. I'm saying though, you been moving around?"

"Yeah, I been mobbing a little bit. I fucked around and did a little research on us and bra, this shit crazy! How bout we ain't got no records of existence at all."

"I was just about to ask you about that and ask you if you heard about that bus shit."

"Hell yeah, I heard about that bullshit! My uncle had all that shit when I got here, but when I tried to look shit up online, I couldn't find shit on us. When I say nothing, I mean *nothing*! No mugshots, no arrest records, No medical records, no birth records, no nothing! Bra, I looked on the computer, I checked the clerk of courts, I called the hospital I was born at. Nigga, I done looked everywhere! It's like we're ghosts!"

"Yeah, I know, my mama showed me the same shit."

"What's all that noise in the background?"

"I'm outside walking down the street."

"Oh yeah? What you up to?"

"Shit, I'm about to grab me some Chinese food from down the block."

"Must be nice."

"It's alright."

"Check it out though, bra, I need to start getting me some fucking money! I ain't been feeling right and it's time to change that. I think I might have a possible play and I'ma need you with me."

"Shit, you already know how I'm rocking. Just let me know when and where and I'm there. I need some money too!"

"Alright, cool. I'm still putting the play together but as soon as I'm ready, I'ma hit your line."

"Say no more, you know where I'm at."

"Alright, well gone ahead and enjoy your precious meal, my nigga. I'ma get up with you. Love, lil nigga."

"You already know. love, bra."

***

After ending the call with Bo-T, Wizz approached the counter at the New China and placed his order. *I wanna fuck a Chinese bitch*, he thought as he sat down at a table to wait for his order. He glanced around the small diner and was surprised to see a petite Spanish woman, sitting at another table talking on her phone. It was only 9:27 in the morning and New China had just opened at 9:00, so he didn't expect to see anyone else this early.

When the woman ended her call, Wizz approached her table and said, "You mind if I take a seat?"

The woman looked him up and down and when he smiled and revealed his glittering teeth, she smiled herself and signaled for him to sit down.

"Good morning, how you doing?" Wizz began.

"Good morning to you too and I'm good, just trying to fill my belly and get my day started."

"That's what's up, so what's your name?"

"Shanice and you?"

"Everybody calls me Wizz."

The older Chinese lady at the counter signaled to Shanice that her order was complete, and she politely excused herself from the table and retrieved her meal.

She reapproached Wizz and said, "It was nice meeting you, Wizz."

"You too fine to only meet once, and I'd love to get to know you a little better. Let me get your number." Wizz reached in his pocket for his phone and extended it to her.

She entered her digits and said, "Make sure you call me." She then turned around and left the diner.

Wizz retrieved his food shortly after and then made the short, ten-minute walk back home.

Chapter 7

Two Weeks Later

"Yooo!" Wizz answered.

"What's up, lil nigga, this Bo-T!"

"What's up, bra? I'm just koolin at the house on this purple."

"That's real. Aye, you got wheels?"

"Hell naw, I'm at the house dolo right now."

"You think you can get a ride out here sometime later?"

"Hell naw! Who the fuck gone drop me off way in Tampa? Only car I could've made that mission in is my sister shit, but she went out of town yesterday."

"Alright, don't sweat it. Just get yo shit together and I'll be down yo way in a couple hours to scoop you up."

"Alright cool, but what's up with the sudden road trip?"

"You remember that lil play I was telling you about a couple weeks ago?"

"Hell yeah, what's up with that?"

"Everything-everything. I done finally put that shit together and it really didn't take much thought. I just had to find out if it was sweet or not, and believe me when I tell you, that shit sweet!"

"Alright, well say less. You remember how to get here?"

"Hell naw, nigga. I'ma hit you back up when I pull off the interstate."

"Say no more, I'm waiting on you."

"Say less."

Wizz ended his call and decided to take a shower. After cleaning himself up he put on a black tank top and some green, black and white Jordan gym shorts. He put on some long black socks and then slipped his feet into some green, black and white Jordan Retro shoes.

He maneuvered around his room and made sure everything was clean and then he packed a book bag with a few more outfits and supplies. He then relaxed in the living room and flipped through the channels on the flat screen while waiting for Bo-T. About forty minutes later, the awaited call came through and he gave Bo-T the final directions to his spot.

Fifteen minutes after that, a white Tesla pulled into his driveway and Bo-T hopped out the passenger seat rocking a fresh fade, no shirt, a crisp pair of black 501 Levi's and a pair of black high-top Air Force Ones.

Wizz stepped out the house and locked the door. He met Bo-T in the driveway, and they embraced in a brotherly hug.

"What's up, lil ugly ass nigga." Bo-T joked and threw a jab that connected with Wizz's mouth.

"Damn nigga, My lip!" Wizz responded and used his hand to see if his lip was busted.

"Nigga, fuck yo lip! Soft ass nigga! If you was on point, you would've weaved that shit. You're losing your touch, lil nigga." Bo-T laughed.

Wizz dropped his bag on the floor and raised his fist. "Try that shit again, tough ass nigga."

Bo-T quickly threw another jab that Wizz quickly side stepped and followed up with a two-piece. Bo-T blocked the two piece and threw a hook that Wizz managed to duck. While ducked down, Wizz threw a body shot and Bo-T blocked it with his elbow. Bo-T threw another quick jab and caught Wizz on the forehead. He followed up with a straight and Wizz ducked it while throwing an overhand that clipped Bo-T over the eye. Bo-T then lunged forward, grabbed Wizz by the waist and scooped him off his feet.

"You lucky we on concrete. If we was in the grass, I would've slammed yo ass, lil nigga," Bo-T stated while putting Wizz back on his feet and breathing heavy.

"That's all you want to do is grab a nigga!"

"I was just about to beat yo ass."

"So, why you grabbed me?"

"Hurry yo ass up, cuzzo! I ain't got all day!" Kat shouted from inside the car.

"Who the fuck is that?" Wizz questioned.

"That's my lil cousin that I stay with, her name Kat."

Wizz picked his bag back up and hopped into the back seat behind Bo-T.

Kat turned around to face Wizz and said, "Damn! You ain't tell me your homeboy was fine as fuck!"

"You told me I was dead wrong when I tried yo homegirl Monica. Now look how you acting with my nigga."

Kat laughed and said, "I'm just saying, damn!"

"What's up Kat, they call me Wizz."

"Pleasure to meet you, but let me get this car back on the road, before I forget where the hell I'm at."

The three of them kicked it and laughed all the way back to Tampa and when they entered the house, Bo-T told Wizz, "Roll up some of that purple shit. You got that gas, nigga."

Wizz crashed on the couch and said, "Yeah, this shit smoking."

"Where you going?" Bo-T asked Kat, who was heading back out the door after grabbing something from her room.

"I've got to meet Monica at the mall and I'm late," she replied and flew out the door.

Bo-T and Wizz smoked, while Bo-T gave Wizz the rundown on the lick he had planned for the morning. After that, they just laughed and joked until Bo-T stated, "Alright, lil bra, I'm about to take it in and get some rest. We moving out early tomorrow, so be ready."

"Say less. So, where I'm sleeping?"

"Right there on the couch, nigga!"

"Works for me."

Bo-T left the living room and quickly returned with a blanket. He tossed the blanket to Wizz and said, "I'll holla at you in the a.m."

Wizz accepted the blanket and stretched out on the long couch. He focused his attention to the movie playing on the television and zoned out. About two hours later, he realized he couldn't sleep and decided to raid the refrigerator. He found some Welch's grape juice and poured himself a glass.

As he finished the juice, Kat walked into the kitchen and blurted out, "Oh, I'm sorry. I didn't know you were in here."

Wizz smiled and said, "It's all good, you act like you just caught me in the bathroom or something."

Kat giggled and said, "Yeah, you're right, I guess I'm just a little stressed out right now."

"Wanna talk about it?"

"It's nothing worth discussing really, but I'm about to smoke to ease my mind, and you can join me if you want."

"Sure, why not?" Wizz stated and followed her down the hall to her bedroom.

Kat handed Wizz a blunt and some weed off her dresser and said, "Roll up and make yourself comfortable."

Wizz looked around the room and didn't see anywhere he could make himself comfortable other than her bed, so he sat down on the edge and begin the rolling process.

Kat wiggled out of her jeans and removed her shirt. Wizz damn near dropped the weed on the floor when he saw how fat her ass looked while she stood there in her panties. Her slim waist only made her ass and hips look even fatter, and when she bent over to remove her socks, Wizz almost stopped breathing.

Kat's ass cheeks jiggled and wobbled like Jello as she yanked her socks off one by one. She tied a scarf around her head and looked at herself in the mirror. She used the reflection to look behind her and she caught Wizz staring at her ass and smiled. When she turned around and faced him, his eyes locked onto the thick and fluffy lips demanding attention between her thick and juicy thighs. She had an average face, but her smooth chocolate skin added to her beauty, and her body looked delicious.

Kat lowered her gaze and saw a twitch in Wizz's shorts. Right before her eyes, his large print grew larger, and she unconsciously bit her lips.

Wizz saw the lust in her eyes, and he broke the lustful silence by saying, "Lighter?"

Kat grabbed a lighter from her dresser and handed it to him. Wizz ignited the blunt and soothed his lungs before passing it over. As she leaned back in her bed, Wizz asked, "So, what had you so uptight tonight?"

"It's a lot really. For one, I've been having a hard time getting approved for an apartment, and then my homegirl had an attitude with me all night because I was late meeting her at the mall today."

"That sounds petty. Where you been trying to move though?"

"I've been looking at a few apartments in your neck of the woods."

"Orlando?"

"Yeah, I like it down there."

"That's what's up. So, who you moving out there with?"

"I'm going by myself. I'm tired of being bothered by people, but I'll let my cousin come if he wants to."

"No man?"

"Naw, I don't have a man. I haven't been with a man in any type of way in nearly a year, believe it or not. I know my cousin be talking trash about me, but I'm really not like that. I'm just grown, and I know what I want and don't want. I do tease and play around a lot, but I just do that for fun."

"It's all good. I don't judge a book by its cover. I get to know people first and then I decide what type of person I think they are."

Kat took one final pull on the blunt and then dropped the remains in the ash tray. Wizz leaned back in the bed with her and they stayed up talking and getting to know each other until the weed mixed in with a long day and they both passed out.

***

"Y'all look real cute right now," Bo-T blurted from the doorway of Kat's bedroom.

Wizz slowly opened his eyes and saw Bo-T leaning in the doorway with an amused facial expression.

"Get yo ass up, bra. It's about time to ride out," Bo-T instructed.

Wizz tried to get up and realized he was trapped under a heavy thigh and an arm. Kat had her leg wrapped around Wizz's lower body and her arm around his waist. Her head was on his chest, and she was slightly snoring.

Wizz shook her leg, and she opened her eyes. She looked up at him and lazily asked, "What?"

"I'm about to slide out," Wizz stated.

"Okay, I'll see you later."

"I can't slide until you let me go," Wizz laughed. "You got your body wrapped around me like an octopus."

Kat smiled and detached herself from his body. Wizz eased out of the bed and took one last look at her before he left. Even under the covers, her full figure was unmistakable. He shook his head and stepped into the hallway.

Bo-T was standing in the hallway with a serious look on his face and said, "Keep it real, lil bra. You popped my lil cousin?"

"Hell naw!" Wizz blurted.

"Come on, lil bra, you ain't gotta lie to kick it."

"Real shit, bra, I ain't hit her. I thought about it, but we ain't take it there. We was just vibin until we fell asleep. She really cool as fuck."

Bo-T's mug turned into a smile, and he said, "Shit, I don't give a fuck if you did or didn't, to be real. I just wanted to know, because if you did that would give me something to fuck with her about."

"Oh okay. But naw, bra, it wasn't nothing like that."

"Alright, well go ahead and get your gear on. As soon as you get right, we riding out," Bo-T concluded and walked away.

Chapter 8

"You understand everything?" Bo-T asked after going over the plan one last time.

"Let's do it," was Wizz's short reply.

"Alright, pull up to the curb right there," Bo-T instructed, while pointing at a house only four houses away from where they were parked.

"Why we ain't riding in a stolo or something? We making yo cousin car hot," Wizz stated while creeping the car forward.

"Because this shit sweet and we ain't got time for all that extra shit. And Kat don't give a fuck as long as I break her off, so fuck it."

Wizz parked along the curb and left the car running. They both hopped out and approached the front door. Bo-T knocked.

"Who banging on my shit?" a voice shouted from beyond the door.

"This Bo-T."

"Slide in, it's open!" the voice shouted.

Bo-T turned the knob and swung the door open. He stepped inside with Wizz on his heels and about ten steps later, they were walking into a dining room.

In the dining room, Big Mike was standing over Mason, who was sitting at a table weighing up ounces of Molly on a digital scale. Big Mike was Mason's younger brother, but he was twice Mason's size. The scowl that appeared on Big Mike's face when he saw Wizz made it very clear he wasn't pleased with the extra party.

Big Mike was about to announce his displeasure, but Bo-T stepped in front of Wizz and blurted out, "What's up, y'all boys?"

Wizz quickly recognized the signal and roughly shoved Bo-T into Big Mike. The force from their contact sent Big Mike crashing into Mason, and their combined weight caused all three of them to fall onto the floor.

"Yo what the fuck!" Mason shouted.

Wham!

Wizz slapped Mason across the face with his 9mm and shouted, "Nigga, shut the fuck up!"

Big Mike was about to jump up when a sharp pain suddenly shot though his head and he shouted, "Ahhh, fuck!"

Wham!

Bo-T smacked Big Mike in the back of the head again with his .357 and shouted, "Lay yo big soft ass down!"

"Ahh!" Big Mike cried.

"Shut yo soft ass up!" Bo-T shouted.

Wham!

Bo-T hit him again.

"It's all in the room!" Big Mike cried.

"It better be."

Boom!

Bo-T sent a bullet flying into Big Mike's skull and his head burst open like a pumpkin. "Go check that out" Bo-T told Wizz while aiming his .357 at Mason. "Sweet ass nigga!" He teased Mason.

"You gone die for this!" Mason spat.

Wham!

Bo-T slapped Mason with the long hard barrel of the .357 and barked, "I bet you die before I do! You better hope that shit back there or I'ma dust yo ass next!"

"Fuck you!" Mason yelled.

Boom!

Bo-T sent a bullet through Mason's chest and blurted, "Fuck you too! Bitch ass nigga!" He then hustled to the back of the house where the two bedrooms were and saw Wizz searching through a closet in one room, so he rushed into the other.

As soon as he stepped into the room, he saw four big boxes sitting right in the middle of the bed. He flipped the boxes over one by one and found himself staring at four large, vacuum-sealed pounds of marijuana, two bricks of Molly, a half-key of coke and an unidentified amount of money. "Damn!" he shouted.

Wizz came stumbling into the room seconds later, with his pockets poking out and two pillowcases full of goodies.

Bo-T stuffed his findings into two other pillowcases and scanned the rest of the room. He started flipping out the dresser drawers, while Wizz searched the closet. They quickly decided nothing else was in the room, so they dashed back towards the front of the house.

When Wizz bent the corner of the hallway, he saw Mason crawling into the kitchen and put a bullet into the back of his head.

Boom!

Bo-T bent the corner next and blurted, "Damn, I thought fool was over with!"

"He over with now."

They dashed out the house and threw their belongings into the back seat of the Tesla. They then jumped into their original seats and swerved off.

"That shit was sweet, lil bra! What you found in there?" Bo-T questioned.

"Man, I found all type of shit! We needed that!" Wizz replied while whipping Kat's car back to Bo-T's projects.

"Let's get this shit back to the house so we can bust this shit down," Bo-T stated eagerly.

When Wizz parked the car and they rushed back into Bo-T's house, everything was quiet. Wizz looked at his phone and the time was only 9:22 a.m.

"Slide in my room. Everybody still sleep," Bo-T spoke.

Wizz peeked inside Kat's room and saw her still dead to the world, balled up under her blankets. Bo-T shut his bedroom door after they both entered and then tossed his two pillowcases on top of his bed. He poured out the new merchandise and began separating everything evenly. Wizz dumped his pillowcases out and produced nearly the same thing, except he also dumped out a machine gun.

"Damn, nigga! What the fuck is that?" Bo-T asked excitedly.

"A MAC-90! Big boy shit!" Wizz boasted.

"Damn, that bitch pretty!"

"Bra them niggas had most of this shit just laying on the bed."

"That's exactly how I found the rest of this shit. Them niggas must've just re-upped or something. I told you that shit was sweet!"

"How long you think it's gone be before somebody finds them niggas?"

"Fuck them niggas! Let's count this paper."

Half an hour later, they found themselves splitting up their come up, twenty-four large to be exact. "Twelve bands, four pounds, two bricks of Molly, half a key and a pretty addition to the arsenal sounds like a damn good day," Wizz cheerfully stated.

"Not bad at all," Bo-T agreed.

"So, what's the plan now?"

"Well, I don't know about you, but that shit got me hyped up and ready to hang out! One of the best feelings in the world is a pocket full of money! I wanna spend some money and grab some gear."

"That might be a good idea for two reasons I can see right now. One, you got blood all over yo shirt, now that I'm paying attention. Two, nobody wear's Levi's anymore." Wizz laughed.

Bo-T examined himself and noticed he did have blood and possible brain residue stuck to his clothes. He then slipped off his crisp, bloody Levi pants and said, "Man, I be seeing a whole bunch of niggas out here wearing Levi's! Fuck you talking bout?"

"That's because them poor ass niggas can't afford the finer things." Wizz laughed. "You should be rocking True Religion jeans at the bare minimum."

"Alright, well let's go sauce up then and grab a lil something to flex in for the night."

"Where we going tonight?"

"Shit, we gone go see some ass and titties! Now that I've got a little money in my pocket, I'm ready to pay to play," Bo-T stated with a grin.

***

Wizz tucked a freshly rolled blunt behind his ear and brought his seat back up. Bo-T turned the car off and together, they stepped out. They looked forward at the line of people waiting to gain entrance to the venue, and noticed the name "SKINS," plastered over the main doorway in big bold letters. They hopped in the short line and waited for their opportunity to enter the bar. As soon as they stepped through the doors, the blaring music became deafening.

"Where you going with all that ass, let me touch it! She say it's mine, so I smack it when I fuck it!" Moneybagg Yo and Megan Thee Stallion screamed through the speakers, while different-sized asses and titties bounced, clapped, jiggled and shook throughout the building.

"Damn! This bitch flooded with pussy!" Wizz shouted over the loud music.

"I done died and gone to heaven," Bo-T commented.

They decided to get some drinks and swaggered over to the bar.

"What you drinking tonight, baby?" a slim but sexy, brown-skinned honey asked from behind the bar.

"I'll drink you if you let me," Wizz replied with a smirk.

The slim honey blushed and said, "That's very flattering but I like women."

"Shit, we on the same page then. You like 'em, I love 'em," Wizz quickly responded.

"Sounds like you got all the game," she stated with a smile.

"Games get played, I'm dead ass serious."

The bartender laughed and said, "Well alright, holla at me before you leave, and we'll go from there."

"Say less," Wizz stated and then ordered his drink.

"You a smooth criminal," Bo-T joked while they bopped away from the bar.

"Look at that thick ass black shit over there!" Wizz shouted and pointed towards a thick chocolate stallion.

"Fuck that black ass bitch. Look at them two thick-ass red hoes over there!" Bo-T shouted back and pointed in the other direction.

"Oh, my God!" Wizz exclaimed when he rested his eyes on two exotic beauties, doing pole tricks on a stage in the far corner.

They approached the stage and made themselves comfortable in two chairs placed a few feet from the stage. Now that they had a better view of the two eye candies, they immediately noticed two things. One, they were even sexier up close and two, they were identical twins.

They were both about five-five and their clearly enhanced body parts made their approximate weight undecidable. They had beach ball booties and perky watermelon titties. They were shaped like inflated hour glasses, and their curly jet-black hair hung down to their waist. The shiny silkiness of their hair seemed to glow against their golden skin. They both had bright green eyes and a series of tattoos that streamed from their shoulders to their ankles.

So far from their vantage points, the only noticeable difference between the twins was that one of them had a tattoo on the shoulder that read "Sugar," and the other one had an identical tattoo that read "Spice."

Bo-T and Wizz watched the twins put on a show and lustfully approved of the way their asses clapped together.

The twin with the "Sugar" tattoo leaned into the other twin and whispered in her ear.

Bo-T and Wizz couldn't hear what the women were saying, but it had to be about them because as soon as they finished talking, they both looked up and stared directly in their direction. Bo-T raised his glass and gave the women an air toast and Wizz flashed his golden smile.

The twins waltzed off the stage and strutted towards them. Their breasts bounced with every step. One twin sat down on Bo-T's lap, and the other made herself comfortable on top of Wizz.

"What's up, papi?" Bo-T's companion asked.

"You tell me . . . what's up, what they call you?" Bo-T slurred. The alcohol was starting to take effect.

"They call me Spice," she seductively whispered in his ear.

"Oooh shit, caliente! I like it spicy!" Bo-T blurted.

Spice smiled and began rotating her hips in Bo-T's lap.

"They call me Sugar," Wizz's partner hissed.

"By the time I get finished with you, I'ma fuck around and have diabetes," Wizz joked.

Sugar started laughing as Wizz glanced over at Bo-T and admired the lap dance he was receiving.

"That's what you want, papi?" Sugar asked and began swaying her hips to the beat of a song that Wizz couldn't focus on.

"If it was left up to me, I'd want way more than just a lap dance."

Sugar placed her hand on Wizz's throbbing manhood and bit her lip. She grabbed his hand next and said, "Fuck it, follow me." She eased off his lap and guided him to a dark secluded area in the corner of the club.

Spice saw Sugar heading towards what they called the "Fun Zone" and whispered to Bo-T, "Come on Papi. Let's go play." She led Bo-T into the same direction and the club became darker and darker.

There turned out to be a barely visible couch in the corner. The whole area was so dark that from a distance, you could tell the corner was occupied, but it was too dark to actually see what was taking place.

"Take a seat, papi," Sugar instructed.

Spice told Bo-T to do the same and together they flopped down onto the couch. The twins winked at each other and then squatted down in front of their hosts.

Sugar ran her fingers across Wizz's lap and tugged on his belt. Wizz quickly got the message and in one swift motion he yanked his pants and boxers down and let them fall around his ankles. His dick was already rock hard and now it was waving in Sugar's face like an extra-large popsicle.

Sugar grabbed the base of his dick and blurted out, "Damn, papi!"

Wizz's dick throbbed in her hand and demanded attention, so she happily gave it the attention it craved and wrapped her warm wet lips around the head. Inch by inch, she slowly eased his dick into her mouth, until his entire dick vanished into her throat. In a smooth steady motion, she began massaging his balls with her soft hands.

Wizz pulled her hair back so he could watch her work her lovely magic. He used his hands to guide her head up and down and made her speed up her pace.

Spice was stroking Bo-T's dick with her spit-filled hands, while sucking on his balls. Bo-T's eyes were about to roll out of his head while he tried his best to hold his nut back.

Spice let his balls drop out of her mouth and then greedily latched her mouth around his dick. She forced her head down until she felt his dick push into her throat, and then she quickly began to bounce her head up and down. She worked her mouth like a hungry hippo and Bo-T was loving it. The warm and wet sensation was too much, and he couldn't hold back any longer.

Spice must have felt his urgency because she pulled him out of her mouth and began quickly pumping his dick with her hands. Seconds later Bo-T erupted, and his semen splashed all over her face.

Less than a minute after that, Wizz thrusted his hips forward and pushed Sugar's head into his lap. He pumped her throat full of his slimy unborn babies, and she gagged while he filled her up.

"Damn!" Wizz gasped while easing his naked bottom back onto the cool leather couch.

Sugar licked her lips and said, "Mmmm, very tasty, papi."

"Damn," was all Wizz could manage.

Bo-T adjusted his pants and said, "Damn, baby! What a nigga owe you for that right there?"

Spice wiped her mouth and said, "Papi, all I want is a number and a house visit."

"Damn baby, I call that, but I left my phone in the car so you gotta put yo number in my lil brother phone," Bo-T lied and felt slightly embarrassed for still not having his own phone.

After Wizz regained the feelings in his legs, he pulled his pants up and smiled.

"Let me give you my number, papi," Sugar offered.

Wizz fished his phone out of his pocket and smoothly handed it over.

After Sugar punched in her digits, Spice blurted out, "Let me put my number in there too!" Sugar passed the phone to Spice and Wizz looked puzzled for a moment. He glanced at Bo-T, and Bo-T winked his eye.

They all stood up and when Sugar looked at Spice, she blurted, "You better not take your ass back out there with all them soldiers marching on your face."

Spice wiped her hand across her face and said, "Damn!" Her hand and face was covered with wads of sticky goo.

Bo-T took his shirt off and handed it to Spice.

"Thanks," she bashfully stated, while using the shirt to wipe the globs of nut off of her face. "Better?" she asked Sugar.

"Much better." Sugar laughed.

Spice tried to hand Bo-T back his shirt, but he denied the offer. "That's alright, you keep it. We're about to bounce."

"So, when will I be hearing from you?" Sugar asked Wizz.

"I really ain't even from around here, but I promise I'll catch up with you. I ain't gone leave you waiting," Wizz replied.

"Make sure you do that, because something about you just made me do something I ain't never did," Sugar admitted.

"Just chill, lil baby. I got you," Wizz assured.

Bo-T and Wizz worked their way back towards the front of the club and made their exit. When they hopped back in the car, Wizz leaned back in the passenger seat and rolled up a fat blunt.

"Bra, we just fell off in a strip club and got some free head! Now, that's what you call saucy," Bo-T joked and peeled out of the lot.

"We like the modern-day Bang Bros.," Wizz joked.

"Shit, the way we skeeted on them hoes we more like the Skeet Bros!" Bo-T laughed.

"Skeet Gang!" Wizz blurted.

"Call me Skeeman from now on!" Bo-T joked.

"Call me Skeecho!" Wizz joked back.

"I'm feeling that, Skeecho," Bo-T chuckled.

"Aye, I got a bunch of missed calls and text from Kat. She saying where the fuck we at because she needs her car back," Wizz informed.

"Oh shit!, Well shit, she'll be alright. Let her know we on the way now."

"Cool."

While they weaved through traffic, they passed the blunt back and forth and had flash backs of their very eventful day.

"Damn! I forgot to get that bartender's number!" Wizz blurted.

Bo-T just laughed.

Chapter 9

Two days later

Wizz felt his phone vibrating in his pocket and slowly stirred awake. He slowly reached into his pocket and answered his phone upon retrieval. "Yooo," he groggily spoke.

"Hey, what's up?" a soft, feminine voice spoke.

"Who this is?"

"Damn Wizz, how many bitches you got calling you this early?"

Wizz looked at the screen of his phone and said "What's up, Shanice? My bad, baby, I ain't look at my phone before I answered it and I was sleeping. "

"Yeah, whatever! I was just calling you to check on you, since you never seem to check on me."

"Quit playing, I just been real busy lately."

"That's what you always say. Well, what you got going on this weekend? Can you make time for me?"

"Uhhh, yeah, I can do that."

"You don't sound too sure."

"I had to think about it but it's all good. I got you."

"Okay. Well, my cousin is hosting a block party this weekend. He's a DJ and I want you to meet me there. Can you do that?"

"Exactly when is it?"

"Saturday."

"Saturday night?"

"Yeah!"

"Alright, I'll be there."

"You sure?"

"Yeah, I got you."

"Alright, thanks, boo. I'll see you then."

"Cool."

"Bye."

"Yooo."

Wizz stretched his arms and yawned while sitting up on the couch he was just knocked out on in Bo-T's living room.

"What's up, Skeecho? Who got you smiling like that all early in the morning?" Bo -T asked while flopping down on the couch next to Wizz with an already lit blunt.

"I was just on the phone with this lil baby name Shanice. Some lil hoe I met at a Chinese store. I fucked the hoe a couple times and now she be acting all clingy and shit," Wizz explained, while accepting the blunt from Bo-T.

"Wake and bake!" Bo-T blurted.

"Hell yeah. Aye, you want to slide to a block party?"

"When?"

"In two days?

"Saturday?"

"Yup. Saturday night."

"Shit, hell yeah! Where that bitch going down at?"

"It's in the O. That's what the lil hoe was just telling me bout."

"Oh okay, well, hell yeah! When should we slide yo way?"

"Shit, we can slide now if you want. We can hang out for a couple of days and then be ready for the party."

"Hell yeah! I'ma ask Kat square ass to drop us off and then I'll get right." Bo-T shot from the couch and quickly burst into Kat's room without warning. "What's up, cuzzo, what you doing?"

"Nigga, don't be busting in my shit like you ain't got no damn sense! I'm painting my damn nails, what it look like?" Kat fussed.

"Fuck all that. Aye, you think you can give me and Wizz a ride back to his spot in the O? We got gas."

"When?"

"Shit, we tryna leave now really. I just want to take a quick shower. "

Kat looked at the time on her phone, it was 10:42 am.

"Well, I definitely can't leave right now. I need to finish my hands and toenails and then shower. After that, you're lucky because I actually need to go out there anyway. I got my move-in date yesterday and I need to go sign some paperwork for my new spot."

"So, we good?"

"Yeah, be ready around 12 or 12:30."

"Alright cool," Bo-T stated and then headed for his room. He made sure his stash was in a good spot and then he peeled five bands off his knot. He showered and then packed a few clothes in a bag, along with his trusty .357, then considered himself ready. Bo-T glanced at his new watch, It was now 12:17 pm. "What's up, Kat? Let's ride!" he shouted while stepping out of his room.

***

Five hours later

Bo-T tossed two handfuls of bags into the trunk of Kat's car and boasted "Now, that's how you blow a bag!"

Wizz tossed his many designer bags into the back seat and added, "Who you telling, my closet about to look real good tonight."

"Where y'all want to go now?" Kat questioned.

"Shit, all we need now is the rental car. You still gone handle that for us?" Bo-T asked.

"Yeah, I'll get it," Kat replied and drove her Tesla out of the Florida Mall parking lot.

About twenty minutes later, Kat pulled into the parking lot at Enterprise and assisted Bo-T and Wizz inside. They looked around for a few minutes and easily decided on an onyx-colored 2018 Dodge Charger. Kat quickly handled the paperwork and deposit, and Bo-T sponsored the finances. After obtaining the keys, they brought the Charger around to where Kat had parked and transferred all their belongings.

"Alright, Kat, I'ma catch up with you. I appreciate you helping us out today," Bo-T stated.

Kat leaned through her open window and said, "It's all good, cousin. You know I do what I can for you. And thank you for buying me them sexy ass heels, Wizz!"

"Ain't no pressure, you gone wear them for me?" Wizz joked.

Kat smiled and replied, "Hell yeah! And I got the perfect lingerie piece to match them with."

"Keep playing and I'ma test that shit," Wizz stated

"And you gone fall right into the trap! I pass all my tests with flying colors!"

"Come on, Skeecho! Let's ride! You and Kat can flirt later!" Bo-T blurted from the passenger seat of the new rental.

Wizz threw Kat the peace sign, hopped in the Charger and pulled them out into traffic. Kat followed behind them until she eventually went one way, and they went another. It wasn't long before Wizz parked in Ashley's driveway.

They entered the house and after locking the front door, Wizz told Bo-T, "Make yourself comfortable, Skeeman. I'm about to put my stash up and take a quick shower."

Bo-T made his way to the living room and before long, he found himself losing consciousness on the couch.

***

Two days later

Wizz looked himself up and down in the full body mirror hanging on the back of his bedroom door and nodded his head in approval. He was wearing eggshell-colored True Religion pants with a red, long-sleeved True Religion shirt that had the label and emblem scribbled across his chest in white. His all-red Givenchy shoes completed his outfit perfectly and the gold ice draped around his neck, wrist and fingers perfectly complemented his golden smile. He turned his head to the side to make sure his nappy high-top fade was cleanly edged and then he exited the room.

As he stepped into the living room, Bo-T stood up from the couch, holding his nuts with a swagger that said, "Yeah nigga, I'm clean too!"

Bo-T was rocking a gray and black striped True Religion shirt that went along with his gray True Religion jeans. His all-black Jordans made his all-black G-Shock stand out and he had a freshly cut temp fade underneath an Oakland Raider fitted cap.

"Yeah, nigga!" Bo-T exclaimed.

"Do ya thang, Skee! I ain't hating!" Wizz joked.

"So, when we stepping out, Skeechabob?"

"We gone slide right now, Skeewee," Wizz replied and snatched the car keys and Bob Marley lighter off the glass table by the couch.

Once they were in the car and on the road, Bo-T rolled up a blunt the size of a quarter roll. After a couple rotations, it seemed as if the car had transformed into a spaceship, and they were headed for Pluto.

Wizz had a Lil Baby track echoing through the car when his phone rang and threw off his vibe. "Yoooo!" he answered.

"What's up, where you at? I thought you were coming tonight," Shanice spoke with a slight attitude.

"Man, calm down. I'm turning off I-4 on Semeron now. I'll be there in like ten minutes," Wizz calmly stated.

"Oh okay, my bad, boo. When you get in my neighborhood, come all the way around to the back by the park. I'm under the fourth pavilion with my homegirls."

"Alright," Wizz simply stated and hung up. He turned the music back up and vibed to the music for the rest of the drive. As soon as he bent the corner by the park, he was forced to slow down and park along the curb.

"Damn! This bitch swole, Skee," Bo-T blurted.

Wizz killed the engine and they hopped out the car.

The DJ had a Drake and Future song booming up and down the block and the crowd was loving it. "Granny, she was standing right there while I catch a play on a brick–woo! I make them lil niggas go haywire, Taliban in this bitch-woo!" Future screamed into the night.

"Let's hop on some of these hoes before my lil bitch start cock blocking," Wizz spoke.

"Let's hang out, Skeecho!" Bo-T quickly replied.

They merged into the crowd and pushed up against two black girls, twerking in the middle of the road, clearly drunk.

Wizz felt a tap on his shoulder and when he turned around, he saw Shanice standing behind him with her arms crossed and a mug on her face. He pulled his crotch away from the black girl's ass and gave Shanice his undivided attention. The black girl simply moved over and shook her ass on somebody else, like Wizz was never there.

"Nigga, I told you I would be under pavilion number four!" Shanice blurted.

"Okay, well what the fuck you doing over here then? Pavillion number four is way over there," Wizz replied and pointed over his shoulder.

"Nigga, I was over there, but I saw you and your homeboy get out that black Charger."

"Well damn, you got some binoculars on you," Wizz joked.

"Nigga, you ain't funny!" Shanice scowled and hit Wizz on the arm with her tiny hand.

"Ouch!" Wizz laughed.

Shanice rolled her eyes and walked back towards the pavilion she had been chilling under.

"Aye Skeeman, I'm about to slide over there with this bitch before she start crying and shit. What you gone do?" Wizz asked.

Bo-T looked around and said, "Shit, I'm staying out here where all the action at, Skee!"

"Alright, Skee, I'll catch up with you."

Once Wizz trotted off, Bo-T bounced around and soon laid his eyes on a tall, thick, chocolate stallion with long dreads. She was wearing an all-black cat suit and some red bottom high heels.

"Damn!" Bo-T said to himself while approaching the dread-headed stallion. "What's good, baby? You looking real edible right now," he flirted.

The stallion gave him a quick head-to-toe inspection and replied with a heavy Jamaican accent, "You looking pretty good yourself."

They began conversating and it wasn't long before Bo-T was pulling out the new phone he was proud to finally have. After getting the stallion's number and placing his phone back in his pocket, he continued getting his mack on. Suddenly, he was roughly shoved from behind.

He stumbled into a parked car and quickly yelled, "What the fuck?" Before he could regain his balance and turn around a fast combination of punches began raining down on the back of his head. The punches caught him completely off guard but once he got his feet firmly planted, he threw a wild elbow, which made hard contact with something that felt like a possible eyeball.

The punches stopped raining for a moment and that was all the time he needed to turn around and face his opponent. The tall black man with long dreads standing in front of him, threw a wild hay-maker and Bo-T ducked it. Bo-T grabbed the man by his shirt and pants and lifted him effortlessly high into the air. He slammed him face first into the hood of the car they were twisting on, and then yoked his head up by his dreads.

Bo-T started pounding his opponent and feeding him a melee of punches while shouting, "What, you thought this shit was sweet, fuck nigga?"

"Oh, my God! Y'all stop!" the stallion yelled.

"Baby, ain't that yo homeboy?" Shanice blurted out and pointed towards the crowd of people surrounding the action.

"Oh, shit!" Wizz blurted and raced towards the crowd.

By the time Wizz bumped his way through the crowd, Bo-T had the dread head on the floor, who was trying to uselessly block the blows he was still receiving. Wizz ran up and swung his foot out like an NFL punter and used the dread head's face in place of the football.

The dread's head bounced off the bumper of the car he was leaning against, and before his head could bounce back into place, he was kicked again. The dread tried to escape by crawling under the car and was suddenly saved when a heavy fist crashed into the side of Wizz's jaw.

Wizz bounced against the side of the car and was lifted off his feet before he knew what hit him. He fell hard onto his back and was punched in the face at the same time.

Bo-T left the dread head alone and grabbed the fat man that was about to kick Wizz by the collar of his shirt and snatched him back. There was still another short stocky nigga on top of Wizz, but he could handle him better than the fat man, Bo-T thought while crashing a right hook into the fat man's temple.

The fat man's head snapped to the left and Bo-T hit him again. A sharp pain suddenly shot through Bo-T's head, and he was falling towards the ground. He threw his arms up over his head just in time to feel a hard object smash into his forearms. He took a quick glance at Wizz and saw him tussling and trying to defend himself from three dudes.

The music stopped playing and the DJ's voice boomed through the microphone. "Y'all niggas chill the fuck out! All this pussy out here and you niggas wanna rub on each other and fuck up the night!"

Shanice ran up to the three dudes jumping Wizz and sprayed them all in the face with a can of mace she carried on her key chain. The three dudes quickly shielded their eyes and scattered.

Wizz quickly bounced back onto his feet and charged the fat man that was throwing heavy blows into Bo-T's rib cage. He kicked the fat man in between the legs, and he went straight down. Wizz then threw a clean hook into a slim dude that was on the verge of hitting Bo-T with a crowbar.

The crowbar flew out the dude's hand and Bo-T was back on his feet. Bo-T scooped the slim dude off of the ground and slammed him headfirst into the curb.

The mace Shanice sprayed was still lingering in the air and causing everyone to cough and scatter. The crowd quickly cleared, and everyone began jumping in their cars and leaving.

The dread head that had originally started the fight was long gone. The dreaded stallion had helped him crawl from under the car and got slapped in the face for her efforts. The dread head called the stallion every type of hoe he could think of and quickly fled the scene while his homeboys handled the beef he started.

Now that the crowd was clear, the only people left in the street were Bo-T, Wizz, Shanice and the slim dude that wielded a crowbar.

The slim dude was balled up in the road, while Bo-T and Wizz feverishly kicked him from his head to his ass.

The DJ approached the scene and said, "Come on, y'all, let the lil nigga get up out of here."

"Fuck this nigga!" Bo-T panted and kicked him again.

Shanice grabbed Wizz by the arm and said, "Okay, baby, that's enough! Tell your homeboy to chill."

Bo-T took one last kick and said, "You lucky I'm tired, pussy nigga!" He took a step back and the slim dude quickly struggled to his feet and limped away.

Wizz looked down at his clothes and shouted, "Oh, hell nawl! These fuck niggas done fucked up a nigga outfit! Bra, look at this big ass scuff mark on the front of my fucking shoe!"

Bo-T looked down at his own wardrobe and shook his head.

"Aye, you know these niggas?" the DJ asked Shanice.

"Yeah, this my nigga Wizz right here, and that's his homeboy. I invited them out here," Shanice explained.

"What's up y'all, they call me DJ Cocaine. I've got to admit, even though y'all fucked up the night, y'all some real ass niggas!" DJ Cocaine laughed and then continued, "I saw how y'all got down tonight and considering how outnumbered y'all was, y'all held y'all ground and put on till it was over."

"I should've shot one of them niggas," Bo-T stated with a straight face. He adjusted the cannon on his waistline and tightened his belt.

"You strapped?" DJ Cocaine asked in disbelief.

"Nigga, I'm always strapped!" Bo-T admitted.

Wizz smiled and adjusted his pistol as well.

"Damn, both of you niggas strapped and y'all ain't shoot this bitch up!" DJ Cocaine blurted.

"I told my lil nigga a couple days ago that the first nigga that try us, we gone whoop his ass!"

Bo-T laughed. "Hand-to-hand combat be an adrenaline rush!"

Wizz smiled and said, "I think we still got it, Skeeman-Heman."

Bo-T laughed and said, "That shit almost got ugly, Skeecho, but we got off."

Shanice shook her head and said, "Y'all niggas is crazy."

"I'm about to roll up, Skee. My neck starting to hurt," Bo-T stated and walked off towards the car.

"So, how long y'all been talking?" DJ Cocaine asked Shanice and Wizz.

"Like three weeks or so," Shanice replied.

"I approve. He a solid one," DJ Cocaine stated.

"So, what's up with your name? You got that Cocaine forreal, or is that just a music reference?" Wizz asked.

"I do my thing a little bit, but shit kind of slow for me right now. My plug just got booked a couple weeks ago."

"Was yo plug out here on the East Side?"

"Yeah, he stayed around Alafaya."

"Well shit, I got some raw beige Molly and some coke," Wizz offered.

"What ya prices looking like?"

"For the Molly or the powder?"

"Both."

"You tryna spend big or grab some ounces?"

"I spend big, my nigga."

"Alright, well I'll tell you what. This what I'ma do for you. Bring me twenty-five and I'll hook you up with a brick of that Molly, and a half a key of coke," Wizz offered.

"Twenty-five grand?" the DJ questioned timidly.

"Price too high for you?"

"Too high? Nigga yo prices so low, you scaring me!"

"This shit come and go. Ain't no pressure. And since you my girl cousin, it's all love."

DJ Cocaine rubbed his chin and looked at Wizz seriously. "Alright, I'm fucking with it. I know you and your partner some thoroughbreds and like you said, since you fucking with my lil cousin, it's all love. So, when can I holla at you?"

"Shit, I'm on deck right now," Wizz quickly stated.

"Alright, well check it, since the party ended early, I've got a lil extra time to spare. So I'ma bend a couple corners real quick and then I'ma link up with you."

"Whenever you ready, just call Shanice. I'ma be with her for the rest of the night, so you can reach me through her, and we'll go from there."

"Say no more, young soulja. I'll hit you up in about an hour or so."

"Say less," Wizz concluded and gave the DJ some dap.

While the DJ was walking away, Bo-T was walking up with a freshly rolled blunt between his lips.

Bo-T sparked the blunt and said, "What's up with that nigga?"

"Fool finna cop that work I brought back from them dummies round yo way," Wizz informed.

"Oh yeah, well what's up?"

"We need to slide back on my side of town, so I can go grab that shit real quick and then we gone link up with fool in about an hour or so."

"Let's do it, Skeecho!" Bo-T ended.

Fly Rock

Chapter 10

Wizz opened his closet and the first thing he noticed was the two UPS boxes he had sitting on the top of his shelf seemed out of place. He had a complex for placing things a certain way, so the UPS labels that should've been pointing towards the right, were now pointing directly at him and that immediately disturbed him.

He reached up for the boxes and when he lifted the first box, it was as light as a feather. "Oh, hell naw!" He tossed the box to the side and quickly reached for the other. He slammed the weightless box on the floor and began tossing shit everywhere. Clothes and boxes were flying over his head as he continued to search for his treasure in frustration. "Fuck!"

Wizz quickly glided over to his dresser and Bo-T rushed into the room and blurted, "What's up, Skeechobean? What the fuck you yelling for?"

"All my shit missing!"

"What shit?"

"Man, all my fucking dope!" Wizz shouted and then sighed with relief when he found his money stash still safely secure and untouched where he had it in his sock drawer.

"Your coke missing?"

"My coke, my Molly and my fucking weed!" Wizz angrily replied and then found an ounce of weed he was smoking on in another drawer.

"Damn, Skee! You sure you ain't misplace it?"

"Hell naw! I know where I had my shit!" Wizz quickly whipped his phone out and called his sister.

"What's up, twin?" Ashley answered.

"You been in my room moving shit?"

"No. Why what's up?"

"Where you at?"

"I'm still out of town. I should be back tomorrow night."

"Where yo ugly ass boyfriend at?"

"I don't know. I think he been staying with his sister while I been gone."

"Alright, I'll holla at you when you get back."

"Okay, but is everything okay? You sound upset."

"Yeah, I'm good, I'll catch up with you," Wizz stated and ended the call before she could pry any further.

"So, what's up, Skeecho?" Bo-T asked.

"I think that ugly ass fuck nigga stole my shit."

"Damn," Bo-T mumbled while shaking his head.

"This shit wild as fuck!" Wizz shouted and kicked his bed in frustration.

"So, what we gone do about the DJ nigga?"

"I ain't got nothing for the nigga! If you wanna drive all the way to Tampa and get yo shit, then you can make the sale."

"Fuck all that. We need that bread, Skeechodee!"

"Well, what we gone do?" Wizz questioned.

"What's understood don't need to be explained, Skeecho. Let's ride!" Bo-T stated and turned around to leave.

They stopped in the living room for a few minutes to come up with a quick plan and then they stomped out of the house. Bo-T jumped in the Charger and Wizz hopped in the passenger seat of Shanice's car. Together, they pulled off.

"What's up Boo, I thought you were grabbing something?" Shanice commented.

"I just brought us here, so I could change out them dirty ass clothes. My nigga on his way to grab the shit for yo cousin from his house. He gone meet us at the spot," Wizz explained.

"Okay boo, so where to now?"

Wizz gave her some directions and in less than ten minutes, they were parking in a large parking lot that was dark and nearly invisible from the world. Wizz leaned his seat back and rolled a blunt. He passed the blunt back and forth with Shanice while they silently waited.

About ten minutes later, a black Honda pulled into a parking lot and parked in a parking spot two spots away from the light blue Taurus Wizz and Shanice were in.

"Who is that?" asked Shanice.

"Oh, that's bra," Wizz plainly replied.

"Wasn't he driving a Charger?"

"Good observation, but he probably left it at his house. That's his Honda."

Before she could pry any further her phone rang, and she answered it on speaker. "What's up?"

"You still with Wizz?" DJ Cocaine asked.

"What's up, Cocaine?" Wizz spoke loud enough to be heard.

"You tell me, I'm ready for you."

"Alright cool, you know where the old Dollar Movie Theatre used to be? Behind the Burlington Coat Factory?"

The phone went silent for a second and then DJ Cocaine answered, "On West Colonial and Dorscher?"

"Yeah, exactly. It's a church now."

"Yeah. Yeah, I know where you at."

"Alright, well, I'm waiting on you then. I'm parked in front of the church in Shanice's car."

"Say no more, I'll be there in about fifteen minutes."

The call disconnected and then Wizz looked over at Shanice and shook his head. *Oh well*, he thought. "Is that your cousin's car?" he asked and pointed on the other side of Shanice.

She turned her head to look out of her window and said, "I don't see anybody."

WHAM!

Wizz slammed the butt of his pistol into the back of her head, and she was instantly unconscious. He then quickly hopped out of the car and ran over to the driver's side.

Bo-T hopped out the Honda with a book bag and gave it to Wizz. Wizz opened the driver's door and Shanice's unconscious body fell out and slammed into the pavement.

"Damn Skeecho, you killed her?" Bo-T asked.

"Naw, not yet." Wizz dragged her to the trunk. "Pop the trunk," he told Bo-T.

Bo-T pulled a lever by the driver's seat and the trunk sprang open. Wizz attempted to lift Shanice into the trunk and dropped her back on the floor.

"Help me put this bitch in the trunk, Skeeman," Wizz stated.

"Weak ass nigga!" Bo-T joked.

"Fuck you!"

Together, they tossed her in the trunk, then Bo-T quickly hustled back into the Honda and concealed himself behind the tinted windows. Wizz sat on the hood of the car with the book bag and rolled another blunt. Right when he finished rolling up, a silver Hummer pulled into the parking spot in between Shanice's car and the Honda.

DJ Cocaine hopped out with a duffle bag and walked around the front of his car to meet Wizz. Bo-T quietly snuck out of the Honda and tiptoed behind the DJ.

"What's up, young soulja?" DJ Cocaine spoke while raising the duffle bag to show he had the money.

WHAM!

Bo-T struck the DJ at the base of his neck, with the butt of his cannon and the DJ crumbled to the floor.

WHAM! WHAM!

Bo-T slapped him two more times in the head and knocked him unconscious. Wizz quickly scooped up the duffle bag and examined its contents.

"Cha-ching!" Wizz blurted. He threw the duffle in the back seat of the Honda and hurried back to the sprawled-out DJ.

Together, they lifted the DJ and threw him in the trunk on top of Shanice. Bo-T lit up the blunt Wizz had rolled while Wizz reached in the book bag he had and retrieved a gas can. Wizz then poured gasoline over the two unconscious bodies and poured the remainder of the can all over the inside of the car. He then slung the empty can in the trunk and wiped his hands on his pants. Bo-T passed the blunt to Wizz and they smoked in silence.

"I should've at least fucked the hoe one more time or got some head," Wizz stated.

"You played, Skee-Skee," Bo-T chuckled.

Wizz took one last pull from the nearly fully smoked blunt and then tossed the remainder into the trunk.

WHOOSH!

The whole car instantly burst into flames. The flames quickly grew higher and brightly illuminated the dark sky.

"Damn, Skee! That's how that shit look in the movies!" Bo-T blurted.

"Usually, in the movies the car always blows up, so I think we need to gone head and clear it, Skeeman!"

They ran inside the Honda Bo-T had quickly hot-wired for the caper, and they quickly swerved away from the hot air and bright flames.

***

Two and a half weeks later

Tampa, FL

"I'm higher than a bitch, Skeeman-Geeman!" Wizz laughed.

Bo-T joined the laughter and said, "Skeecho, we have lift off!"

"Planet Skee is approaching," Wizz joked.

"One small step for Skee, one giant step for Skee kind," Bo-T laughed.

"You want bacon or sausage with your eggs, papi?" Sugar asked from the kitchen.

"Bacon, bacon and more bacon!" Wizz shouted.

Bo-T and Wizz were chilling on the couch in the living room of Sugar and Spice's small duplex in Highland Pines. Like always, they were smoking like chimneys and laughing about nothing. Sugar was in the kitchen cooking breakfast for Wizz, and Spice was sitting on a single sofa doing laundry.

After adding twenty-five grand to their stash, they decided to cool off in Tampa and after one thing led to another, they found themselves spending the night with the twins. One night led to two nights, and two nights led to two weeks, and now they were comfortable.

The twins loved their company and the Skee gang didn't mind their company either. To make it all better, they had been serving all their product, not only around the twin's neighborhood, but also in the strip joint where the twins worked. They would give the twins a package every night to take in and every night they would come back with no work and bundles of cash. Their new set-up turned out to be a gold mine. Great pussy and consistent money circulation. Win-win situation.

The television in front of them was on *Bay News 9*, and the image of the dirty home on the dirty street looked so familiar, Wizz had to pick up the remote and turn up the volume.

"The two victims that were found murdered yesterday in their home have now been identified as thirty-two-year-old Mason Wilmer and his younger brother, twenty-nine-year-old Michael Wilmer. Investigators are saying the decomposition of the bodies suggest the victims may have been deceased for nearly three weeks. Neighbors and other residents in the West Tampa neighborhood claim to have not heard or seen anything suspicious in the last three weeks. Police say they have fingerprints for two possible suspects, but those fingerprints haven't produced any information so far. Police are now asking for help in bringing justice to a horrible crime. If anyone has any news or leads, then please call in with any useful tips that may help bring justice to the family."

The red-haired white woman then politely ended her segment, and the screen changed to a middle-aged white man, talking about some new plague going around the world called COVID-19, or the Coronavirus.

"Oh shit! Sugar, did you hear that? That's Mason and Big Mike!" Spice blurted from the sofa.

"Yeah, I heard, fuck them niggas! Big Mike was okay, but he tips like a broke nigga and Mason was always so damn disrespectful," Sugar replied, while bringing Wizz his breakfast.

"Did y'all know them?" Spice asked Bo-T and Wizz.

"Never heard of them," Bo-T calmly answered. He gave Wizz a quick look and Wizz responded by shrugging his shoulders and stuffing his mouth with bacon and eggs.

Spice shrugged as well and said, "Well, on another note, it's supposed to be a big party going down at Whisky North, and I think Lil Baby supposed to perform."

"That shit gone be live!" Sugar added.

"Y'all wanna go?" Spice asked everybody.

Bo-T looked at Wizz for his opinion and Wizz blurted out, "Hell yeah! That nigga Lil Baby got dumb sauce! I'm fucking with fool."

"Alright, when is it?" Bo-T questioned.

"Friday night," Spice answered.

"Sounds like a plan," Bo-T ended.

Fly Rock

Chapter 11

Tallahassee, FL

One day later

Former federal agent Matthew Fisher leaned back in his recliner and ran his hands through his salt and pepper hair. He loosened his belt and allowed his gut to hang more freely. He wasn't entirely out of shape, but he hadn't been in the field for so long that he had unconsciously let himself go, and his newly given free time had given him the opportunity to notice.

Fisher had no wife, no kids, and he lived by himself. He was basically a recluse and the agency had been his entire life for the past twenty-three years.

"I've got to get my fucking job back," he mumbled out loud. "Shit ain't making no sense. I know for a fact that not a single person was left behind. I personally watched the obliteration of every life form on that whole compound. I've got to figure something out . . . I just need to relax and think things through. I'm a thinker. That's what I've always gotten paid for. Thinking! So, calm down and start thinking."

He opened up the newspaper folded on top of his coffee table and searched for the article he had read earlier in the morning.

"It's a shot in the dark, but it seemed kind of interesting. So, fuck it, why not?" He dialed the phone number given at the bottom of the article.

"Hillsborough Homicide Unit, how may I help you?" a woman, with boredom in her voice answered.

Fisher looked at the name printed next to the phone number, then said, "Good afternoon, ma'am. I'm looking for Detective Jeremy Jenkins."

"May I ask your purpose, sir?" the woman asked.

"Yes, ma'am. I'm trying to deliver possible information on a homicide case your detective is in charge of. His name and this number were given out to the public if anybody had tips," Fisher explained.

"Okay, hold for a minute please and I'll connect you through."

Fisher waited patiently for about two minutes and finally a husky male voice spoke into his ear. "Hillsborough Homicide Unit, Detective Jenkins, how may I assist you?"

"Good afternoon, Detective, I'm with the FBI. My name is Agent Fisher and I'm calling with interest of a homicide investigation you're in charge of. I have a few questions on the double homicide if you don't mind me asking."

"Why would the FBI be even slightly interested in a Tampa homicide?" Jenkins curiously asked.

"Well, I read your news article and I have strong interest in these mysterious fingerprints you claim to have. Could you give me a little insight on that?"

The phone went silent for a moment while Jenkins contemplated discussing his case. He quickly decided he had nothing to lose, since he had no leads anyway, so he broke the silence. "Well, it's simple really. We're assuming nobody came in the house after the murders, and the cell phones we have from the victims, show us how long they've been missing calls. With that being said, we found two sets of fingerprints around the house and on the door handles, that do not belong to the deceased, and overlap the other groups of prints on the door handles.

"So, we're assuming our suspects were the last to enter and exit, and therefore the two sets of prints must be theirs. We also have ballistic reports that confirm two different weapons were used in the crime. That increases our assumptions. Now, the problem with the prints is, they appear to be nothing more than prints. No history behind them at all. No records on either print, and that brings us to a dead end."

"That's interesting. Do you have any ideas on why the prints are producing no leads?"

"Well, the only sensible assumptions would be that my perps clearly don't have an arrest record. And all that means is it will take more time to find them. It's a very large world and the identity of my prints could belong to anybody. We would have to trace the fingerprints back to birth and that's a little out of our league. Maybe you hot shots in the bureau could help us with that?"

"I'll check with my sources and see if we can give you a hand on that. If so, I'll give you another call. Other than that, I appreciate the insight."

"Did my insight give you any further interests?"

"Unfortunately, Detective, no. No, it didn't. But there was no harm in making sure. You know how it is."

"Yeah, I guess so. Well, remember to keep me in mind if you can give me that hand."

"Will do," Fisher replied and ended the call. *Definitely interesting, but not nearly interesting enough. Oh well, worth a try*, he thought.

Fly Rock

Chapter 12

Tampa, FL

Three Days Later

Bo-T slipping into his peanut butter brown Timberland boots and completed his outfit. He had on some beige Christian Dior jeans, and a peanut butter brown Christian Dior shirt. His Louis Vuitton belt was beige and brown and his jewelry game was the icing on the cake. His pockets were on swole, and he was ready for a good night.

Wizz was sitting next to Bo-T on the couch and scrolling through his phone. He had on a cocaine white Versace V-neck t-shirt that fit him perfectly, and was neatly tucked behind a large Medusa head belt buckle. His belt was looped through his platinum-colored Balmain jeans and his jeans were perfectly perched on top of his brand-new cocaine white Timberlands. His teeth were gleaming, and the rest of his shiny accessories made him look like a rapper.

"What's up with the Skeebabies?" Bo-T questioned.

"They playing, let me check," Wizz replied then rose from the couch. He walked up to Spice's bedroom door and lightly knocked.

"Come in!" Spice shouted.

Wizz stepped into the room and saw Spice sitting on her bed, with her thick thighs on full display. Her thick pussy was peeking out under her short, black strapless Gucci dress. She had a red Gucci bag hanging off her bare shoulder and her bag matched her red Gucci heels.

"Sugar's in the bathroom taking forever," Spice informed.

Wizz tapped on the bathroom door and Sugar shouted, "I'm almost ready!"

Wizz opened the door and stepped in.

Sugar was sitting on the toilet rubbing a strawberry scented lotion up and down her thick golden legs. She had on the same exact outfit as Spice, but her dress came with spaghetti straps that made her dress hang slightly lower. That small feature made it seem like her big juicy titties were about to burst out at any moment.

"Damn, them some big titties!" Wizz blurted and laughed.

Sugar jiggled her breasts with her hands and said, "They 38-DD, papi . . . You like?"

"Hell yeah! I call double-D's, da-dayums!" Wizz laughed.

Sugar laughed and then pulled her dress down and her 38 da-dayums fell out. She lifted one of her breasts and licked her large pacifier nipple. She then lifted her other breast and gave her other nipple a lick. She pushed her breasts together with both hands and said, "Slide your dick between them, papi."

"Damn baby, we gone be late," Wizz spoke while unbuckling his belt. As soon as he wiggled his pants and boxers down, his dick sprang out and bounced in her face.

Sugar kissed the tip of his dick and spit on the shaft. She rubbed her spit around his dick with one hand, until it was completely wet and shiny. She then spit on her titties and rubbed the spit between her cleavage. "Come on, papi," she hissed.

She squeezed her wet breasts back together and Wizz slipped his dick right between them. His dick disappeared under her breasts and then reappeared on the top. He pulled back and began stroking her breasts like a pussy.

Sugar stuck her tongue out and licked the head of the dick every time it popped out the top of her large breasts. Wizz pulled his dick away from her chest and aimed it for her mouth. She opened her mouth wide, and he stuffed his dick straight into the back of her throat. She made a gagging noise, and then his dick slipped further into her throat and disappeared.

"Damn!" Wizz whispered. He pulled back and began slowly stroking her throat with his dick.

She kept her eyes locked on his face and accepted every stroke into her throat. Spit began dripping and leaking down her chin and soaking her breasts. His dick started to throb in her throat, and he picked up the pace.

Sugar moaned and made choking noises every time his dick stuffed her throat. Wizz grabbed the back of her head and pushed her face into his lap while still pumping her mouth.

"Will y'all hurry up!" Spice shouted from the bedroom. "I can hear y'all!"

Sugar's throat felt amazing but for some reason, Wizz's dick wouldn't release its slimy dessert. Wizz slowly eased his dick out of Sugar's throat and her mouth made a plopping noise as his dick escaped her lips.

"Damn, papi! My throat feels loose as fuck," Sugar spoke, while wiping the saliva off her lips and chin. "You fucked up my make-up!" she added.

"Bend over, bae," Wizz lustfully stated.

"No papi, we gone miss the show!" Sugar spoke while wiping her breasts with a baby wipe and fixing her dress. She stood up over the sink and started reapplying her lipstick.

"Come on, bae," Wizz whispered while pushing his dick against her forty-eight-inch ass. He tried to lift her dress up and she swatted his hand away.

"No papi," she giggled.

"Alright, don't worry about it. I got something for yo ass when we get back," Wizz mumbled while stuffing his dick back inside his Versace boxers.

They quickly got themselves back together and then hustled out the bathroom.

"About damn time!" Spice blurted when they entered the living room.

Sugar simply laughed and together, everybody left the house.

"We'll meet y'all there," Spice stated and hopped in the driver's seat of her cherry red 2019 Mustang GT 5.0, as Bo-T and Wizz hopped in their latest rental car, which was a 2019 black and white Challenger.

Thirty minutes later, they were creeping through the parking lot in front of Whisky North, looking for a parking spot. The sea of cars was a clear indication that the club was beyond packed.

The twins found a slot in the middle, and Wizz and Bo-T found an available spot way in the back. They met up at the front and headed for the VIP line.

The twins looked so juicy in their Gucci dresses, they caused the entire line to break their necks as they walked by. Everybody wanted a chance to see the way their asses jiggled with every stride. Both men and women had their eyes glued to the ass cheeks threatening to burst out the bottom of the black dresses.

"It's kind of late for the line to still be wrapped around the building," Spice stated.

They approached the bouncer and Wizz paid a healthy tip that got the four of them quickly ushered inside with no hesitation. As soon as they entered the building, they could feel the loud music vibrating in their chests.

The twins immediately dashed towards the dance floor and started turning up. Since they were already well-experienced strippers, it was no surprise to see the way they made their basketball booties bounce and clap together. They shook their asses but only danced with each other. Even though they didn't have a relationship status with Bo-T and Wizz, they didn't want to disrespect the relationship they were building on, so they sometimes politely and sometimes arrogantly denied every man that approached them.

Wizz and Bo-T bopped through the crowd and were just as turnt up as everyone else. A flock of hoes kept gravitating towards them everywhere they went, and they acknowledged all the attention by grabbing handfuls of ass from every chick that pushed up on them.

A bunch of shouting suddenly emerged from a crowd of people by the bar, and it grabbed Bo-T's attention.

"Check it out Skeebo, that red nigga over there kind of look like you!" Bo-T shouted over the music and pointed towards the bar.

A slim red nigga with wavy hair was standing on top of one of the counters with a duffle bag going nuts. He was reaching inside the bag and pulling out wads of cash. He threw the wads into the air and before the bills hit the floor, he was showering the crowd with more.

"Bra, that nigga don't look like me at all. You got me fucked up" Wizz seriously stated.

Bo-T started laughing and before he could say another word, the entire club went black. Bright blue lights popped up on the stage over the dance floor, and the crowd went wild when Lil Baby stepped into the lights.

"How y'all doing tonight?" Lil Baby asked into the mic.

The crowd erupted with noise.

Lil Baby lifted up his wrist to show off his diamond flooded watch and right on cue, the DJ dropped a beat and Lil Baby started rapping. "All of my diamonds they VV's! They don't want to see us on TV unless it's the news, I got something to proove! Yeah, I'm young but got something to lose! In these streets I done paid all my dues! No extortion, ain't talking bout lyrically. I be walking on beats is you hearing me! I just pray that my kids be as big as me they can't get rid of me! My diamonds they VV's!"

Wizz and Bo-T rushed into the crowd and started bouncing to the music.

When the song was over, Lil Baby quickly switched over and began singing. "We started off as close friends. Somehow, you turned into my girlfriend. We used to tell each other everything. I even went and bought her diamond rings. Matching earrings. Everything was so cool. Lately, baby been acting so rude. I don't know what somebody told you. But I ain't gone lie I miss the old you."

Wizz and Bo-T felt hands suddenly wrap around their waist and they found themselves being held by the twins. They pulled the twins closer and began slowly dancing to the lyrics.
Niggas were silently envying them, and bitches were quietly hating on the twins.

When that song went off and Lil Baby began to rap his next song, Bo-T tapped Wizz and said, "Aye, check it out, Skee. That lil red nigga sliding with them duffles."

Wizz looked around and caught the red nigga exiting the club with two duffle bags in hand.

"We'll be back," Bo-T quickly stated to the twins. He and Wizz then rushed away through the crowd. They quickly made their exit and began looking around. "Where that nigga at, Skee?" Bo-T questioned.

"There he go right there!" Wizz blurted and pointed across the parking lot.

"Bring the car around, Skee! I got him!" Bo-T blurted.

Wizz quickly dashed across the parking lot in the opposite direction towards the Challenger, and Bo-T quickly but quietly snuck up on the red nigga.

The red nigga was bent over leaning inside his car through the driver's side door when Bo-T crept up behind him.

WHAM! *WHAM*!

Bo-T slapped the red nigga in the back of the head with his trusty cannon and the red nigga fell face-first into the car.

"Ahh shit!" the red nigga shouted.

"Shut yo soft ass up before I smoke yo mothafuckin boots out this bitch!" Bo-T grimaced. "Where the fuck them bags at?"

"They in the trunk, bra!"

"Well, why the fuck yo scary ass ain't pop the trunk yet?" Bo-T shouted.

The red nigga pushed a button, and the trunk made a quiet "pop" noise.

"Get the fuck up!" Bo-T ordered.

"Come on, bra, don't kill me!" The red nigga pleaded.

"Nigga, shut the fuck up, and I'll think about it! Now go get them bags out the trunk!"

Wizz pulled up behind the money green Camaro and came to a halt.

The red nigga reached inside the trunk and pulled out the two duffles he had just put in, and handed them to Bo-T.

"Get yo soft ass in the trunk! Sweet ass nigga!" Bo-T demanded.

"Come on, bra, I gave you what I got."

"Nigga, shut the fuck up and get in the trunk!"

WHAM!

The red nigga fell backwards and fell halfway into the trunk, so he grabbed his face and climbed the rest of the way in.

"Sweet ass, nigga. Fuck you!" Bo-T blurted.

BOOM! BOOM!

Two shots to the head guaranteed a closed casket. Bo-T dove into the Challenger and Wizz mashed the gas. They swerved out of the lot and merged into the midnight traffic.

"Where you wanna go?" Wizz questioned while checking the rearview mirror to make sure they didn't have any unwanted company.

"Get us back to the twins' spot," Bo-T decided.

While Wizz put them on course, Bo-T leaned back in his seat and sent a quick text to Spice. "Y'all go ahead and hangout. Wizz wasn't feeling well, so we're heading back to the house. Enjoy your night."

When they parked in front of the twins' house, Bo-T grabbed the two duffles and they entered the house.

"Let's see what we got, Skee," Bo-T stated and sat down in the living room. He unzipped both duffles and dumped them out.

"BUMMMMBACLOT!" Wizz screamed.

Bo-T grabbed a handful of cash and jumped up, singing, "I really run it up! Baby! If the topic is money, I'm coming up!"

Wizz grabbed a handful of cash as well and started singing "Heart been broke so many times, I-I-I don't know what to belieeeeve!"

"Let's add it up, Skeecho-Freethrow!" Bo-T blurted.

"We looking good, Moneyman-Skeeman!" Wizz blurted back.

"Damn right, Skeecho-Peepshow."

"Absolutely right, Freakman-Skeeman."

"Skeecho-Macho!"

"Jumpman-Skeeman!"

Bo-T burst out laughing. "Alright, alright, Skee. Real shit, let's count this paper. Roll up!"

Wizz rolled up a blunt thicker than his thumb and put it in the air. When the blunt went out they were still counting up money so Wizz rolled another blunt and put it in rotation.

They were damn near too high to concentrate, but they made it through and bust their new riches evenly down the middle. The total came to forty-two thousand apiece. "We're moving up Skeecho!" Bo-T slurred.

"Hell yeah!" Wizz replied and tossed his half into one of the duffles. "I'm about to take it in, Skee." He grabbed his duffle bag and walked towards Sugar's room.

Bo-T grabbed his healthy duffle and wobbled his way to Spice's room.

Wizz threw his bag under the bed and crashed onto Sugar's soft mattress. As soon as his head hit the pillow, he was dead to the world.

Chapter 13

"Good morning, J.J.," the busty blonde receptionist cheerfully greeted.

"Good morning," Detective Jenkins somberly replied.

"Is everything okay? You don't sound too happy this morning."

"Everything is fine, Joyce. I just had a long night."

"Alright. Well, a new file came in this morning and I put it on your desk," Joyce informed.

Jenkins nodded his head and entered his office. He sat down at his desk and released a heavy sigh. "I've got paperwork stacked to the fucking ceiling! I'm still struggling with my last case and now I've got to deal with this bullshit! Fuck my life!" He grabbed the new stack of paperwork and pulled the sticky note off the cover of the file and read the address. "Might as well move now," he sighed.

He straightened out his sloppy desk and rose to his feet. He threw on his jacket and stepped back out the office. "Forward all my calls, Joyce. I'll be back by lunch."

He hopped on an elevator and on the way down to the garage, he thought, *my wife would kill me if she knew I had this big-breasted bimbo working for me.*

He breezed through the garage, climbed into his Ford Explorer and cruised towards his destination.

Twenty-three minutes later, he was cruising into a parking lot flooded with police cruisers, medical examiners and forensic specialists. He drove through the maze of yellow tape and quickly found parking. All attention appeared to be on a green Camaro.

Jenkins approached the crime scene and quickly produced his badge. "Homicide Unit, Detective Jenkins. What've we got?"

A uniformed officer took a quick glance at the detective's credentials, then replied, "Black male found murdered in his trunk. Two shots to the head. No bullet casings. No witnesses. Club owner was locking up this morning after a long night and noticed the green Camaro parked over here. Claims he sees this type of thing all the time. People get drunk and hitch rides with people a little more sober. They come back for their car later. He says he approached the car to make sure there wasn't a drunk driver behind the wheel passed out and ended up finding a trail of blood, in between the driver's side door and the trunk. He rushed back into the club and called 9-1-1."

Jenkins scribbled notes on a pad and then asked, "No witnesses at all? Nobody heard anything? Camera footage?"

"Owner says his cameras haven't been working for the past three weeks and apologizes for the inconvenience."

"Alright, I'll come back to you if I find something interesting."

Jenkins approached the Camaro and was confronted by a short and toned brown-skinned woman, with a black jacket that had "FO-RENSICS" written across the back. He flashed his badge again. "Homicide Unit, Detective Jenkins."

Without looking at his badge, she said, "How can I assist you, Detective?"

"Who's leading the forensics team?"

The black woman looked insulted for a moment, then answered, "That would be me. So again, how can I assist you, Detective?"

"My apologies. What can you tell me so far?"

"It's all pretty much black and white. Two gunshot wounds to the face. No shell casings indicate a possible revolver was used, unless we have a smart suspect, but then again, smart suspects don't stuff people in a trunk at the club, possibly in front of everybody. Blood DNA around the vehicle, more than likely belonging to the victim. Most probable motive would be robbery. We'll know more in a day or so. The only possible trace left by a possible suspect is the large handprint located on the trunk where the suspect probably slammed the trunk closed. Like I said, we'll know more in a day or so."

Jenkins transferred all the verbal information onto his note pad and politely thanked the specialist for her time. He swiftly walked back to his truck and made his way back to his office to review his notes and think things over.

***

Sugar turned the volume down on the television and blurted, "Wow! Papi, that's crazy! We were all there last night and didn't even know someone got killed."

"If what they just said on the news is true, then it sounds like nobody knew," Wizz commented.

"Black people can't never end a good night peacefully," Spice stated.

Bo-T looked at Wizz and shrugged.

Wizz's phone started ringing and he glanced at the screen. He quickly answered the phone and said, "What's up, mini-me?"

"I miss you, twin! Where the hell you been at?" Ashley shouted.

"I been out here fucking off with Bo-T. What's up, though? You good?"

"Yeah, I'm good. I really just wanted to let you know that Mikey's here. He got here last night. I don't know how long he'll be here though. I told him you wanted to talk to him, and we got into a big argument."

"Oh, shit. Alright, well try to keep that nigga there and I'll be down there tomorrow."

"Alright, I'll try. Love you!"

"Love you too, mini-me." Wizz unsteadily slid his phone back into his pocket and leaned back on the couch.

"What's up, Ocho-Skeecho? What you shaking for?" Bo-T asked from the other side of the couch where he was weighing up nine ounces of coke.

"That was twin. She say that ugly ass, baboon-looking-ass nigga at the house right now," Wizz informed.

"Oh, yeah! Shit, what you wanna do?"

"I told her to keep that nigga there and we gone pull up some-time tomorrow."

"Say less. Aye, I'll be back though. I need to serve a nigga these nine ounces real quick." Bo-T scooped up Spice's keys and said, "I'm taking the Mustang, I'll be back." He exited the house and then eased into the Mustang. He adjusted the seat to make room for his legs and then began his short journey.

Before long, he was pulling into a neighborhood, and up to a white house. He eased the car up by the mailbox and came to a halt.

The red lever on the side of the mailbox was standing up, so he pulled the flap down and reached inside. He pulled out a brown bag and peered inside. "Looking good," he said to himself and placed the bag of money under his seat.

He replaced the brown bag holding the money, with the brown bag containing the coke and lowered the red lever, which signaled to the people in the house the transaction was complete.

He pulled away briskly and noticed a dark green Yukon cruising behind him. He bent two corners to see if he was being followed and by the time he turned the second corner, the green Yukon was joined by two police cruisers with red and blue lights flashing on the top.

"Oh shit!" Bo-T blurted. He mashed his foot against the gas pedal and the Mustang's engine began roaring as he turned another corner and gunned it down a straightaway.

The cruisers and the Yukon began slowing down and giving him distance, because they didn't want to drive recklessly through a residential neighborhood.

Bo-T swerved around two more corners and then punched the Mustang through traffic across an intersection and entered another neighborhood. The police screeched to a halt at the intersection to avoid crashing and Bo-T lost them.

He quickly made his way to the twins' neighborhood and parked by the entrance. He grabbed his pistol and the bag of money, and quickly wiped the car down with some baby wipes Spice kept in her glove compartment. He then jumped out the car and sprinted back to the twins' house.

As soon as he burst through the door, he blurted out "Skeecho, we cho need to go-go! Like right now!"

Wizz noticed Bo-T's heavy breathing and the urgency in his voice and said, "Like right now, as in right-right now?"

"Right now, as in right-right-right now!" Bo-T shouted and threw the keys at Spice. "Aye, call the police and tell them yo car just got stolen!" he told her.

"What? Why?" Spice blurted in confusion.

"Let's ride, Skeecho!" Bo-T blurted and jetted for Spice's room.

Wizz sprang off the couch and ran to Sugar's room.

Second later, they were both sprinting out the door with their duffle bags of cash and jumping in the rental Challenger. Bo-T urgently swerved away and while they were exiting the neighborhood, the police were turning in and blitzing the bright red Mustang with the door swung wide open.

"Damn, Skee! What happened?" Wizz questioned.

"I think them niggas tried to set me up or something! I don't know, bra. After I made the play, troll jumped behind me and I had to skram, Skee!"

"Alright, so where we going now?"

"We might as well slide to yo city now and crash at Kat's new spot," Bo-T suggested.

"Let's do it," Wizz replied and leaned his seat back to make himself comfortable for the ride.

***

Ding-Dong! Ding- Dong!

"Give me a second, I'm coming!" Sugar shouted from the living room. She slowly cracked the door open and poked her head out. "May I help you?"

Two uniformed officers were standing on her porch, and one was holding a piece of paper, with a photo printed on the front. The officer glanced at the photo, glanced back at Sugar and said, "Stephanie Santiago, mind if I ask you a few questions?"

"My name isn't Stephanie Santiago," Sugar replied.

The officer looked at the photo again, and then turned it around for Sugar to see. "So, you're saying this isn't you?"

Sugar glanced at the photo and said, "That's exactly what I'm saying."

"Listen, we don't have time for your bullshit!"

Sugar opened the door wider and revealed Spice sitting on the sofa. "That's Stephanie, my sister. My name is Samantha," Sugar stated with an attitude.

The two officers looked back and forth between the twins and shared a surprised look. "I'm very sorry, Ms. Santiago. Well, can I have a word with your sister please?"

"Yes?" Spice asked.

"Good evening, Ms. Santiago, can you please tell me who was last driving your car?" the officer quizzed.

"What kind of question is that? Nobody drives my car but me," Spice answered.

"So, where is your car right now?"

"Right there," Spice pointed to an empty slot behind the officers. "Hold on, what the fuck! Where the fuck is my car?" Spice shouted and ran out the door. She began screaming and making a scene and acting like she had no idea her car was missing.

The officers calmed her down and began asking her a series of questions. After about twenty minutes of going in circles with questions, the officer stated, "Okay, so let me make sure I have this correct. You went grocery shopping this morning and after that, you've been in the house all day with your sister? Neither one of you left the house, or stepped outside in between then and now, and you had no knowledge your car was missing until just now?"

"That's right," Spice plainly stated.

"You don't seem to be upset anymore," the officer noted.

"That's because now I'm trying to figure out why y'all ain't brought me back my shit yet? You show up at my door, telling me my car was stolen, but you have it and you haven't brung it back yet. How that sound?"

"It's kind of funny though how we found your car right in the front of your neighborhood though, isn't it?"

"I wouldn't give a damn if you found it stuck up yo ass! I said what I had to say, now where is my car?"

"It was being fingerprinted. Got wiped down pretty good apparently, because they barely found your fingerprints, let alone the suspect of the high-speed chase. But your car should be returned within the next hour."

"Alright, well, is that it?" Spice asked.

The officer looked at his notes and said, "Yeah, that's all for now. I guess we'll just leave the situation alone."

The officers then thanked them for their wasted time and left.

Fly Rock

Chapter 14

Orlando, FL

Bo-T pulled into the Nassau Bay apartments in Rosemont and made his way to Kat's new apartment.

"I used to live in these apartments. It was called The Brittanys back then though. This shit rachet," Wizz spoke.

"I heard a lot of hoes stay out here," Bo-T commented.

"Hell, yeah!" Wizz blurted.

Bo-T parked the Challenger and told Wizz, "I'ma return this rental tomorrow and see if I can grab us a new one."

"Works for me," Wizz commented.

They walked up the stairs to Kat's third floor apartment and Bo-T lightly knocked on the door.

Bo-T looked around and said, "This shit look kind of clean out here."

"Fuck no! It's just dark right now. This rachet ass shit dirty as fuck," Wizz informed. "This shit Section Eight."

Kat opened the door with a baby in her arms and stepped to the side to let them in. She locked the door behind them and followed them into the living room. "Make yourselves comfortable."

Wizz sat down on the couch and Bo-T walked into the kitchen.

"What you got to eat in this bitch? I'm starving like Marvin," Bo-T spoke.

"It's all type of shit in there. Hang out," Kat replied while taking a seat on the couch next to Wizz.

"You had a baby?" Wizz joked.

"Nigga, when you seen me pregnant?" Kat stated.

"Shit, it look like yo big ass booty was pregnant," Wizz laughed.

Kat started laughing and said, "Boy, whatever! I'm babysitting for my neighbor while she's at work."

"Oh, okay. So, where I'm sleeping at?" Wizz questioned.

"In the bed with me, duhhh!" Kat stated with a grin. "Aye cousin, I forgot to tell you. Our lil cousin World called me earlier. I told him you had come home from prison, and he was so excited. He told me to give you his number and for you to call him ASAP," she told Bo-T.

"You talking about Lil Petey?" Bo-T asked.

"Yeah, you know he lives in West Palm Beach now."

"Damn, that's what's up. I ain't seen that lil nigga since he was a youngin. How old that nigga is now?"

"He twenty-five now."

"Damn, you think he gone answer this late?"

"Hell yeah, call him," Kat said and pointed to her phone on the counter.

Bo-T picked up the phone and scrolled through her contacts. He found the number for World and headed to one of the back rooms he would be sleeping in.

Wizz was staring at Kat's dark juicy thighs on full display and his eyes locked in on the fat pussy print her tiny purple shorts couldn't hide.

"You ain't got to stare. It ain't gone bite you unless you want it to," Kat joked. She then spread her legs open a little to give him a better view of how her shorts were jacked up in her pussy.

"Damn! You gone fuck around and get yoself in trouble if you keep playing," Wizz joked.

"In trouble with who? Nigga, I'm grown. I do what I please and who I please."

Wizz shook his head and said "How you been doing out here in your new spot? You like it?"

"Yeah, it has pros and cons. I like the privacy and I like being independent, but this shit be sucking me dry and that's frustrating. After I pay my bills and everything else, I don't ever have anything left over for myself. I've got a shit load of free time and can't even enjoy it," Kat vented.

Wizz reached in his pocket and pulled out a thick stack of blue hundreds. He peeled two grand off his knot and handed it to Kat." Here. Enjoy yourself."

"You ain't gotta give me nothing. I'll manage."

"That ain't the point. I want you to be able to hang out a little bit. You deserve it."

Kat accepted the money and said, "Thank you, Wizz. I really appreciate it."

Bo-T walked back into the living room with a blunt hanging from his lips and said, "I think I left my lighter in the car. Throw me a light, Skeechobob."

Wizz reached in his pocket for his lighter and Kat blurted, "Oh, hell naw. You know I love to smoke too, but you can't smoke in here while I'm babysitting. You gone have to take that shit outside, cuzzo."

"Why I gotta go outside? Why the baby can't go outside?" Bo-T joked.

"Not funny," Kat stated.

"Alright, whatever. Let's step outside, Skeewee," Bo-T spoke and headed for the door.

Wizz jumped up and followed him out. They took the stairs down to the second floor and sat in the middle of the staircase. Bo-T fired up the blunt and they began to relax their nerves.

Bo-T looked down the steps and saw an older, strung-out-looking white man smoking a cigarette. The white man threw his head up at Bo-T, and Bo-T nodded back.

"You on the clock?" the white man asked.

"What you mean by that?" Bo-T questioned.

"You got any work? I'm tryna party."

"Your party hard or party soft?"

"I like to party like a rockstar."

"Alright, what you looking for?"

"Think you can hook me up with a seven?"

"Yeah. I got you, give me a minute," Bo-T stated and handed Wizz the blunt. He walked back up the stairs and disappeared.

Wizz stayed seated and enjoyed the blunt until Bo-T returned and walked down the steps to meet the white man.

After making the exchange and receiving the money, the white man said, "You got a number I can reach you at if I enjoy the party?"

"Yeah, take this number down," Bo-T replied and gave the man his number.

The white man walked inside an apartment on the first floor and Bo-T rejoined Wizz.

"Damn, Skee! You smoked the whole blunt! Roll up another one," Bo-T stated.

"Man, I'm higher than a kite. Go ahead and hang out, I think I'ma lay it down," Wizz spoke.

"Alright. Say less, I'll catch you in the a.m.," Bo-T replied.

"Aye, I think yo lil cousin wanna fuck me," Wizz blurted.

"Shit, duhhh. Her hot ass talk about you all the time."

"So, you don't care?"

"Hell naw, nigga! That's on y'all. Shit, show her that Skee-chomeatshow!"

Wizz laughed and said, "I'll catch you tomorrow, Skee!"

***

The loud ringing from Bo-T's phone caused him to jump up out his sleep. He clumsily felt around the bed for his phone and then looked at the caller ID. He didn't recognize the number, but he answered anyway. "What's up?"

"Is this Bo?" a raspy voice asked.

"Bo? Who the fuck is this?" Bo-T questioned.

"It's John."

"Who the fuck is John?"

"I met you on the staircase in front of my apartment last night and you invited me to a party, remember?"

"Ohhh, yeah yeah, what's up John?"

"Dude, I ain't been to a party like that in years! I ain't been to sleep yet! I'm tryna see if you can keep me going?"

"Where you at?"

" I'm sitting at the bottom of the same staircase."

"Alright stay there and I'll come holla at you." Bo-T ended the call and sat up in bed. He grabbed a blunt off the dresser, some weed from his pocket and rolled up. He then stepped outside and took the stairs down to meet John. "What's good? What you looking for?"

"Listen, I gave you all my cash last night, but I've got a fully loaded Visa and I'll get you whatever you want," John offered.

"How much you trying to actually spend though?"

"Whatever you can supply, I'll cover! I'm falling asleep and I need to wake back up!"

Bo-T thought about it for a second and said, "Alright, check it out. Can you get me a rental car?"

"Fuck yeah, dawg! Absolutely! Just let me know what kind and for how long."

Bo-T gave John a model and a time frame, and John quickly fumbled for his keys and hustled to his car.

"I'll be right back with it. Treat me right, dog," John spoke.

"Everything will be ready when you return," Bo-T replied.

John hurried off and Bo-T sparked his blunt. His phone rang again, and he quickly answered. "What's up, Spice?"

"Are you okay, papi?"

"Yeah, I'm good. Did everything go fine on your end?"

"Yeah, it's all good. The police showed up at my door before I could call them, but they eventually dropped the subject and brought me back my car. No worries."

"Did they say who they were looking for? Did they have a description?"

"No papi, they said the car got wiped down so good, they couldn't even find my prints. Everything is cool."

"Alright, that's good news then."

"Papi, I found a book bag in my closet full of your stuff. What do you want me to do with it?"

"Damn! I forgot all about that shit. I thought I had that shit in the car. I was moving so fast. Uhh, I tell you what. Just move everything in the club and have the bread waiting on me when I come back. Can I trust you with that?"

"Of course, papi! I got you, but when will you be back?"

"I'm not sure yet. Me and Wizz still got a few things to handle, but I'll let you know."

"Okay. Well, I'll talk to you later, papi. I know it's early, I really just wanted to ask you about the bag real quick."

"It's all good. I'll holla," Bo-T stated and hung up. He tossed the remainder of his blunt on the floor and stared off into the distance. *I can't believe I left all that dope over there*, he thought.

Wizz came walking out the apartment and joined Bo-T on the steps. "What's good, Skeeman? I missed the wake and bake?" Wizz asked.

"You got yo own weed, nigga. Smoke that shit," Bo-T joked.

Wizz pulled out a blunt and began the rolling process, while Bo-T told him about all the dope he left at the twins' house.

Wizz fired up the blunt and said, "Well, if they handle business, then we've got ourselves a pair of keepers. If they play, shit, we throw 'em with the fishes."

Bo-T nodded his head and said, "I'm saying though. So, you finally gave Kat freaky ass what she looking for?"

"Man, hell naw! That shit went sour, Skee. She had that flaw ass, cock-blocking ass baby laying there crying the whole damn night!"

"Aww man, you played, Skee." Bo-T laughed.

The moment Wizz finished his blunt, a black Dodge Charger Hell Cat pulled in front of the building and parked. John hopped out and tossed Bo-T the keys.

"You got it for two weeks," John stated.

"Alright, cool. Give me a five minutes," Bo-T replied and winked at Wizz.

They both walked back into the apartment and Bo-T quickly put together a care package in exchange for the rental. Bo-T stepped back outside and was back inside in seconds.

"I'ma tell Kat to return the Challenger later. A nigga hungry as fuck right now though. You wanna slide out and grab something?" Bo-T spoke.

"Hell, yeah! This the perfect time to slide through Judy's!" Wizz replied.

"What the fuck is Judy's?"

"Just chill, Skee. It's a lil hood spot that serve breakfast and lunch."

"Alright, well put some clothes on and we out of here. I'm about to put all our shit in the Charger," Bo-T stated.

"You damn sho don't mind riding dirty," Wizz joked.

"Tell the feds if they coming, they better come now!" Bo-T joked back.

Wizz stepped into Kat's room to gather his clothes and saw Kat sitting up on the bed, feeding the cock-blocking cry baby a bottle of milk.

"Where you going?" Kat questioned.

"I'm about to grab some breakfast. You want me to bring you something back?"

"Hell yeah! I'd appreciate it."

"You need to get rid of the flaw ass baby," Wizz stated with a straight face.

Kat laughed and said, "It's okay, we'll be all alone in a few more hours, and I won't be babysitting again until next weekend."

"Yeah, whatever. I'll be back, I got you," Wizz stated and left. He met Bo-T at the Charger and caught him putting the last bag into the trunk.

"Let's ride, Skeecho, you're driving!" Bo-T stated and tossed Wizz the keys.

They began making the drive to the food joint and chit-chatted back and forth about whatever came to mind.

Wizz's phone rang, and he fished it out of his pocket. Without looking, he answered, "Yoo!"

"Twin!" Ashley blurted.

"What's up, mini-me?"

"Are you still coming over today?"

"Yeah, I'll be there sometime later. What's up?"

"I don't know if Mikey will still be here. I just heard him on the phone talking to somebody, and it sounds like he's tryna get a ride."

"Alright, well hold him as long as you can. I'ma try to slide through right now," Wizz stated and hung up. "Change of plans,

Skeeman. It's clobbering time!" Wizz stated while making a U-turn in the middle of the road.

"What's up, Skeecho?" Bo-T questioned.

"Twin says she thinks the ugliest nigga on the planet might be about to leave, so it's now or never."

"Alright, let's go get 'em Skee JoeFrazier!"

Ten thoughtless minutes later, Wizz was turning onto Ashley's street. As soon as he bent the corner, he saw Mikey jump in the passenger seat of a blue Toyota and pull off.

"Don't let that ugly ass nigga get away!" Bo-T blurted.

"I got 'em, Skee!" Wizz assured. His phone rang again, and he quickly answered. "Yoo!"

"I'm sorry, twin, but I couldn't hold him. He just left," Ashley stated.

"It's alright, twin. I'll catch up with fool another time," Wizz spoke while trailing the Toyota.

"Alright, well are you still coming over?"

"Yeah, I'll be there later on. I'm handling something right now, so I'll call you later."

"Alright, love you."

"Love you too!"

Wizz ended his call and followed the Toyota for twenty minutes, until it finally made a right onto Mercy Drive, and then turned into the projects known as The Palms. When the Toyota finally stopped in a parking space in front of one of the project buildings, Wizz quickly stopped his car behind it and boxed them in.

Mikey jumped out of the Toyota, screaming, "What the fuck is yo problem!"

Wizz and Bo-T both quickly hopped out the Charger and Mikey's eyes instantly grew bigger then two golf balls.

Mikey threw his hands in the air in an "I surrender" gesture and said, "Listen, Wizz, I can expla—"

BOOM!

Wizz sent a bullet flying through Mikey's right hand and quickly closed the gap between them.

"Ahh, fuck! What the fuck, man? You shot me!" Mikey cried.

"Shut the fuck up, you ugly ass, thieving-ass fuck nigga!"
WHAM!

"Ugly ass, Daffy Duck ass nigga!" Wizz shouted after another strike.

A crowd quickly began to form as people began to watch the show.

Bo-T decided to get in on the action and slammed his pistol into the bloody face of the thief.

WHAM!

"Dirty ass, Dave Chapelle looking ass nigga!" Bo-T blurted.

WHAM!

"Marshmallow ass nigga!" Wizz blurted.

The driver's door to the Toyota swung open, and a very ugly black woman sprang out, shouting, "Oh, my God, stop! I'ma call the police!"

"What bitch!" Bo-T blurted and quickly pounced on the black woman. He forcefully swung his hand out and slapped the woman across the face harder than Ike slapped Tina. The black woman flew backwards and fell on her bony bottom.

Bo-T stood over her and shouted, "Bitch, if you ever say the word police again, I'ma slap the shit out yo ugly ass until you die! Ugly bitch, if you even dream about the police, I'll show up in yo dreams and make that shit a nightmare! Now sit yo flat booty ass right there and shut the fuck up!" Bo-T cocked his hand back and the thin woman flinched. "That's what I thought, bitch!"

Bo-T then quickly hopped back over to the nearly unconscious Mikey and rejoined the action.

WHAM!

"Ugly ass nigga! Being ugly runs in yo ugly ass family! Look at that ugly ass bitch over there!" Bo-T shouted.

WHAM!

"Ugly ass, black ass, dolphin looking ass nigga!" Wizz blurted.

WHAM!

"Ugly ass, hammerhea—"

"Aye, somebody called the police y'all boys!" someone in the crowd shouted.

"Oh, shit! Skram, Skee, skram!" Bo-T blurted and jumped back in the car.

"If it wasn't so crowded out here, I'd take yo ugly ass on a journey to Atlantis!" Wizz shouted while hopping back in the car. He leaned out the window and shouted, "Soft ass fuck nigga! You softer then a wet piece of bread! I can't even think of nothing softer than that! That shit soft as fuck! And you just got the ugliest, softest nigga in the world award! Fuck nigga!" Wizz mashed the gas and swerved off.

As he turned out of the one-way in the one way out complex, the police were turning in and they slipped right by.

"Alright, now we can swing by Judy's," Wizz chuckled.

"Hell, yeah. I'm extra hungry now! Let's go eat, Skeeli!"

Chapter 15

"I might fuck around and eat Kat shit," Wizz said while smelling the food inside the Judy's bag.

"Kat gone sell yo ass out if you eat her shit! But we can bust that bitch down though and act like we forgot," Bo-T laughed.

"She lucky I'm full," Wizz joked.

Bo-T changed lanes on Pine Hills Road and said, "So what you want to do after we drop this plate off?"

"Probably pull up on twin for a minute and after that, it's whatever."

"Say less. Let's gas up real quick," Bo-T stated while turning into the 7-Eleven gas station on Pine Hills and North Lane. He pulled up to a gas pump and said, "I pay, you pump!" He then hopped out and headed into the convenience store.

Wizz slid out of the passenger seat and walked around the car to the gas tank. He leaned against the trunk and waited on Bo-T while looking around at his environment.

An old school Chevy Impala swerved into the gas station lot and pulled up to the gas pump directly across from Wizz. The Impala had its music blasting and two short, stocky black dudes exited the vehicle. One of them leaped onto the trunk of the car and was occupied with a phone conversation while the other entered the store.

"You don't want this Arizona Tea?" the store clerk asked Bo-T.

"Naw, I changed my mind. I'm good on that," Bo-T replied.

"Alright, well three-ninety-one is your change, sir."

Bo-T accepted his change and headed for the door. The short stocky dude was entering while he was exiting and since the short man made it through the door first Bo-T gave him a little space to walk by.

The stocky man was either very clumsy, or very disrespectful. Either way, he boldly leaned over and stepped directly on Bo-T's foot. Bo-T roughly shoved the short man with so much force, he went flying into a candy rack and sent Skittles and Snicker bars flying all over the floor.

The short man rolled over on the floor and reached for his waistline and that action caused Bo-T to reach for his as well. The store clerk watched the whole scene unfold like an old Western movie as both men pulled out their pistols as quickly as they could.

BOOM! BOOM!

"They call me Quick Draw McGraw, fuck nigga!" Bo-T chuckled. The two shots that pierced the short man's chest left him on the ground gasping for air.

Bo-T turned towards the clerk and saw him hanging up the phone behind the counter. "You just called the police?" he questioned.

"No way, man, no way! The phone just rang, and I hung it up!"

"Lying piece of shit. I ain't hear no damn phone ring!"

BOOM!

A bullet exploded into the clerk's face and sent him crashing into the shelf behind him.

"Fuck!" Bo-T shouted in frustration and ran out the store. He hopped over a dead body in the parking lot and dove into the back seat of the car, while Wizz burnt rubber out of the area.

"Damn, Skee! What the fuck!" Wizz blurted.

"Man, that shit wasn't my fault! Some lil no-neck ass nigga stepped on my new Jordans, so I had to get the lil nigga right! After that, the nigga tried to up on me, but I beat him to the punch. . . or should I say I beat him to the shot!" Bo-T laughed.

"Damn," Wizz simply stated.

"Who the fuck that was outside?"

"Outside where?"

"Nigga, the dead nigga in front of the store!"

"Oh, that was the no-neck nigga's homeboy. I saw them niggas pull up. When the first couple shots rang out, we both looked at the store and the nigga ran towards the entrance. He ain't know I was with you though, so he ran right past me, and I smoked his boots!"

"Damn, this shit wild as fuck! Swerve back to Kat's spot real quick so I can throw her the keys to the Challenger, and then we got to hit it."

"Alright, where we gone slide to?" Wizz asked while racing through traffic.

"We'll figure it out when we get on the highway," Bo-T answered.

***

Wizz turned off on the exit ramp and followed the directions given by Bo-T.

"I ain't never been in West Palm Beach before," Wizz stated while cruising down the busy streets.

"Shit, me neither, but this seems like the perfect time to check it out," Bo-T responded.

They spent about half an hour on the road before finally entering a gated housing community.

"That's the house right there," Bo-T spoke, while pointing to a well-kept, two-story, light green home.

Wizz pulled into the driveway and shut the car off. Bo-T sent a quick text on his phone and seconds later, the front door popped open and a muscular, brown-skinned nigga with a bald head stepped out to greet them.

"Long time, no see, cuzzo! What's good!" Bo-T greeted.

World clapped hands with Bo-T and then threw his arms around him and gave him a brotherly hug. "Welcome home, fam! Damn, it's good to see you."

"I count my blessings every day."

"Man, I thought them crackaz gave you life, cuzzo!"

"Yeah, that's what it was looking like, but God sent me an angel," Bo-T replied.

"What's up, fam?" World said to Wizz and gave him some dap.

"What's good, my nigga, they call me Wizz."

After getting quickly acquainted, World ushered them inside and told them to make themselves comfortable on the couch, while he went upstairs to grab a few blunts.

When World re-entered the living room, Bo-T said, "You got a big ass house, lil bra! You must be moving bricks or something."

"Naw, fam. I used to do my thing, but I done gave all that street shit up. I fucked around and did a three-year bid and that jail shit was for the birds. I'm legit now and I've been doing pretty good for myself. No complaints."

They all smoked two blunts back-to-back and conversated about life until World looked at his watch and said "Oh shit! I got to get ready for work."

"Alright cool, so what is there to do around here?" Bo-T questioned.

"Shit, y'all can hit the mall. It's right down the street. It be plenty of hoes floating around in that bitch."

"Sounds like a plan. What time you get off?"

"I get off around 10:00 pm, so I should be back around 10:30-10:45pm." World then ran back up the stairs and changed into his work clothes. About twenty minutes later, he was walking out the door, saying, "I'll fuck with y'all later on."

**

"I see I'ma have to roll another blunt, because yo wet-mouth ass tryna tax a nigga shit," Bo-T blurted.

"Nigga, whatever! Ain't nobody tryna hog up yo blunt and it ain't my fault my mouth stay wet! I bet yo ass won't complain later," Nina joked and passed Bo-T back the blunt.

Bo-T took the blunt and shook his head. Wizz was sitting on a couch across from Nina and Bo-T, smoking his own blunt with Nina's homegirl Chiquita. They met Nina and Chiquita at the mall earlier, along with another girl and decided to kick it with them at World's spot.

Nina was short and slim, dark and had a pair of pillow-sized titties hanging from her chest. Chiquita was short, thick, high yellow and had a pumpkin booty and golds at the bottom of her mouth. They were both ghetto as hell, but their ghetto attitudes were attractive since Bo-T and Wizz were both into that type of vibe.

Some keys started rattling in the door and World walked into the house with a puzzled look on his face. He looked at Nina and couldn't help but notice that she probably had the largest breasts he had ever seen. He then looked at Chiquita, and his eyes instantly fell down to her wide hips that were sinking into his couch.

"Damn, y'all throwing a party and I wasn't invited?" World joked.

"You looking in the wrong direction, cuzzo. This a personal party," Bo-T blurted.

World grinned and said, "Damn, bra, it's like that?"

"Nigga, you blessed! You got a left hand and a right hand! A lot of people can't say that," Bo-T joked.

Everybody in the room started laughing.

"Ha-ha, very funny," World stated. He dropped down onto a single sofa across from everybody and was about to say something else when the sound of the toilet flushing in his downstairs bathroom grabbed his attention. "What the fuck? It's somebody else in here?"

A pale white woman stumbled out of the bathroom with water splashed all over her face and looking sick.

"Damn girl, you okay?" Nina asked.

The white chick was too dizzy to respond. She just shook her head and held her stomach.

"We need to take her home!" Chiquita blurted.

"It's probably something she ate at the mall" Nina guessed.

"I'm sorry, Wizz, but we need to go," Chiquita announced.

"It's all good, but y'all need to hurry up though! It looks like snowflake about to throw up everywhere," Wizz commented.

Nina jumped up and helped the white girl wobble to the door. Chiquita held the door open, and they helped her to the car. Wizz and Bo-T joined them outside and let them know they would chill another time. After the women drove off, World accompanied them outside and fired up a cigarette.

"Who that white bitch was?" World questioned.

"Shit, that was supposed to be a lil action we picked up for you, but that hoe fucked everything up with her sick ass," Bo-T replied.

"Damn, at least y'all tried. I thought y'all left me hanging for a minute. I'm saying though, why y'all ain't take them hoes to a hotel or something?"

"Because my lil cousin house was free! Duh!" Bo-T laughed.

"Real shit though, these hoes out here shiesty! You gotta watch these Palm Beach hoes."

"I'll remember that next time. Aye, where you work at though?"

"At a check cashing store."

"A check cashing store!" Bo-T blurted.

"Yeah nigga, a check cashing store. No big deal, nothing major."

"Why you ain't been say that shit?"

"What does it matter? I ain't know it was that serious."

"Hell yeah, it's that serious! Me and my nigga might wanna run off in that bitch!"

World looked dumbfounded for a second and then said, "Shit, if y'all niggas dumb enough to rob a check cashing store, then y'all probably dumb enough to rob the money truck that loads it up on the last Friday of every month."

Bo-T looked at Wizz and smiled. Wizz acknowledged his smile with a wink.

Chapter 16

Milton, FL

I don't know why the fuck I even come here, Agent Fisher thought, while walking up the stairs of one of the dorms in the now vacant prison. He slowly walked down the aisles and looked carefully into the cells as he passed by.

He stepped inside one of the cells and looked out the window. There wasn't anything in sight except for gates, trees and a quickly setting sun.

"I've been walking around this bullshit for hours and I ain't seen anything even slightly close to a clue that suggests we may have made a mistake. This is bullshit," Fisher huffed. "Fuck this place. It's getting late and my legs are starting to hurt." He sighed deeply and turned on his heels to leave.

He took a step forward and felt a snag on his feet. He looked down and saw a piece of string snagged on the heel of his left boot. He tried to wiggle off the string and noticed something strange. The string had a weighted tension to it that made it feel like it was possibly attached to something else.

He leaned over, tugged on the string and heard something rattle under the bunk. He got down on his hands and knees and peered under the bunk behind the lockers.

In the midst of dust and spiderwebs was a bundled-up blanket in the far corner behind the bunk. He stretched his arm back as far as he could and felt the blanket on the tips of his fingers. He forced his arm to stretch another inch and was able to grip the blanket.

He yanked the blanket from under the bunk and began coughing when a cloud of dust invaded his nostrils. He got his breathing under control, wiped the cobwebs off his sleeve and untied the blanket.

"What the fuck is all of this?" he spoke to himself. He carefully inspected the small amount of items with interest and quickly gave all his attention to a small photo inside of a blank envelope.

The photo was actually a prison face sheet, which is a black and white mugshot the officers place on the outside of the cell doors to identify who is inside the cell. A face sheet usually has a picture and the name of the inmate, along with other information, but this one had all the information torn off and was a simple cut out of the photo only.

Fisher stared into the colorful eyes of the light-skinned young man and took in his features. It was only a face shot, but the nappy afro and heavily tattooed neck made the young man very distinctive. He folded up the phone and placed it in his pocket. He poked around through the other items and saw nothing else of interest. He then decided that continuing through the prison would be useless now under the dark sky, so he exited the building and made the moderate walk back to his car.

Once he was back inside his Jaguar, he backed away and drove off the prison grounds. He passed a sign that read "Warning! Radioactive zone!" and shook his head.

While driving down a nearly deserted street and turning on to the interstate road that would take him back towards his Tallahassee home, he considered his next move. He fished his phone out and placed a call to one of his old friends that still worked in the agency.

"Yello!" A man answered cheerfully.

"What's going on, Josh?" Fisher responded.

"Fish? Is that you?" Agent Josh questioned.

"Yup, it is I."

"Jesus, Fish, I haven't heard from you since you left the agency. What's going on?" Josh whispered.

"I'm just taking it day by day. Why are you whispering?"

"Because my ass would be grass if I got caught talking to you! You're not exactly a celebrity around here, you know."

"Yeah, well... I need a favor, Josh. Can you help me or not?"

Agent Josh nervously fidgeted at his desk and looked around. "What exactly do you need, Fish? What kind of favor?"

"It's simple, really. I just need you to look up every unsolved crime committed between Milton and Tampa. I only want crimes that have pictures of the suspects and only crimes with two suspects.

Time period between now and the experiment. Can you do that for me, Josh?"

There was a long pause over the phone before Agent Josh said, "Alright, Fish, I'll do it. I'll get what you need, and I'll call you in a few days."

"Thanks, Josh, I appreciate it."

The line went dead, and Fisher quietly finished his ride home.

***

Agent Josh looked around at all his coworkers and watched them as they answered calls and did paperwork. He weighed his options and decided the best thing for him to do would be to cover his own ass.

"Me and Fish are cool, but not that cool," Josh mumbled while reaching for his desk phone. He dialed an extension line and waited.

"What's up, Josh? This better be important," Bossman stated.

"I'm sorry to bother you, Bossman, but I thought you might want to know Fisher just called me."

"Okay... so fucking what! Sounds like you're wasting my time."

"He asked me to help him look up some crimes in some distinctive areas. I don't know what he's getting at, but he's clearly still looking into the experiment."

"Do you seriously think I would let Agent Fisher's dumbass just walk around with all that knowledge in his head? We've been watching Fisher and we know exactly what he's been up to."

"So, you're not worried about him?"

"Fuck no! If anything, his constant snooping and determination might lead him in the right direction and guess what that means? That means if he finds our ghost, then we find our ghost."

"So, do you want me to give him what he requested?"

"Sure, help him out. It might do us some good and if not then oh well. No harm, no foul."

"Alright, Bossman. Sorry to bother you."

"Yeah, whatever."

Chapter 17

West Palm Beach, FL

One week later

"Ooooooohh, yes! Fuck me, baby! Fuck me! Shit… damn! Fuck!" Nina shouted. She bit down on her bottom lip and stuffed her face in the pillow to try and conceal her loud shouts of pleasure, while Bo-T continued to slam himself into her from behind.

"Don't run now! Keep on screaming!" Bo-T grunted and yanked Nina's hair so her head lifted from the pillow.

"Oh, my God, baby! Yes! Fuck me harder, baby! Fuck me!" Nina continued shouting.

The loud shouts from Chiquita caused Bo-T to turn his head and look towards the other bed in their small hotel room.

"Give me that dick, daddy! Give me that dick! Oooh shit, this dick feel so fucking good, daddy, damn!" Chiquita was shouting while bouncing her ass up and down on top of Wizz.

Wizz was holding her by the waist and helping her slam herself up and down on his pole.

Nina tried to stop her heavy breasts from swinging back and forth, but Bo-T was punishing her pussy so good, all she could do was grip the sheets and keep screaming while her body shook, and her pussy leaked from her back-to-back orgasms.

"Damn, I'm to bout nut!" Bo-T blurted and pumped her faster.

"Give me that nut, baby, please!" Nina encouraged him.

He took two final strokes and then buried his seeds deeply inside her very warm garden. "Fuck!" he blurted and then fell backwards on the bed.

Nina let her face fall into the pillow and kept her ass tooted in the air, while breathing deeply and trying to regain control of her shivering body.

Bo-T's phone was on the small table between the two hotel beds and had been vibrating and lighting up for the last hour. The phone had just stopped vibrating when he lifted it from the table. He mumbled to himself, "Who the fuck blowing up my phone."

Forty-one missed calls were flashing on his screen, and they were all from the same person. He was about to toss the phone back down, but it stared to vibrate and flash again. He used his thumb to slide the green icon to the right of the screen and blurted, "I sholl hope somebody died, because I'm obviously busy, and you steady calling my shit like it's my damn birthday or something! What's up?"

"Nigga, I been calling yo stupid ass for over an hour and you got the nerve to say you busy! Nigga, when you see me calling yo black ass, then yo dumb ass need to answer!" Kat shouted in his ear.

"Man, who the fuck you talking to? Matter of fact, fuck that, what the fuck you want? I'm busy!"

"You need to take yo nasty ass on somewhere so I can talk to you, because whatever bitch you got around you gone get yo stupid ass fucked up! And why the fuck yo nasty ass got me on the phone while you fucking!"

Bo-T looked over at Wizz and started laughing. Chiquita was still shouting at the top of her lungs with her legs in the air, and Wizz jumped inside her like a pogo stick.

"That's how you do it, Skee!" Bo-T blurted and laughed. He then let out a sigh and eased off the bed. He put on some shorts and walked out the door. Once everything was quiet, he spoke into the phone. "Alright, happy? Now what the fuck is so important that you got to fuck up my private party?"

"Nigga, yo freedom! That's what! What the fuck is wrong with you? Are you stupid, or are you fucking stupid?"

"Man, what the fuck you want! I'm getting impatient!"

"Nigga, yo face is getting broadcasted on every damn news channel in the world, and you really wanna ask me that? Why the fuck would you do something so fucking stupid? They got the whole thing all over the fucking TV! Clear as day! You killed two people in a fucking gas station and walked out with a dumb ass smile on yo face! You—"

"Whoa! Whoa! Hold up, Kat! Okay, I'm on camera, but what are they saying?"

"Nigga, that's why I been calling yo slow ass! The police came to my damn house and flipped my shit everywhere looking for yo black ass! They—"

"What the fuck! They came to yo shit? How the fuck?"

"Stop opening yo fat ass mouth and listen! They said the getaway car was rented by some white man named John Crosby. And when they tracked him down in my damn building, the white man said he rented the car for a man named Bo that he met over here, and he saw you come in and out of my house!"

"Alright, so what happened? What you tell them?"

"I told them that that cracka must have lost his damn mind, and when they showed me the picture of you from the gas station, I said I've never seen you a day in my life! So, they came in, trashed my shit, and left. They said they'd be back through and now I'm scared!"

"Damn. This ain't good. Okay, listen. Hurry up and clean yo shit! Top to bottom! When they come back, they might try to do all type of fancy forensic shit, so make sure yo shit clean! Stick to your story! Don't know me! Never seen me! And that cracka is a dope head that probably saw a unicorn! Other than that, shit might get a lil shaky for a while, so you might not hear from me or see me in a long time. Everything gone be straight though, I just need to figure things out."

"I already lost you for too long and I don't wanna lose you again!" Kat cried.

"It's gone be alright, Kat. Just do what I told you and never call this phone again. I'll holla at you when I can. I got to go now."

"Alright, cousin, I love you!"

"Love you too, jit." Bo-T ended his call and shouted "Fuck!" He quickly ran back into the room and slammed the door. "It's time to go, Skeecho! Things are bad!" Bo-T urgently blurted.

"What's up, Skeeman?" Wizz asked while keeping his eyes on the pretty face choking his dick.

"I just got a call from Kat. Shit done hit the fan, Skee! I'll explain later. Right now, we need to haul ass!"

Wizz wasn't sure what the problem was, but he could detect his homie's urgency, so he pulled his dick out of Chiquita's throat and pushed her to the side. He scrambled for his clothes and began dressing.

"Y'all keep the room and we'll holla at y'all another time," Bo-T stated to the naked women.

Nina looked puzzled and Chiquita looked annoyed.

"I'm still horny!" Chiquita blurted.

"Well, go get a dildo and watch a flick! You'll be alright," Wizz responded.

Chiquita rolled her eyes and watched them sprint out of the door. Wizz and Bo-T hustled into the wanted Charger and nearly crashed into a parked car while backing out of their parking spot.

Bo-T broke his phone and slung it out of the window, while Wizz put them en route back to World's house. Bo-T explained the situation to Wizz, and all Wizz could do was shake his head and keep driving.

***

Orlando, FL

Next Day

"Black! Attorney visit! Get dressed and step out into the sally port!" a male C.O. screamed into the dorm over the intercom.

Michael Black had been sitting in his cell, eating a shrimp flavored Ramen Noodles soup, when he heard his name get announced. He balanced his liquidy soup on the corner of his bunk and removed his now-brown, formerly white T-shirt. He slid into his navy-blue jumpsuit and carelessly exited his cell.

While gliding down the stairs, he cupped his hands and smelled his breath, and shrugged his shoulders.

"Dirty ass nigga!" one of the inmates blurted as he walked by.

Michael kept his mouth shut and exited the dorm. Once he got into the sally port, the C.O. that had called him out shouted at him. "Get yo raggedy ass back in there and put some damn socks on before I cancel yo visit!"

Michael quickly ran back in and did as he was told. Once he was back in the sally port the guard looked him up and down, then led him down a fall.

After passing through a few control-booth-operated doors, the C.O. opened a heavy door surrounded by glass that allowed you to see in, but not out. When Michael stepped inside the room, he was slightly surprised to see two black men and not his female public defender.

"Michael Black?" the older of the two asked.

"Yes, sir."

"We're here in response to your call on the TIP line about a homicide suspect we're looking for. You claim to have information on his whereabouts, is that correct?"

"The gas station killer?" Michael questioned with eagerness.

"That's right. Now what can you tell us?"

"Do I get some kind of get out of jail free card or reward money or something?"

"Depends on how useful your information turns out to be. All of that could be a strong possibility."

A wide grin spread across Michael's face as he began to explain how he knew the man wanted for murder. After about forty minutes of Q and A, the two detectives told Michael they would follow up on his story and be back to ask him further questions if they needed to.

Before leaving, Michael told them they could call his sister and she would be able to confirm his story. They told Michael to sit tight, and they would investigate his story. With nothing left to discuss, they gathered their notes and exited the jail.

Less than half an hour later, the detectives were parking in front of a corner house and checking their notes to make sure they had the right house. Together, they approached the house and politely rang the doorbell. They waited for two short minutes and were greeted by a short, light-skinned woman with curly hair and green eyes.

"Ashley Watson?" one of the detective's asked.

Ashley looked puzzled for a moment, then nervously replied, "Yes. Is there a problem?"

The same detective that appeared to be the voice of the two held up a mugshot photo and asked, "Do you know this man?"

"Uhh, yes. That's my ex-boyfriend, Mikey."

"Okay, thank you. Do you mind if we come in and ask you a few questions in regards to your boyfriend?"

"He's not my boyfriend, he's my *ex-boyfriend* and we don't have any dealings with each other anymore, so I don't think any questions will be necessary."

"We promise not to take up too much of your time. Just a few minutes please and we'll be on our way. It's very important."

Ashley released a sigh and moved to the side so the detectives could enter. She led them over to the living room and offered them seats on the couch. She sat down across from them and said, "Okay, can we make this quick please? I have company coming over soon."

"Who are you expecting?"

"That's a little personal. Does it matter?"

"Actually, it does. Our whole purpose for the visit is based off some information we received from your boyfriend."

"*Ex-boyfriend.*"

"Yeah, okay. Well, do you know this man?" the detective asked and held up a photo of Bo-T looking straight at the camera while exiting the 7-Eleven gas station.

With no hesitation, Ashley quickly replied, "I've never seen him in my life other than on the TV since that looks like the man that's been all over the news for the past week."

"Well, your *ex-boyfriend* claims he met this man at this house and that he often comes here, because he hangs out with your brother. Mikey claims he and your brother have even assaulted him on numerous occasions and with that being said, I believe we have a very good reason to be interested in your company."

Ashley started lightly sobbing at first and then her sobs turned into full streams of tears, and she shouted, "Get the hell out of my house! How dare y'all come into my home and disrespect me!"

"Whoa-whoa! Calm down, young lady! What's the problem?" the detective asked with shock from Ashley's sudden outburst.

"I think she's on drugs like her boyfriend," the other detective spoke.

"How dare you disrespect me like that! I should slap yo ass right back into yo mama's pussy! How dare y'all come in here talking about my brother? Everybody knows my only brother has been dead for nearly half a year, and y'all wanna come in here and remind me of my problems because of what some junkie made up in his fat ass, junkie ass head!"

The two detectives looked puzzled as they considered this new revelation they were clearly unaware of.

"Do you have any proof of what you're saying?" the lead detective said.

Ashley continued to cry and stormed off into her bedroom. She came back moments later with a folder and opened it up to show them the obituary and news article.

"This is my only brother, and I would appreciate it if he could rest in peace!" Ashley shouted.

The two detectives both appeared dumbfounded and then one of them broke the awkward silence and said, "I'm very, very sorry. We appreciate your cooperation. Please forgive us, and we'll get going."

Ashley quickly escorted them out of the door and then let out a huge sigh the moment the door slammed. She placed her back against the locked door, slid down to the floor and continued to cry.

***

The two Orlando homicide detectives stood outside the interrogation room and stared through the glass at Mikey. They had driven directly back to the Orlando County Jail and had the guards quickly call him back for another meeting. This time Mikey entered an empty room and the detectives watched him carefully through the one-way glass.

Mikey was fidgeting in his seat and looking around while scratching himself in weird places. The older detective looked at his watch and right on cue a young, skinny black woman appeared, nervously strutting down the hall with a female C.O. leading her way.

The detectives quickly introduced themselves to the young woman and politely asked her, "Do you know this man?"

The woman looked into the room through the glass and stared at Mikey. The sight of him shaking and scratching his ashy arms caused her to frown and she replied, "Yes, that's my little brother."

"Can you give us his name?"

"Michael Black."

"Alright, well, here's the deal. Your brother here needs some help, and he claims you can help him."

"I don't have any money. I already told him I can't bond him out."

"That's not what we meant. See, Michael here has given us some information and a few stories that could help us out greatly and by helping us, we can help him. Only problem with his stories so far is, they're not adding up! We followed up on his claims and we're honestly disappointed and insulted, quite frankly. But he claims you personally witnessed one of the scenes he's told us about. He claims he was assaulted by two men, and it just so happens, one of these men are wanted for two counts of first-degree murder.

"This is a very dangerous man that we must have apprehended. Michael claims you were with him when this happened. You can help your brother out here, and also help us capture a fugitive. So, to make this fast and simple can you tell us, have you ever seen this man?" The detective speaking held up the photo of Bo-T, and the woman's hand reflexively shot to her face where Bo-T had slapped her. She rubbed her cheek and became quiet.

The detective wiggled the picture in her face to snap her out of her sudden trance and repeated his question. "Have you ever seen this man?"

She glanced into the room at her brother and considered her options. *I'm sick and tired of being put in these horrible situations behind his dumbass actions! I can't keep getting hurt behind his bullshit! This dummy gone get me killed one day*, she thought.

"Well?" the detective questioned.

"No, sir!" she blurted. "I've never seen him."

"Are you positive? This is very serious."

"I'm positive. I don't know what kind of stunts my brother tryna pull, but I don't want to be a part of it."

"Well, what took you so long to answer? If I'm not mistaken, I think I may have seen some sort of recognition in your eyes."

"Definitely not! I hesitated because a part of me wanted to lie and go along with whatever he's tryna do, but after giving it a quick thought, I can't do it."

"Well, alrighty then. Thank you for your time. Your free to go," the detective stated.

I'll never take another slap like that in my life, the slim woman thought as she was being escorted away.

The two detectives looked back at Mikey.

"What a lying piece of shit," one of them blurted.

"A complete waste of time," the other stated.

Fly Rock

Chapter 18

West Palm Beach, FL

Four days later

"I can't wait for this shit to fall through, so we can hurry up and get the fuck up out of here," Bo-T spoke with a mouth full of smoke.

"I'm about to see what's up with this hoe brother," Wizz stated, while pressing the dial icon on his phone.

"Hey, boo!" Chiquita answered.

"What's up, banana clip? Aye, what's up with yo brother? Where that nigga at?" Wizz asked.

"His annoying ass around here somewhere. I think he downstairs with one of his lil chickenheads."

"Alright, well, get yo lazy ass up and take him the phone. I need to holla at bra."

"Child, boo, I ain't going down there! I ain't got my hair done, and I ain't bout to have these lil hoes out here thinking they doing better than me."

"Man, fuck yo hair! Yo bald headed ass should've had yo shit done! Now take yo apple headed ass downstairs, give bra the phone, and I'll get yo nappy ass hair done when I slide back over there later."

"My next hairstyle gone cost three hundred and—"

"Did I ask yo poor ass how much it would cost? I'm bout to hang up on yo dumb ass! I'll holla at you another ti—"

"Okay-okay, damn! I'm going downstairs now, damn. I can't stand yo ass sometimes. You so aggressive." Chiquita had a smile on her bright face and once she descended the stairs, she realized her brother wasn't there. She looked outside and saw him waving at his chicken head that was driving away.

As he came back into the house, Chiquita stuck her phone out for him. "Here!"

"Who this is?" he asked her before taking the phone.

"Just take the damn phone and find out! I ain't got time for y'all."

He annoyingly snatched her phone and said, "Hello?"

"What's up, il bra, this Wizz."

"Ohh, what's up, fam? What the play is?"

"Aye check it out, you still got them sticks on the market?"

"I sold one last night. I still got two left though, what's up?"

"What you want for both of them?"

"For you . . . give me seven hundred."

"How bout an ounce of coke?"

Chiquita brother paused for a minute and quickly calculated the profit he would make with an ounce of coke as opposed to seven hundred and decided the choice was obvious.

"Shit, hell yeah. I call that, big bra. When you want them bitches?"

"You on deck right now?"

"Got to know that."

"I'll be over there in bout thirty minutes."

"Say less."

Wizz disconnected the call and told Bo-T to weigh up an ounce.

"Nigga, you weigh it up."

"You the muhfuckin dope boy! Let me do it and jit gone get a brick!" Wizz joked.

Bo-T got up and stepped into the garage. He popped the trunk to the Charger, pulled out a book bag filled with dope, grabbed a scale as well and went back into the living room.

After carefully weighing out an ounce, he wrapped it up in a sandwich bag and handed it to Wizz. "You owe me a thousand bucks, El Skeecho," Bo-T joked.

"Just add it to my tab," Wizz joked back and rose from the couch. "Is it cool if I ride in yo wheels?" he asked World.

World didn't open his mouth to answer. He simply tossed Wizz the keys and kept watching the television. Wizz exited the house and casually drove away.

About an hour and a half later, he was walking back into the house with two big, brand-new machine guns hanging from his shoulders.

"Damn, Skee! What the fuck! That's how you walking around? No bag, no nothing? You thuggin like that? Bo-T laughed.

Wizz let out a chuckle and said, "Crackaz got a law called ten/twenty life. Streets got a law called ride with ya fye!"

"Damn, them bitches pretty! Let me get one!"

Wizz tossed him one of the rifles and sat down next to him and examined the other.

"What these called?" Bo-T questioned.

"These AR-15's!"

"Damn, these hoes raw! "

"Hell, yeah! Right on time too. Now, we just gone duck off until it's time to handle up."

"Say no more, Skeecho Pablo, say no more."

***

Two and a half weeks later

"Yes, Lord, yes! Fuck me, daddy, fuck me! Just like that, daddy! Kill this pussy!" the other white woman moaned. She had her back against the wall, and her legs wrapped around World's waist.

Her head bounced against the wall as World added more power to his thrust to answer her moans. World raised her higher and slowly eased along the wall until he reached a door.

This particular door was an exit door to the back of the check cashing store they worked in, and it led to an alleyway loaded with dumpsters. The store was positioned in the middle of a "L" shaped plaza, so that placed the door in the middle of the alley.

It was 9:20 at night and since somebody had recently shot out all the streetlights, the alley was pitch black.

World slowly eased his hand onto the door and felt around for the locks. Once his hand made contact with the locks, he quietly unlocked the door while still carrying and powerfully thrusting himself into his co-worker.

He knew due to his position, the cameras in the two corners of the room wouldn't reflect what actually took place. Anyone who reviewed the cameras later, would only see a man and a woman fucking like horny teenagers. Nothing more, nothing less.

World then removed her from the wall and carried her over to a pile of large wooden crates. He slipped his dick out of her wide walls and placed her back on her feet.

She quickly turned her back to him and bent over with her hands stretched out over the crates. World grabbed her soft hips and re-entered her large, loose pussy. He roughly pounded her from behind, while she screamed with pleasure for the next ten minutes.

Before he lost control, he quickly pulled out of her and then shot his sperm all over her ass and back. "Damn!" he blurted with a deep breath. He pulled his pants up and wiped the sweat off his forehead.

The white woman pulled her skirt back down over her hips and looked around for her panties. "I fucking love your young energetic cock," she admitted while slipping her panties back on.

"We still on for dinner after work?" World asked.

"Absolutely! Hell, we might have to skip dinner and go straight for the dessert!"

"Sounds like a plan. I'ma go home and change, and I'll meet you at your spot a little later. You wanna close up or do you want me to do it?"

"I'll handle it. I've got to do paperwork and sign off anyway. The truck comes tonight, so I couldn't leave if I wanted to."

"Alright, well I'ma clock out then, and I'll catch you in a few." World walked through the door that led to the front of the store where the counter was behind the glass. He used his key to step through another door and then headed out the front door and crossed the dark parking lot.

He climbed into his car and nervously sent a text message that had already been saved in his phone as a draft. He looked at the time, the message was sent at 9:52 pm. He drove away and prayed his slight involvement wouldn't come back to bite him in the ass. He needed an alibi and that meant his plan on sitting alone at a restaurant, while waiting for a date he'd just fucked and would probably never show, was perfect.

***

Bo-T reached for Wizz's vibrating phone and read the message that flashed across his screen. "OPEN" was the only word visible. He looked over at Wizz and said, "*Showtime at the Apollo,* Skeemask-Skeecho."

"Let's do it, Bandman-Skeeman," was Wizz's reply.

Bo-T cocked his .45 Springfield and checked the magazine on his AR. He tapped his hip to make sure the extra clip was firmly in place and then he opened his car door.

Wizz slung his AR over his shoulder and gripped the MAC-90 he still had from the hit on Mason and Big Mike. He wasn't sure if he would ever get a chance to use the big boy MAC, but now seemed like the perfect time.

They stood on the side of a Dollar Store, which was the last store on the far-left corner of the plaza. They looked around to make sure they were alone and then ran behind the building towards the back door of the check cashing store.

Bo-T lowered his ski-mask and then twisted the doorknob. When the door silently opened, Wizz pulled his mask down as well and together they quickly dashed into the back of the store. They ran across the concrete floor and hid behind the stack of crates.

They got comfortable and patiently waited in a crouch while the clock continued to move forward.

About fifteen minutes later, the door to the front of the store opened and World's white co-worker appeared with a clipboard. She stood in the middle of the floor and ran her fingers through her long blonde hair. She looked around the room and froze when her eyes landed on the pile of crates. She rubbed her ear and slowly approached.

Wizz tightened his hands around the MAC-90 and Bo-T slowly raised his .45. They peeked through the cracks in the crates and watched the woman get closer and closer.

The woman stopped directly in front of the crates and squinted her eyes. She bent over and picked something up off the floor in front of the boxes and said, "That man is an animal." She placed her earring back in her ear and thought about how it must've fell off during their lustful session.

As soon as she turned around, Bo-T noticed a long white stain on the back of her shirt that looked like snot. *This white hoe nasty as fuck*!

Before any other thoughts could invade his brain, a loud steady knock at the door caused his tension level to rise tremendously.

The woman opened the door and immediately handed the clipboard to the two men that stood on the other side.

These niggas look like the damn SWAT team, Wizz thought when he saw the two heavily armed men.

The men signed papers and then handed the clipboard back to the woman, before vanishing from their view. A loud rattling noise could be heard and then they reappeared with a dolly cart and entered the room.

The woman mumbled something that wasn't clear and pointed to a stack of crates, next to the crates Bo-T and Wizz were crowded behind. The men loaded five crates onto the dolly and rolled them out the door.

Bo-T carefully listened to the wheels going up the ramp and continued to listen as the wheels came back down the ramp and re-entered the room.

Two entirely different men entered the room with the original two men, but the two new equally armed guards each had a silver suitcase handcuffed to their left wrists. The woman pulled out a key, unlatched both suitcases and set them to the side.

Bo-T whispered to Wizz, "Do we just take them two suitcases, or do we wait to see if they bring more?"

"Shit, they might come grab these crates next and blow our cover before they bring more suitcases," Wizz whispered back.

"Alright, well do we just settle for them cases, or do we try to rush the truck?"

"Do you feel lucky?" Wizz questioned.

"I had a dog name Lucky."

"Did he chase after trucks?"

"Yeah, ice cream trucks."

"Well, let's go get that ice cream truck!"

Bo-T held up his hand and whispered, "On the count of three." With his fingers he signaled the countdown and as soon as he raised his third finger, they both jumped from behind the crates and began firing their weapons.

One of the armed men lost his head and a second man lost his head and arm. The woman shouted at the top of her lungs and dove out of the way. The two other guards that originally had the suitcases tried to quickly draw their weapons but ended up faceless on top of each other.

Bo-T and Wizz rushed the door and began emptying their clips into the back of the armored truck.

Tat-Tat-Tat-Tat! *Ting-Ting-Ting*!

Bullets bounced off of the truck and put holes in the metal. Bo-T was about to take a step through the door when a large chunk of concrete exploded next to his head. Another bullet whizzed by his ear, and he realized the truck was shooting back.

Wizz dropped down on one knee and unloaded the rest of his clip into the back doors of the truck. He ducked behind the wall to swap out his MAC for the AR and a hail of bullets began raining into the room.

Tat-Tat-Tat-Tat-Tat!

Bo-T quickly dove to the floor and swapped out his clips. Boxes were exploding in the room. Paper, wood and pieces of concrete were flying everywhere. Once his clip was successfully swapped out, he looked up and noticed the white woman pinned to the front door, with multiple holes oozing blood out of her lifeless body. He stuck the gun out the back door and began shooting blindly.

Wizz swapped his AR clip out and shouted over the loud gun battle, "I'm almost out of bullets, Skee! This shit ain't looking too good!"

Bo-T kept his finger on the trigger until a clicking noise told him his luck had run out. "Fuck!" he shouted.

The bullets never stopped raining through the door, and it seemed like they never would.

Wizz heard the click on his AR and shouted, "Bra, we gone die!"

"Abort mission, Skee! Abort! Abort! Abort!" Bo-T shouted.

Wizz dove past the open back door and slid across the hard floor. He and Bo-T quickly snatched up the suitcases and jumped over the dead white woman, while running through the front door. They ran through the front of the store and bolted out into the darkness.

Police sirens began wailing in the distance and growing louder by the second.

They sprinted across the dark parking lot towards the corner of the building where they were parked, and dove into their life saver. The armored truck zoomed from around the other end of the plaza and screeched out the empty parking lot.

When the truck went one way, they quickly got the car started and zoomed out the other way. They merged into traffic and mashed the gas back to World's house. It took them twenty minutes to make it back successfully and run inside the house.

"Bra, we might as well hit the highway now. Fuck the bull-shit!" Wizz suggested.

"Yeah, you right, Skee! Let's just break off World real quick," Bo-T reasoned. He popped open the suitcase he was carrying and almost lost his mind when his eyes drifted into the sea of crispy blue money. His mouth got dry, and his hands got sweaty, but he quickly unloaded half of the suitcase and stuffed the banded -up money under one of the couch cushions in World's living room. He snapped the suitcase back shut and said, "Let's ride, Skeecho!"

They sprinted back out the house and decided on the highway that their best bet was to go back to the twins' spot, so they could lay low and consider their next step. They weren't exactly sure what their next step would be, but they now knew one thing for certain.

They were obviously willing to get rich or die trying!

Chapter 19

Tampa, FL

It was 3:00 in the morning when Bo-T pulled into the twins' driveway and shut off the car. He looked over at Wizz's unconscious body and slammed his fist into the steering wheel. "Fuck!" he shouted.

Wizz quickly leaped out of his sleep and groggily said, "What's up, Skee? What's going on?"

"Nothing, bra, I'm just frustrated as fuck!"

"Man, fuck that shit. Ain't no sense in crying over spilled milk. At least we made it out with something."

"Fuck all that. Bra, do you know how much money we left in the back of that truck? That shit could've been life changing!"

"As long as life ain't over we'll catch another break."

Bo-T smacked the steering wheel one more time and mumbled something under his breath. They each grabbed a suitcase and quietly entered the twins' home with the spare keys they got months ago.

"What if these hoes got some niggas in here?" Wizz questioned.

"Then that's they fault for giving us keys. Them niggas gone take they ass on somewhere. How I'm feeling right now, I'll fuck a nigga up!"

"I'm finna just crash on the couch. I don't even feel like being bothered," Wizz stated before sinking into the couch and sliding his suitcase underneath.

Bo-T headed straight for Spice's room and entered without warning. He shut the door behind him, and that was all Wizz remembered before falling back asleep.

***

Wizz slowly stirred awake and woke up to an aroma he knew all too well. When he opened his eyes, he was instantly blinded by a cloud of smoke and when the smoke cleared, he saw Sugar squatting down in front of him with a big Kool-Aid smile on her face.

"Oh my God, I missed you, papi! Here," Sugar stated and passed him the blunt.

He accepted the blunt and allowed the smoke to invade his lungs. While puffing the blunt, he couldn't help but notice Sugar's extremely fat pussy print bulging out of her boy shorts.

"Why you sleeping way out here, papi?"

"What time is it?"

"It's 7:19 a.m."

"I had a long night, Sugar. I'm going back to sleep."

"Wait, at least come to the room. I want to show you something."

"What is it?"

Sugar spread her legs slightly wider to give him a clearer view of her puffy lower lips and grabbed his dick through his pants.

"Come on, papi. I need you," Sugar whined.

Wizz rolled off of the couch and rose to his feet. He followed Sugar into her bedroom, and kept his eyes glued to her fat wobbling booty the entire way. As soon as they were privately in Sugar's room with the door shut, she stripped out of her shorts, removed her bra and crawled onto the bed.

Sugar assumed the position on her knees and elbows and began making her big round basketballs bounce. She looked back at Wizz and licked her lips while giving him a show. Every time her ass cheeks clapped together, her pussy made a wet smacking noise and the view caused Wizz's dick to instantly rise in his pants.

Wizz stripped down to his birthday suit and stuffed his face in between Sugar's wobbly cheeks. He used both his hands to spread her ass apart and slid his tongue up and down the slit of her juicy lips.

Sugar released a soft moan and pushed her ass back onto his face. Wizz flicked his tongue back and forth across her swollen clitoris, while using his hands to rub and massage her thick cheeks.

Sugar remained faithful to Wizz during his absence and was feening for his touch. Her body needed this attention so bad, she couldn't stop herself from gushing and releasing her first orgasm all over his lips.

Wizz sucked her flowing juices into his mouth and then stood all the way up. He dragged her to the edge of the bed and pushed her back in, so she was face down and ass all the way up. He aimed his throbbing dick towards her soaking wet pussy and slowly pushed himself inside of her.

"Oh, my God! Damn, that feels so good, papi!" Sugar moaned.

He slowly eased his dick out until only his swollen head was left inside her, and then he pushed all of his inches back into her.

"Yes, papi! Yesss!" Sugar continued to moan.

Wizz grabbed her by her slim waist and began roughly pounding himself into her pussy. He pushed himself deeper and harder with every stroke, and Sugar couldn't stop herself from shouting.

"Fuck! Fuck! Fuck! Yesss, papi! Yesss!" Before she knew it, she was cumming for the second time and creaming all over his dick. "Please don't stop, papi! Please don't stop!" she begged.

Wizz slapped her on the ass, and she shouted, "Yes, papi! Slap it again!"

He complied with her wishes and slapped her again, and then told her to look back at him. She kept her face buried in the bed, so Wizz slapped her harder and shouted, "I said, look at me!"

She lifted her head and looked at him over her shoulder and tried to suppress her moans by biting down on her lip. They stared into each other's eyes, while Wizz continued to slam his dick balls deep into her leaking pussy.

The look on Sugar's face sent Wizz over the edge and he busted his nut deep into the bottom of her pussy. She felt his dick throbbing inside her tight walls while his nut continued to splash her insides. He slowly slid his dick out and crashed onto the bed.

Sugar crawled up beside him and kissed his lips. "I love you," Sugar whispered.

Wizz started to say something, but Sugar placed her index finger over his lips and said, "Shhh. You don't have to say anything. I'm just letting you know how I feel."

Wizz closed his eyes and in a matter of seconds, he was back inside the dream world.

***

After waking up a little later in the morning, Wizz eased his way into the shower and slowly scrubbed away the sweat from last night and this morning. Once he was cleaned up, he got dressed in something comfortable and stepped into the living room. He joined Bo-T and Spice on the couch and left Sugar in the bed still asleep and heavily sedated from the morning sex.

"What's up El Skeecho-chopo," Bo-T blurted with a chuckle.

Wizz didn't answer. He just reached for one of the strawberry Dutch blunts on the coffee table and began busting it down.

"The twins got that paper for us," Bo-T stated.

"How much they got?" Wizz questioned while filling the gutted blunt with sticky nuggets of weed.

"Twenty-nine bands! They sold everything and spent nothing. They held it down for the Skeegang!" Bo-T laughed and pointed to a Victoria's Secret shopping bag on the table.

Wizz didn't notice the bag until now and he peeked inside. Bundles of wrinkled-up money stared back at him, and he nodded his head in approval. "Looks like the Skeebabies handled business."

"I think their loyalty should be rewarded. . . I say we let them keep it," Bo-T suggested.

"All of it?" Wizz questioned.

"They kept it solid, fuck it, why not?"

"Well, congratulations, Spice. Looks like you've earned your money and earned our trust," Wizz stated.

Spice started smiling like a kid in a candy store and said, "Gracias, papi."

Bo-T clapped his hands together and said, "Well, I've been waiting all morning for you to get yo ass up, Skeecho. It's time to count our blessings."

Wizz lit the now fully rolled blunt and reached under the couch until his fingers made contact with the suitcase, he stashed last night. Spice kept her eyes glued to the shiny box as Wizz pulled it from under the couch. She didn't even blink until she saw Bo-T pull another shiny box from the other side of the couch.

Bo-T winked at Spice and slowly popped open the suitcase. Wizz popped the top on his suitcase as well and together, they stepped over to an empty spot on the floor and poured out the money. The never-ending bundles of crispy blue money flowed out of the suitcases like a waterfall, and the sight caused Spice's jaw to drop open like somebody broke it.

"Oh, my God!" Spice shrieked and clutched her chest.

"Breadwinners, baby!" Bo-T blurted.

Wizz passed Bo-T the blunt and then took a seat on the floor. Bo-T joined him on the floor, and they added their riches. Since all the money was already stacked and labeled, it didn't take long for them to realize they had just added three hundred and twenty grand to their pockets. Each suitcase carried two hundred grand, so that meant Bo-T's cousin World had a healthy eighty grand stuffed in his couch.

"Skeecho for three!" Bo-T blurted.

"Swish!" Wizz blurted back.

They laughed for a minute and then separated the money evenly.

"Y'all robbed a bank?" Spice blurted.

"Somewhat," Bo-T joked. He stuffed his bank back into his suitcase and then told Spice, "I need help with a few things real quick."

"Whatever you want, papi! You know that!"

"Alright, well first, after me and Wizz unload the car, I need to finally get rid of it. So, I need you to follow me across town so I can burn this shit in the woods." He paused to make sure she knew he was serious and then added, "Then I wanna grab something to eat because I'm starving and then, I need you to rent something new for us."

"Alright, papi, whenever you're ready."

"Good. Now let's unload," Bo-T said to Wizz, and they headed out the door.

They looked around and carefully removed two book bags full of money from past adventures, another book bag filled with weed, coke and Molly, from the trunk. They threw the bags over their shoulders and looked around one more time. Noticing the coast was clear, they quickly pulled out two AR-15's, a MAC-90, two Glock 9mm's, a .357 revolver and a .45 Springfield.

They hustled everything into the house and then made one final trip to retrieve their clothes.

"Alright, let's ride," Bo-T said to Spice.

Bo-T hopped inside the Charger and Spice climbed into her Mustang. Together they drove away and Wizz locked the front door.

***

Bo-T kept his head on the swivel as he cautiously weaved through traffic, with Spice on his trail. After driving for almost half an hour he found a heavily wooded area and drove directly into it. Once he felt like he was deep enough to be unseen from the road, he parked and stepped out.

Spice didn't follow him into the woods, but she parked along the edge and waited. About three minutes later Bo-T came rushing to the car like a mad man and yanking on the door. He hit the glass and his force damn near broke the window. Spice pushed a button on her door and the passenger door unlocked.

Bo-T jumped inside the car and shouted, "What the fuck you got the door locked for? Are you crazy?"

"I'm sorry, papi, I didn't realize the—"

"Hurry up and drive off! What the fuck you doing?"

Spice shut her mouth and quickly drove back onto the road. She drove back towards her side of town while listening to Bo-T cuss her out for having the door locked during a mission. She rolled her eyes and pouted, but she didn't respond because she knew she was wrong.

She eventually pulled into a Steak N Shake drive thru line and ordered food for them, while trying to avoid Bo-T's gaze. After retrieving the food, they drove towards a rental car service, and Spice asked the question that had been on her mind for a while now.

"Papi, is that you they've been having all over the news for killing those men in the gas station?"

Bo-T looked at her carefully and didn't speak for a moment. Spice kept her eyes on the road and waited for his response.

Eventually, he said, "What you think?"

The fact that he didn't deny it instantly let her know it was him, but she didn't care. She only wanted to know so she could be careful about where they went and what they did. She honestly loved Bo-T and the last thing she wanted was for him to get caught and be locked up. She wanted him with her and not locked up in a cell doing life.

"I think since you didn't say no, that means the answer is yes."

"And how would you feel about that?"

"Bo-T, I love you!" Spice blurted with tears falling from her face.

Bo-T stared at her and was caught off guard by her sudden revelation and burst of emotions. He hadn't been this close or connected to a woman in so long, and he wasn't sure how he should feel. He definitely cared about Spice, but he never thought about his real feelings towards her.

For one, she was a stripper, and he didn't think in a million years he would be in love with a stripper. But she had shown him love and loyalty, and he couldn't overlook that. Being in prison for so long had taught him that love and loyalty meant everything.

"Damn," was all he could manage to say.

"I don't want you to get in trouble, papi! That's all I care about. I'll do anything for you. I don't care what you do or what you've done. I'll hold you down through whatever. You can kill somebody right now, and I'll help you hide the body," Spice admitted through tears.

Bo-T could hear and see the sincerity in her words and simply replied, "Well, I guess what's understood don't need to be explained."

Spice got her emotions under control as they made it to the rental car place. Bo-T stayed in the car and Spice picked them out an all-black new model Cadillac. She drove the Cadillac and Bo-T drove the Mustang as they headed back home.

They had a serious conversation together before making it to the rental car shop, and Bo-T couldn't wait to fill Wizz in on the new information he had received from Spice.

Things were about to get interesting.

Chapter 20

Spice unlocked the door to her home and entered with Bo-T on her heels. They walked inside laughing like somebody just told the world's funniest joke. Sugar and Wizz were sitting in the living room eating when they stepped inside and joined them.

"What's so fucking funny?" Wizz asked with a mouthful of Sugar's deliciously cooked bacon.

"Why this nigga always getting served these fat ass plates like a king and I always gotta order pizza and eat burgers?" Bo-T questioned Spice.

Spice looked embarrassed for a moment then replied, "I don't know how to cook, papi."

Bo-T laughed and said, "Yeah, I figured that out a long time ago."

"I'm still tryna figure out what the fuck was so funny. I wanna laugh too," Wizz insisted.

Spice started laughing again and said, "Every time I think about that shit, I can't help but laugh. Y'all niggas a trip!"

"What happened?" Wizz questioned.

"It's really not supposed to be a funny story, but you know this nigga be so animated when he describes shit, he got me dying laughing! I can't believe you crazy ass niggas tried to rob a Brinks truck!" Spice blurted.

Wizz looked at Bo-T and said, "You can't be serious, bra. Why would you tell her that?"

Bo-T pushed his hands out in a "calm down" motion and said, "It's all good, Skee. We had a long talk and everything's cool. We got certified riders, Skeecho. Nothing to worry bout. We in good hands, like Allstate. Plus, they actually did us a favor much greater then handling that money."

"Oh yeah, and what's that?" Wizz sarcastically asked.

"They found us a sweet ass lick! This lick right here might fuck around and be so successful we won't have to hit nan 'nother lick," Bo-T explained.

Wizz looked at Sugar and said, "Seriously?"

Sugar looked shy for a second then said, "Yeah, papi, I was gonna tell you later. I ain't think Spice was going to spill the beans that fast."

"Alright, well what's up?" Wizz loudly blurted. "Somebody fill me in, and stop beating around the bush!"

Bo-T explained to Wizz how the twins had run into an older guy named Fly while they were at work, and how the dude Fly has been consistently trying to get in their panties.

"He's infatuated with us," Sugar chimed in.

Bo-T continued to explain Fly's resume and apparently, he was the top of the food chain.

"So basically, he's the brickman," Wizz stated.

"I wouldn't call him the brickman. He's the man that serves and supplies all the other niggas you would call the brickman," Spice corrected.

Wizz took in the information and then asked, "Okay, so what's the plan?"

Sugar and Spice explained their ideas in detail and proudly waited to be praised for their work.

Bo-T looked at Wizz and asked, "What you think Skeecho?"

Wizz considered their plan for a moment, then spoke. "Well, it's not bad, but there's a few loopholes I can see possibly going wrong. Slippers count and we ain't got time for that."

Wizz carefully explained all the flaws in their plan and then tweaked their plot and came up with a plan of his own. Once he finished discussing the new plan, he sat back and asked, "How bout that?"

Bo-T nodded his headed and blurted "Perfecto! It's evil, it's diabolical and pure genius!"

The twins didn't expect their plan to be twisted into something so serious, but they couldn't back out now, so they gave their approval and agreed it was a great idea. Truth be told, it really was a better plan, and the new plan had a higher success rate of being accomplished. They wanted the big fish and not the tadpoles. Once their flaws had been pointed out, they realized they hadn't put much thought into every detail. There was obviously a craft to this profession that they were unaware of.

"It's gone take some time, but we can definitely pull it off," Wizz stated.

"Nothing to it but to do it," Bo-T replied.

The twins shrugged their shoulders and decided they were all in. Whatever made Wizz and Bo-T happy, made them happy.

Wizz ate the last piece of food on his plate and said, "Well, let the games begin."

***

"Good news or bad news?" Jenkins asked his secretary through the receiver of his office phone.

"I'm not sure. There's an Orange County homicide detective on line two, waiting to speak with you. He claims it's of the upmost importance."

"Orange County? Orlando? What the hell does he want?"

"I'm not sure, he wouldn't say. But if you'd like to find out, then I'll gladly link the call for you."

Jenkins let out a heavy sigh and said, "Put him through."

About twenty seconds later, a deep voice spoke. "Hello? Detective Jenkins?"

"This is I, good evening, Detective. How may I assist you?"

"My name is Detective Morrisson and I'm with the Orange County Homicide Unit—"

"That's Orlando, right?" Jenkins interrupted.

"Correct. My purpose for calling is favored by the fact that I believe we are both in a great position to help one another."

"And how is that?"

"Well, me and my guys over here have been doing a lot of research, and our crime lab's stumbled upon some very interesting information. From what I've heard and read, you have a few cases with a couple of mystery men that can't be found. Am I right?"

"I won't say they can't be found, more like they haven't been found . . . yet."

"Do you have photos or descriptions of your suspects?"

"At this moment, unfortunately, I do not."

"Are you aware of the homicide case at the gas station that has been vividly broadcasted throughout the state for the last month or so?"

"I'm not familiar with the details of the case, but yes, I am aware of it."

"Okay, where this is where things become interesting, Detective. I'm the lead detective for that case and during that incident, the suspect that you've seen all over television actually attempted to purchase a few things. He purchased gas, blunts and a Fruit Punch Arizona Tea can, which he apparently decided at the last moment that he no longer wanted. We know this because we have him on camera, of course. He took the beverage to the counter but then, left it on the counter and walked away without it. Of course, my forensics team was able to lift a few fingerprints from the can, and to our amazement, after being run through the criminal system and wanted criminal system, our prints produced a ninety-nine-point-nine percent match to the mystery prints in all your cases. And—"

"Get the fuck out of here! Sweet Jesus! You've got to be kidding me," Jenkins shouted and nearly fell out of his chair with excitement.

"This isn't a joke, Detective. Now, this is where I feel like we can really help each other. Since the majority of his crimes have been committed in your jurisdiction, we believe that means he has some form of residence or ties to your city. Now, since we have him on camera, there's no way he can avoid a conviction and guilty verdict from an Orange County judge. We offer our assistance in any way possible. Forensics, labs, notes, anything! When the suspect is captured, you'll get full credit, but we want him held and convicted in Orange County. How do you feel about that?"

Jenkins thought about it for a moment and frowned. This new revelation was a dream come true, but how could he pass on the chance to convict the man in his own city?

"What about the other guy?" Jenkins asked.

"The other guy had prints he left on the gas pump and those were also a perfect match. Fortunately for him, he stayed off camera. He couldn't be seen from the angle he was at, so we don't have a face for the fingers."

"Justice must be served in my city," Jenkins firmly stated.

"And it will be, after we deal with him first. Once we convict him, he will be extradited to your county jail and rightfully charged for his crimes. He's got a lot of music to face…and face it he will."

"Sounds like we've got a deal," Jenkins accepted.

"Let's set up a date sometime this weekend, so we can sit down and go over what we've got. In the meantime, I have a few photos and other information I'll be faxing to your office. I expect the same courtesy."

"No problem, Detective." Jenkins placed the phone back on the hook and couldn't contain his smile.

This was a breathtaking moment, and he was finally feeling as if his hard work was paying off. He picked the phone back up and pressed the extension to connect him to his top-heavy secretary.

"What's up, J.J., how'd it go?" she answered.

"I'll explain later. Aye, do you see Detective Young anywhere?"

"Yeah, he's at his desk. He just came back in from lunch."

"Send him in here please. Tell him it's urgent. Also, there should be a fax coming in from Orlando. I need that brought to me immediately."

"Okay, the fax is coming now and as soon as I grab all the papers, I'll tell Young to come in."

"Thanks," Jenkins stated before ending his quick call.

Two minutes later, his secretary entered his office and placed a stack of papers on his desk. Her milky breasts nearly fell out of her top when she bent over, and Jenkins was almost hoping they did. She quickly turned on her heels and strutted back the way she came.

Jenkins picked up the large stack of papers and the very first page was a colored photo of the man that would soon be held accountable for his deadly actions in Orlando, as well as Tampa. The next few pages were detailed about the crime, photos and lab reports. He quickly scanned through the paperwork and began feeling better.

Detective Young stepped into his office about ten minutes later and took a seat in front of his desk. "What's going on, J.J?"

Jenkins handed Young the photo of their suspect and said, "I need you to place an all-points bulletin on this man right here, and I need that done immediately."

Young examined the photo and eventually recognition glittered in his eyes. "Isn't this the guy that killed those people in Orlando at the gas station?"

"One and the same," Jenkins replied.

"So, why on God's green earth would we be placing an APB out in Tampa, for a guy that committed a crime way in Orlando, and is probably in Mexico by now?"

Jenkins slowly walked him through his latest discovery and filled him in on the connection between their mystery man and the man that made himself famous in Orlando.

"Okay, so we've finally gotten a positive ID on our guy. That's absolutely wonderful, but like I stated a few minutes ago, this guy is probably in Mexico, or maybe even China at this point. So, why should we waste our time on an APB at this very moment?"

Jenkins smiled and said, "This is the really juicy part that I didn't mention yet, nor did I tell the detective from Orlando."

"Well?" Young impatiently asked.

"There was a 9-1-1 call placed this afternoon, but the call had gotten forwarded to the fire marshals. It really didn't mean much at the time, but now it's music to my ears. It says right here in the police report that our suspect fled the scene of the crime in Orlando in an all-black Dodge Charger Hellcat. The car was reported stolen by a guy that apparently rented it for the suspect. The car was never found, however.

"This afternoon, when the fire marshals responded to the 9-1-1 call, they later reported that somebody had torched and abandoned a presumably black, new-model Dodge Charger. It could either be a coincidence or it could be our suspect returning home and trying to cover his footsteps. Either way, there's no way the connection can be disregarded. I want an APB and I want it now! I want every patrol officer in the county on high alert for this man!" Jenkins pointed at the evil man in the photograph and shouted, "Now!"

"I'm on it, right away!" Young blurted and jolted from the office.

Detective Jenkins picked up the picture and smiled. "I've got you now, motherfucker!"

Fly Rock

Chapter 21

Three weeks later

"So, what we doing today, El Skeecho?" Bo-T asked Wizz from his usual spot on the couch at the twins' house.

"The same thing we do every day. Take over the world." Wizz chuckled.

"Alright, Skeechobrain," Bo-T laughed.

"But forreal though, it really ain't shit to do. The police been every fucking where for whatever reason lately, and everything else in the world been going crazy with all this Coronavirus bullshit. Niggas walking around looking like nurses and shit with all these masks on. Ain't shit to do but sit here and smoke this weed!" Wizz stated. "A nigga got all this money and nothing to do with it."

Sugar stepped out of her room and Wizz asked her, "What's up, bae, you working tonight?"

"Yeah, might as well. Ain't shit else going on," she replied on her way to the kitchen.

"I don't understand this shit. Y'all got two young fly rich niggas at home. So, why y'all still shaking y'all ass for niggas?" Bo-T questioned.

From the kitchen, Sugar said, "Well, for one, we love our young fly rich niggas, and we wouldn't trade them for anything. Two, we really still do it just for fun. We like to dance, and we appreciate that y'all don't judge us or look at us differently. Y'all let us do us, and still support us and show us love. We don't do no foul shit. We dance, show a little ass, show some titties and come home. We have fun and get paid. No harm, no foul."

"How we met y'all?" Bo-T asked.

"Don't do that," Sugar blurted.

"I'm just bullshitting. It's all good," Bo-T laughed.

Wizz whipped out a blunt and some weed and started rolling up, while Sugar ate a bowl of Honeycomb cereal and Bo-T flipped through the TV channels. Once the blunt was rolled, Wizz sparked it up and began to calm his early morning nerves.

***

Spice strutted through the club with her ridiculously curvy body on full display. She broke almost every neck she walked by. She was headed towards the bar to get some water for her and Sugar, when somebody reached out and grabbed her ass. When she turned around to see who groped her, she crashed into somebody else and fell flat on her ass.

"I'm so sorry, beautiful! I wasn't paying attention and a woman with your beauty should never be humiliated in such a way. Please forgive me," a man spoke and reached his hand out to help her back on her feet.

Spice looked up into the stranger's face and instantly noticed who the stranger was. "It's okay. Sometimes these heels can be a nightmare," she stated while taking his hand and getting back on her feet.

Fly looked her up and down and like always, he was amazed by her beauty. "Are you Sugar or Spice?" he asked.

"Spice," she replied while straightening her hair.

"I'm sorry, it's hard to tell who's who in the dark."

"It's okay and thanks for the wakeup call," Spice stated and continued towards the bar. Fly followed her to the bar and waited for her to retrieve her drinks.

When Spice turned around and saw him behind her, she said, "Are you stalking me, Mr. Big Baller?"

"Come on, Spice, you know how bad I want a private show with you."

"Okay, well buy a private room and you'll get your private show. Simple."

"How about we leave for the night and have a personal party? I'll pay to play."

"How many times do I have to tell you I'm in a relationship, and I refuse to get caught up for some chump change. My man takes great care of me, and I don't think your pay will be worth it."

Fly arrogantly twisted his face and said, "Baby, don't you know who you talking to? I'll buy this whole club if I feel like it! You ain't gone get caught, I know how to be discreet."

"I'm listening..." Spice stated, with her erect nipples causing a major distraction to the conversation.

"I want you and your sister at the same time. I know a nice quiet place, and I have plenty of money. What you say?"

"I'll have to check with Sugar, but what's your idea of a nice quiet place, and how much money is plenty of money?"

"I know a nice hotel on the other side of town and—"

"Not gonna happen!" Spice interrupted and turned to leave.

Fly reached out and grabbed her arm while saying, "Hold up, baby! What's wrong with that?"

"Nigga, we need a secure location, not no hotel. We ain't no hotel freaks!"

"Alright, listen, I got a house on the other side of town that nobody knows about. Not even my wife. And I'm willing to give y'all ten grand. . . a piece!"

Spice nearly laughed at his offer, but she managed to keep her poker face on and said, "Now, we're getting somewhere. I'll ask Sugar and see if she's up for it."

"We can leave in my ride, and I'll bring y'all back here when we're done."

"Wrong again! I told you, we have boyfriends. What we look like leaving the club with some other nigga? These hoes gone tell on us in a minute! We will follow you in our own car and when we're done, we will leave. Simple."

"Alright I'm cool with that. Well, I'll give y'all ten grand now and the other ten when the party's over."

"Alright, Mr. Big Shot, let me see if I can make your dreams come true." Spice turned around and slowly bounced away, ass cheeks shaking and bouncing with every step. She knew Fly was watching her, so she added a little extra bounce to her step and kept him hypnotized until she was out of sight.

Fly discreetly pumped his fist with joy as his mind flooded with images of what could possibly be in his near future. He had been coming to the club for nearly two months and had been instantly obsessed with the twins the moment he saw them.

Fly was known for tricking and although he had a beautiful wife and plenty of pussy, he had never seen a pair of twins so thick and so sexy. He had been attempting to add the twins to his hit list since he met them, but they continued to play hard to get. Fly figured tonight might finally be his night, and he was feeling lucky.

Spice entered the locker room and found Sugar changing into a new costume.

"Bitch, I think I got him!" Spice eagerly shouted.

"Got who? And give me my damn water!" Sugar spoke.

"Fly! He's here and I just talked to him. He wants to take us to his house! I think this might be it! Do we call the guys?"

"No, not yet. We shouldn't call them unless we're sure we have the right place. They already explained that to us. And how do you know it's the right spot?" Sugar questioned.

"I don't, but it sounds about right. He said he wants to take us to a house on the other side of town that nobody knows about."

"Bitch, tell me everything!" Sugar demanded.

Spice gave her the whole conversation, from the moment she was knocked down to the moment she walked away, and Sugar listened to every word.

"Alright, well tell him we agree, and we'll meet him in the parking lot in twenty minutes," Sugar stated.

Spice quickly left the room and found Fly in the same place she had left him. She gave him the good news and strutted back to the locker room.

Fly couldn't contain his smile as he exited the club and waited by his car. Twenty-two minutes later, the twins came out with their clothes and bags and headed for their car. They saw Fly and nodded their heads. He jumped inside his Escalade and pulled out, and the twins followed suit in the fire-red Mustang.

They nervously drove around for thirty minutes and when it became obvious they were being led to the right place, they became even more nervous.

"Should I call them now?" Spice asked.

"Hell yeah! It's now or never," Sugar replied, while keeping her foot on the gas and her eyes on the Escalade.

Spice quickly called Bo-T and waited for him to answer. He didn't answer the first time, so she quickly hit the redial and called again.

"What's up?" Bo-T answered in a husky voice that let her know he was sleeping.

"Bae! It's time to make it happen! I'm in the car with Sugar right now and we're following Fly!"

"Huh? What the fuck y'all following Fly for? I told you not to do no suspicious shit! You gone blow the whole operation!" Bo-T yelled.

"No, bae! He was at the club, and he came to me with a proposition for me and Sugar. I played it cool just like we planned, and now we're following him to the house," Spice explained.

Now fully awake, Bo-T asked, "Is it the right house?"

"Yeah, bae! This is it! We're turning into the gate right now. We should be in the house in about four minutes."

"Damn!" Bo-T blurted. "Alright what time is it?"

Spice looked at her phone and said, "It's 1:22 a.m."

"Alright remember the plan and stick to it! Do not fuck this up! Time starts now!" Bo-T shouted and hung up the phone.

Bo-T quickly ran inside Sugar's room and woke up Wizz. "Get yo ass up, Skee! It's time to ride!"

"Where we going?" Wizz asked with annoyance.

"The twins at Fly's house right now! Time already started! Come on, nigga!" Bo-T shouted.

Wizz instantly shook off his sleep and jumped out the bed. Together, they scrambled for the things they would need, and once everything needed was in their possession, they jetted from the house.

Chapter 22

Bo-T looked at his watch and saw it was 1:49 a.m. "Alright, Skee, we need to move fast. We behind schedule a lil bit, so let's make it quick," he urged, while throwing a backpack over his shoulder and quietly easing out of the car.

They were parked at a stop sign in a middle-class neighborhood they had been carefully watching for the past few weeks. This was the type of neighborhood that usually promoted a neighborhood watch program and had civilians doing the most, like calling 9-1-1 if a dog was being walked without a leash. Stealth was very important.

Wizz exited the car behind Bo-T and left the engine running, while they quietly jogged down the dark street towards a two-story home, about seven houses away from where they parked. As they approached the house, they causally looked around to make sure everything was normal, and then quickly dashed across the front yard and swiftly jumped the wooden fence.

They landed in the backyard of the two-story home and eased along the fence. They stepped around a line of bushes and were now facing the sliding glass door that would give them entrance into the back of the house. The only thing in-between them and the glass door was a nine-foot-deep swimming pool and a few pool chairs and tables.

Bo-T put his index finger to his lips and signaled with his other hand for Wizz to quietly follow him. They tiptoed around the pool and once they were about ten feet away from the house, a bright porch light came on and nearly blinded both of them.

Bo-T quickly leaped into the bushes and Wizz dove under a pool table. They sat still for two minutes and when the light went off, they crawled the rest of the way to the glass door. Attached to the sliding glass door was a small, rectangular-shaped doggy door, with a flap that allowed the owner's small cocker spaniel to come and go as she pleased.

Wizz adjusted his arms together in front of him and slowly inched his slim frame through the small door until he was on the other side. He slowly rose to his feet and quietly unlocked the glass door for Bo-T.

Bo-T slid the door to the side just enough to squeeze his solid frame through and then handed Wizz the backpack he had been carrying. Wizz pulled out his .357 revolver and Bo-T clutched his Ruger 9mm. They quietly continued forward through a back room and then entered a living room area, with Wizz leading the way.

Wizz bumped into a table and knocked something on the floor. "What the fuck, Skee!" Bo-T whispered.

Wizz froze for a second and heard a bell jingling in his direction. As the bell noise got closer, he felt something furry brush past his legs. "Don't move," Wizz whispered. He quietly stretched his right leg back as far as he could and as soon as the little bell jingled in front of him again, he swiftly swung his foot forward like an NFL punter and felt something crunch against his foot.

A loud squeal followed the crunch and a solid thud against a nearby wall followed the squeal. They remained silent for another minute and then proceeded forward.

The house was pitch-black, so Wizz used his memory to navigate them through the layout. They reached a carpeted staircase and slowly began taking the steps up, two at a time. When they reached the top, there was a hallway with four doors.

One was a master bedroom, one was a hallway bathroom, one was a closet and the last was another bedroom.

"Let's take the bitch first and double-back on the kids," Wizz suggested.

Bo-T nodded his head in agreement, and they quietly headed towards the master bedroom. Wizz grabbed the doorknob and twisted it open. When he peeked inside the room, he was delighted to see a woman and two small children, all laying down and sleeping in the same king-sized bed.

"Lady Luck to the rescue, Skeeman. The Easter Bunny left all his eggs in one basket," Wizz whispered.

"Let's do it," Bo-T whispered back.

Wizz slung the door open, and they quickly rushed the room with a force that changed the whole temp. Bo-T grabbed the sheets and flung them to the side while grabbing the woman by her hair.

The woman instantly awoke with a scream and was quickly silenced with a blow that broke her jaw and knocked her to the floor.

Wizz flipped on the lights in the room and emptied the book bag on the floor by the bed. The lights illuminated the room and revealed a beautiful, nearly naked dark-skinned woman, a pre-school-aged boy that looked to be about four or five, and a toddler girl that was maybe two, if that.

The little boy screamed and tried to jump away, but Wizz grabbed him and slammed him back on the bed. Wizz pinned the boy down and taped his mouth closed. He then tied his arms and legs and pushed him to the side.

Bo-T had just finished successfully doing the same thing to the woman, and now the baby girl was screaming at the top of her lungs. Wizz picked her up and tried to calm her down and she slapped him in the face, so he taped her mouth shut as well and tossed her next to her brother.

"Ready?" Bo-T questioned.

"Yeah, I got it from here," Wizz replied.

"You sure?" Bo-T asked again.

"We're running out of time, Skee. Let's do it!" Wizz blurted.

With nothing left to be said, Bo-T quickly rushed out of the room and jumped down the stairs. He bolted out of the back door and retraced his footsteps to the back fence and jumped into the front yard. He dashed across the lawn and sprinted down the street back to the car that was still running and waiting. He dove into the front seat and swerved away in a hurry. He looked at his watch and checked the time, now 2:01 a.m. "Damn," he whispered to himself.

***

Spice and Sugar were both fully naked and putting on a show for Fly, who sat on the couch in his spacious living room.

Fly had a total of three houses. He used one house to cook and distribute his dope amongst his main workers, who then supplied the local trap houses around the city. His second house, which was also his primary house, was his family home. He lived there with his wife and two kids. That house was now occupied by Wizz, and he would soon realize that in a disturbing way.

His last house was a safe house. He used this house to hide and stash his riches. All of his money and coke were hidden inside his safe house, and not even his wife was aware of this. She had no knowledge of where he kept his dope, and she always assumed he held his money in a bank.

He kept a few thousand in a bank account but avoided suspicion of his small fortune by simply keeping his money to himself in his safe house. With careful and consistent observation, Bo-T and Wizz were able to find out about all three of his homes and their purposes. They watched him so hard over the past few weeks, they even knew what type of cereal his son ate and what type of toilet paper his wife wiped her ass with.

For someone with so much money, he didn't put a lot of effort into security or safety, and to top it all off, his awareness was pathetic. Bo-T and Wizz were actually surprised that nobody else had attempted to snatch this nigga up yet, but whatever the reason for that, they were happy to be the ones to do it.

Spice bent over and made her large ass cheeks bounce one at a time. Fly licked his lips and enjoyed the view of her bright yellow booty vibrating in his face. Sugar was next to Fly on the couch in doggy style position, making her equally large cheeks clap to the beat of some music.

Fly had been waiting for this moment for a very long time and he planned on making the most of it. He stuck his tongue out and licked it across Spice's glistening clit.

Spice bit her lip and moaned with pleasure while she continued to bounce her booty against his face. Fly pulled his pants down and kicked them to the side. He was now only in his boxers and his dick was pressed firmly against the material.

Sugar rubbed her hands across his lap and stroked him through his boxers. He lifted his hips and slipped his boxers down to his ankles. Sugar gripped his short dick in her hand and began rubbing his pre-cum around his dick head.

Fly leaned his head back and allowed his body to enjoy the soft touch of Sugar's hand as she stroked his dick up and down. In Sugar's mind, she laughed at the size of his small penis but in reality, she acted like he was everything.

Spice lowered her ass onto his lap and rubbed her pussy against his stiff dick. She leaned forward and tapped her finger on the screen of her phone that was resting on the table in front of her. When the screen lit up, she looked at the time and saw it was 2:20 a.m.

Spice looked at Sugar and signaled with her hands the time. She then reached between her legs and grabbed Fly's dick. She rubbed his tip against her asshole and moaned.

Fly was so horny and turned on, he was at a loss for words. He just continued to sit back and let the twins take the lead.

"Mmmm, do you have any Vaseline, papi?" Spice moaned.

"Uhh, no . . . but, I got a whole bunch of other shit and I'm sure we can find a substitution. What you got in mind, baby?"

Sugar quickly rose from the couch and blurted, "Oh, don't worry, papi. I've got some in the car."

Fly was immediately about to protest, but before he could speak, Spice shoved her big bright booty into his face and began making her ass cheeks clap against his mouth.

Spice's big round booty blocked his entire view and before he knew it, Sugar was skipping out the front door.

Chapter 23

After violating almost every traffic law, Bo-T quickly came to a halt in front of the home they had mapped out as Fly's safe house. He parked in the road behind Spice's Mustang and checked the time, 2:21a.m.

One of the twins were scheduled to open the front door exactly one hour after their mission timer started and that left Bo-T with a single minute. He sprinted onto the front porch and crouched down beside the front door. He had the same backpack from earlier over his shoulder, and his 9mm gripped tightly in his grasp.

He looked at his watch one last time and saw it was now 2:22 a.m. He gripped his tool tighter and whispered to himself, "Do not fuck this up."

Seconds later, the front door flew wide open, and Sugar bolted through the door in her birthday suit. She saw Bo-T crouched by the door and gave him a quick thumbs' up as she scurried to the Mustang and hopped in.

Bo-T peeked around the door and saw Spice bent over with her ass waving in front of a naked dark-skinned man. Spice locked eyes with Bo-T as he held up his hand and mouthed the words, "Don't move."

Bo-T quickly dashed inside the house and in one swift motion, he pushed Spice to the side and made Fly's biggest nightmare a reality, as he brought his pistol down hard over Fly's temple.

"Ahh, fuck!" Fly shouted.

"Shut the fuck up!"

WHAM!

Bo-T crashed his pistol into Fly's forehead and created a deep gash that instantly gushed blood over his face. Spice bolted for the door and disappeared into the darkness. She jumped into the passenger seat of her Mustang and Sugar sped them away.

WHAM! WHAM! WHAM!

Bo-T continued to mercilessly bash his pistol into Fly's head, until Fly was sprawled across the couch, clearly unconscious. Bo-T then quickly removed a roll of duct tape from the backpack and taped Fly's mouth. He taped his hands behind his back and then reached into his pocket for his phone.

Bo-T quickly scrolled through his apps and pressed on the *WhatsApp*. He went to the dial pad and made a video call. Seconds later, Wizz popped up on the screen and smiled.

"What we looking like, Skeedawg?" Wizz's voice blurted through the phone.

Bo-T angled the camera toward the couch and Fly's bloody face popped up on the screen of Wizz's phone.

"Looking good, Fly, looking good," Wizz joked.

"Give me a second, Skeecho," Bo-T stated and sat the phone down on the table. He cocked his hand back and used all of his force to slap Fly across the face.

Fly's head rolled to the side and Bo-T slapped him again. Fly opened his eyes and began gagging into the tape. Fly's eyes frantically looked around as he quickly remembered what had just happened to him.

"Get yo soft ass up and pay attention!" Bo-T ordered.

Out of instinct, Fly's legs shot forward and he tried to kick Bo-T away.

WHAM! WHAM! WHAM!

"Soft ass nigga, is you stupid?" Bo-T shouted and beat him to the floor. "Try that dumb ass shit again and I'ma smoke yo dumb ass!"

Bo-T rotated his arm around to relieve the soreness from his constant striking and said, "Now, like I was saying, fuck nigga, pay the fuck attention and listen closely. This is important. You might die, and if you die, yo family die. If you live, then yo people might live. It's all on you, so you need to do exactly as you're told. People counting on yo soft ass!"

Fly looked defeated and confused as he watched Bo-T pick his phone up off the table and stick the screen in his face.

"What's up, Skee? This bitch ass nigga hear me?" Wizz asked.

"Loud and clear," Bo-T replied.

"Alright, check it out, Fly. You got something I want, and you gone give it to me. Simple as that. This is not a debate. Let me show you how serious I am," Wizz stated and then pointed the camera towards Fly's naked wife.

Fly began blinking rapidly when he saw his exposed wife appear on the screen. Suddenly, a loud bang erupted and echoed over the phone. Fly watched in complete horror as his wife's head exploded on the screen. The camera quickly left her lifeless body and in the blink of an eye, Wizz was back in the view.

"You ain't gotta worry bout her no more, but if you listen then you can still save the *Flintstones*," Wizz blurted and pointed the camera at the two kids laying taped up on the bed.

A stream of tears began sliding down Fly's face and he dropped his head in disbelief.

"Don't insult my intelligence. I know it's a treasure chest buried somewhere in that big ass house, and I want it! You got five minutes to get it. Time starts now, bitch ass nigga!" Wizz shouted.

Bo-T placed the phone in his pocket and yanked Fly off the floor. He balanced Fly on his feet and shouted, "Hurry up, fuck nigga, before my nigga start trippin!"

Fly wobbled on his feet and groaned something that wasn't understandable.

Bo-T ripped the tape off of Fly's mouth and shouted, "Stop wasting time, soft ass nigga . . . move!"

Fly started coughing up blood and wobbling on his legs.

"Four minutes!" Wizz shouted through the phone in Bo-T's pocket.

WHAM!

Bo-T slapped him with his pistol, and he fell back to the ground. "Get yo fuck ass up!" he shouted and yanked Fly back up.

Fly got his balance under control and began to run through the house like the floor was on fire. He burst through the door of a bedroom in the back of the house and collapsed to the floor. Blood leaked all over his face and upper body from the many gashes and splits all over his head.

Bo-T pulled his phone back out and waved it in Fly's face.

"Two minutes! Nigga, you better tell me something!" Wizz blurted. He grabbed Fly's son and threw him off the bed.

181

The little boy landed next to his headless mother and look terrified. Fly couldn't stop his tears from falling as he tried to yell. His words were useless and unidentifiable through his bloody and broken jaw.

Fly frantically nodded his head towards a large portrait hanging on his bedroom wall. The portrait was a painted picture of *The Last Supper*, and it was about eight feet long and four feet high.

Bo-T pointed at the picture and Fly nodded his head.

"One minute!" Wizz shouted.

Bo-T yanked the picture off the wall and revealed two large wall safes with a number pad in between them. He aimed the camera at the safes, so Wizz could see them.

"What the fuck you sitting there all quiet for, fuck nigga? What's the code, nigga?"

Fly tried to speak but couldn't make his words comprehendible.

Bo-T slapped him in the back of the head and shouted, "Nigga, do it look like I understand Chinese? What's the fucking code!"

Fly groaned in pain and rolled over onto his stomach. He used his hands behind his back to signal the five-digit code number and as soon as Bo-T pressed the "ENTER" button, both safe doors popped open like microwave doors.

"Bingo!" Bo-T blurted with a grin.

"Time's up!" Wizz shouted.

"I got it, Skeecho! I got it!" Bo-T blurted and waved the phone over the safes. One safe showed a mountain of money and the other showed a mountain of coke.

"Bring home the bacon, Skeeman!" Wizz chuckled and ended the call.

Bo-T turned around and without a word, he put a bullet in Fly's head. A thick mist of blood and brains splashed over the floor and Fly was officially of no more use.

Bo-T quickly ripped the pillowcases off the pillows and began filling them up with the money. After filling up five pillowcases of money, he quickly realized he wasn't prepared for the amount of money he had in his presence.

He snatched a sheet off the bed and laid it across the floor. He threw the stuffed pillowcase into the middle and began shoveling the rest of the money onto the sheet.

After that, he tied the sheet into a knot and yanked another sheet from the bed. He threw all the block-shaped white packages onto the sheet and dashed through the rest of the house.

He found four jewelry boxes and threw them all on top of the bricks. He then tied up the sheet and looked around. He was dripping with sweat and excited as he lifted one of the sheets over his shoulder and hustled it outside to the car. He slung the heavy sheet into the back seat and sprinted back in the house for the second sheet.

The sheets were both about the size of the bags you see Santa Claus carrying across the world, and they were too difficult to carry at the same time. He stumbled through the house with the last sheet and tossed it into the passenger seat.

He jumped into the car and without second-guessing his actions, he drove away into the night.

***

After ending the video call, Wizz quickly sprinted through the house and stumbled out the front door. The twins had the Mustang parked directly in front of the house waiting for him, and when they saw him coming, Spice swung open the passenger door. Wizz dove across her lap, and she slammed the door behind him.

Sugar screeched away as Wizz climbed over the center console into the backseat. They drove back to their home in silence and when the three of them entered the duplex, they all crashed onto the couch.

Sugar and Spice were still naked and nervously fidgeting.

Spice eventually broke the silence first and said, "Do you think he's alright?"

"Of course, he is! Just relax and let my nigga work his magic," Wizz assured her.

The twins went to their rooms and put on some shirts and shorts.

When they came back into the living room, they flopped back onto the couch and Sugar asked Wizz, "Do you want to smoke, papi?"

"Smoking is a celebration and we ain't doing no celebrating until my nigga make it back safely," Wizz replied.

They silently waited for another ten minutes, and then finally heard a car swerve into the lot. A pair of headlights flashed through the front window, and everybody became anxious, excited and relieved.

Wizz got up to open the door and stepped to the side as Bo-T wobbled inside, looking like a tired ghetto Santa Claus.

Bo-T dropped the sheet on the floor and quickly hustled back to the car for the second sheet. Wizz locked the door behind him and then stated, "Now, you can roll that shit up, Sugar."

Bo-T looked exhausted but managed to smile. "I think we're finally rich, Skee!"

"Man, it look like you stole a bunch of pillows and blankets," Wizz joked.

"Well, unwrap the gifts then, Skeecho," Bo-T huffed.

Wizz untied one of the sheets and an avalanche of bricks tumbled around the floor. "Damn!" Wizz blurted.

Bo-T stepped over to the mountain and together they quickly counted out thirty-seven bricks of cocaine.

"White world," Bo-T chuckled.

"From now on, call me Skeecho the snowman," Wizz laughed.

Bo-T then dragged the second sheet over and untied it.

"Oh, my God!" Spice blurted.

"Jesus!" Sugar added.

"Whoa!" Wizz joined.

"Rich Gang!" Bo-T concluded.

"It's gone take us days to count this shit! What the fuck?" Wizz blurted.

"Ain't no sleep tonight!" Bo-T stated.

The twins quickly hurried over to help count the money but before they sat down, they both dove on top of the piles of money and started acting like they were swimming.

"This has to be at least a million dollars!" Sugar beamed.

"You ever had sex with a millionaire?" Wizz asked.

Not that I know of," Sugar purred.

"You ever had sex on a million dollars?" Wizz asked again.

"Definitely not" Sugar answered.

"Well get naked!" Wizz stated while removing his shirt.

Sugar quickly stripped and tackled Wizz to the ground over the money. They rolled around in the money until their laughs turned into moans.

Spice looked at Bo-T and Bo-T licked his lips. She quickly stripped and they joined the party.

The entire living room floor was covered in money and cocaine and for the next hour, they filled the air with sweat and moans. After their million-dollar sex scene they pushed all the money into one large pile and took turns jumping in it like kids.

"It's time to find another city," Wizz stated.

"We can leave this bitch as soon as we get done counting," Bo-T spoke.

Wizz looked at Sugar and said, "We gone make sure y'all get y'all cut, but I'ma ask you a serious question and I'ma only ask you one time. Me and Bo-T leaving, and when we leave, we ain't coming back! So, here's the question . . . are you staying or going?"

Sugar looked at Spice and together they screamed, "Going!"

Wizz smiled and said "Well . . . let's count this paper and get the fuck from around this bitch!"

Chapter 24

Ocala, FL

Three and a half weeks later

Sugar ran up and down the stairs of her new home like a kid on a playground. "Papi, I love it," she shouted with pride and joy.

Wizz and Bo-T were sitting on a pair of matching brand-new black leather sofas in their new living room, watching the twins run around like puppies. After adding up one-point-seven million dollars in cash, they decided to make a few long-term investments.

The first thing they purchased were two cars. For the twins, they bought a 2020 Convertible Porsche. The Porsche was a dark purple and the insides were all white. For themselves, they bought a 2020 Bentley truck. All-black paint job with blood red guts.

The Bentley sat up high on thirty-inch black Forgiatos and the Porsche sat pretty on twenty-four-inch chrome Asantis. Both whips were registered in the twins' names, and after they picked out their rides, they went searching for a new home.

They found a two-story home deep in the country with a "For Sale" sign out front and approached the owners with cold hard cash. Money talks and bullshit walks. They were able to move in almost immediately.

The twins handled all the paperwork and today was finally their move-in date. The house was surrounded by five acres of land, and the land was surrounded by a tall black iron gate. Their closest neighbor was nearly a mile away and the privacy added to the reason they chose the home.

A well-paved, long and curvy driveway split into two directions as it approached the home from the gate. One way led to a spacious, three-car garage and the other way led to the front door of the marvelous, two-story, red brick home.

A giant Swarovski crystal chandelier sparkled in the center of the cathedral ceiling as soon as you entered the foyer, and a large living room sat on the left. Double doors led to a kitchen and a staircase to the right led to the five bedrooms and three bathrooms upstairs. The entire flooring was mahogany wood, except for the bedrooms, which had plush pearl-colored carpeting.

The kitchen had marble counters and wooden cabinets. All the kitchen appliances were made of stainless steel. Beyond the kitchen was a second living room in equal size to the first and another bathroom. A dining room and a game room were off to the side of the second living room and in the very back was a small studio that led to a back screened-in porch.

Carefully placed concrete slabs created a path from the back porch to a ten-foot-deep swimming pool. The pool came with a gazebo styled pool lounge and a diving board. Another set of concrete slabs led to a shed and another set wrapped around the side of the house and led to the garage.

These large expenses didn't even put half a dent in their very wealthy pockets, and with thirty-seven bricks of cocaine to fall back on, it was safe to say that they would never go broke again.

Sugar ran across the living room and leapt onto Wizz's lap.

Wizz braced himself for the impact and blurted, "Damn, bae! Calm yo happy ass down! You gone put wrinkles in my damn Versace!"

"And if I do, you'll just buy some more."

"Money don't grow on trees," Wizz joked.

"That's because all the money growing in yo pocket!" Sugar joked back.

Before Wizz could counter Sugar's remark, she blurted, "I wanna go shopping, papi!"

"Yo ass always tryna go shopping! Tell me something I don't know."

"Not for clothes, papi. I wanna get some bedroom accessories, lamps, tv's, things like that."

"When you tryna do that?"

"I wanna go now papi" Sugar stated with a pout and a grin.

Wizz looked down at his new Patek Phillipe watch and said, "Man... alright, but we gone have to make it quick."

"It won't take long, papi, come on. I wanna drive the truck!" Sugar quickly stated while jumping off his lap and snatching the Bentley keys off the table.

Wizz hopped up behind her and they stepped out of the house. They jumped inside the truck and zoomed away. Spice watched the black and red Bentley weave down the long driveway and once it was out of sight, she stepped away from the window and fixed her eyes on Bo-T.

Her lustful stare said more than she could say with words, but Bo-T kept his cool and played along.

"It's rude to stare," Bo-T joked.

"Sugar and Wizz left, papi."

"And . . . so what?"

"So, I was thinking we should use this free time to break in the new house." Spice seductively wiggled out of her dress and stepped forward.

It was physically impossible to look at Spice in her bra and panties and not be instantly aroused. Spice turned her back to Bo-T and slowly bent over while removing her panties.

Her thick bald pussy and her inflated booty was an amazing sight and by the time she stood up, popped her bra off and turned around, Bo-T was already butt naked on the couch with his rock-hard dick standing at attention.

She walked over to him and got on her knees between his legs, gripped the base of his thickness and slowly lowered her mouth over his mushroom head. She then began to stroke his shaft up and down while gently sucking on his tip.

Bo-T rolled his head back and closed his eyes. It seemed like Spice's oral skills got better and better every time and she never failed to please him.

Once his dick was wet and shiny from her spit, she removed her hand from his shaft and slowly eased his full length into her throat. When her lips made contact with his body, she stuck her tongue out and licked his balls.

She then raised the tempo and began to bob her head up and down over his dick. Every time the head of his dick slipped in and out of her throat, she made a gagging noise but never hesitated or slowed her pace.

She slurped his dick until he was throbbing in her mouth but before he blew his load she pulled back and took a deep breath. She stroked his dick with both of her hands and said, "Damn, papi. I love your dick!"

Bo-T didn't respond, but he grabbed her by the wrist and pulled her onto his lap. He turned her around and with her ass cheeks and pussy facing him, she bent over and placed her hands on the floor while straddling his lap.

She slowly eased her pussy over his dick and let out a loud moan as he slipped into her soaking wet tunnel. Bo-T slapped her on the ass, and she began bucking like a horse. He grabbed her ass and slammed her down on his dick with force and every time he slammed her down, she made her ass pop back up.

The sight of her ass clapping and her fully filled pussy was more than enough to send him over the edge, but he held his composure and kept throwing his dick into her sweet spot.

He slowly stood up from the couch, with his dick still inside of her and kept stroking. She kept her hands glued to the floor and put her feet around his waist. She locked her feet together behind his back and he pounded her pussy from behind.

"Oh, my God, papi! Yes, papi! Yess!" Spice shouted.

Bo-T was pounding her so hard that she began crawling forward on her hands, trying to keep her balance, and eventually bumped into the coffee table. She unhooked her legs from around his waist and dropped them to the ground. She put her hands on the table and arched her back.

Bo-T slipped back inside her warm pussy and pulled her hair back.

"Oooooh, shit! Shit! Fuck . . . fuck . . . damn! I love it, papi. I love it!"

Her loud moans and her facial expressions gave Bo-T more encouragement as he continued to ram her pussy. Her pussy was soaking wet and started making squishy noises every time he pulled in and out. Her legs began to buckle, and her thighs began to tremble.

"I'm cumming, papi! I'm cumming!" she screamed.

Bo-T rammed her harder and a thick stream of liquid squirted from her pussy.

"Fuck, papi! Fuck!"

Bo-T slowly pulled out of her and slapped her on the ass. She fell forward onto the coffee table and knocked everything over. Bo-T flipped her over and laid her on her back. He positioned himself between her legs, threw them in the air, and dove back inside of her.

"Ooooooh, fuck!" she shouted.

"Damn, this pussy good," Bo-T whispered in her ear as he mounted her. He began to fuck her and kiss her, and she felt so in love.

"Cum for me, papi!"

"How you want it?" he grunted.

"I want it in me! Cum in me, papi! Please!"

He quickened his pace, and the table began to rock back and forth with his rhythm. He pinned her legs back and started slamming his dick into her like a jackhammer.

"Please, papi, please! Cum for me!" she begged.

Sweat dripped off of his forehead as he continued to stroke her and with a final powerful thrust, he filled her pussy with his semen and the table crashed to the floor. They fell to the floor with the table but managed to stay locked together in their passionate embrace.

Bo-T stayed inside of her and made sure he emptied everything he had. The ecstasy from his brute force and the shock from crashing with the table, caused Spice to shake into another orgasm. She locked her legs around his waist and continued to shake.

They laid still for a few minutes while breathing deeply and quietly catching their breaths.

Eventually, Spice said, "Damn, that was great!"

"Facts!" Bo-T agreed.

"We gotta buy another table," Spice giggled.

"Shit, we can buy ten tables and break all them bitches!" Bo-T joked.

Spice simply laughed.

***

An hour later, Sugar and Wizz re-entered the house with bags full of bedroom supplies and plopped down on the couch.

"Every time this chick say she wants a few items, she fuck around and buy the whole store," Wizz blurted.

"I can't help it, papi, I'm sorry. What happened to the table?" Sugar questioned and pointed to the pile of wood in the middle of the floor.

Bo-T shrugged and Spice began to laugh as they continued puffing on the blunt they were smoking on the other couch.

"Aye, I came up with a saucy ass plan while we was out driving around," Wizz spoke.

"Talk to me," Bo-T stated.

"On the way back, we drove by this big ass warehouse with a 'For Sale' sign out front. I started thinking and check it out. . . we could buy the warehouse, remodel it, and turn it into a brand-new strip club! Think about it, that's a great investment and legitimate way to keep this money flowing. The twins know all the ropes when it comes to the strip club venue, and from what I saw, it really ain't no strip clubs out here. Not no major ones anyway. What you think?"

Bo-T rubbed on his chin and pondered the idea for a moment. "I like it, Skeecho, I like it a lot! How much for the building?" Bo-T questioned.

"They want eighty thousand, but when you considered the profit that's a win, Skee!"

"Alright, so what exactly do we need to do? I like the idea and I'm all for it, but I don't know how this shit supposed to work."

"Well, first we get a lease for the building and permission from the state to buy the building. Then, we get a permit to make it a strip club. Shit… after that, we just need a liquor license, and everything gone be legal. Then we hire some hoes and shit. Shit, we can hire like twenty hoes and get it poppin! I'm sure it's a little more to it, but that's the basics though."

"Y'all up for this?" Bo-T asked the twins.

"Hell, yeah!" Sugar replied.

"I've always wanted to have my own strip club," Spice agreed.

"Well, it's settled then . . . Let's do it, Skeecho!"

Fly Rock

Chapter 25

Two and a half months later

"Well, it took a little time and a lot of effort, but we did it, Skeeman. And we did a mighty fine job, if I do say so myself," Wizz stated while gazing out of the floor to ceiling glass window in their newly made office.

"This shit really crazy when you think about it… Not even a year ago, we were sitting in a hot ass jail cell smoking needle-thin joints and living like losers. Look at us now," Bo-T beamed and blew out a cloud of thick smoke.

They had just put the final touches on their new establishment the day before, and now they were admiring their work. They had painted the old warehouse solid black on the outside and at night, the neon sign hanging over the front door, appeared to float in mid-air against the black walls.

Once you entered through the large double doors in the front, you would be standing on a red carpet. The red carpet was roped off and directed you to the center of the club.

In the middle of the club was a large, oval-shaped bar with a black marble stage in the middle. The stage had three gold stripper poles that went all the way up to the ceiling.

To the right was a spiral staircase that led to the VIP section. The VIP had three small, similar stages to the one inside the oval bar, but they were angled in a triangular format. Eight black leather couches circled the stages so the patrons could watch all three stages in unison. There was also a balcony that overlooked the main floor behind the bar, so a VIP participant could see the entire club from above.

Directly beyond the bar was a wide-open space, with eight large stages with dual poles. All the stages were exactly alike in the black and gold theme. The stages were scattered about and randomly placed, so there was plenty of room for people to move about and enjoy themselves.

Behind the stages in the far back was the locker room where all the strippers could change, shower, relax or do whatever as the night progressed.

To the left of the oval bar was a large area with booths, so people could chill and order drinks or receive lap dances and table dances.

Next to the lounge area along the wall was a door that led to a handful of private rooms, and next to that was two restrooms. One for men, one for women.

Attached to the corner of the restrooms, there was a roped off staircase that led to a door with a keypad lock. Beyond that door was the office that Wizz and Bo-T were now standing in.

The office had two white leather sofas and a glass table in the middle. A wide seventy-inch smart TV hung on the wall in front of the couches and that TV was for entertainment. Another seventy-inch TV rested on the other end of the room over a desk and that TV was for monitoring the club.

Cameras had been carefully placed everywhere throughout the club and every camera could be seen on the screen of the seventy-inch television. The desk held all the files of their business agreements, files on all their workers and all the other licenses they needed.

They held auditions a few weeks ago and had hired a total of forty women. Thirty of the women were dancers and the other ten were bartenders and bottle girls. They had chosen the most alluring and exotic women they could find.

They also hired eight, licensed security guards, but Wizz and Bo-T also posed as security, so that made a total of ten males on the staff. Bo-T and Wizz were head of the security detail and to everyone else, the twins were the owners of the club.

Nobody knew of the relationship between the two duos, and they did that purposely to maintain their elusiveness. After all, Bo-T was still a wanted man, and he didn't intend on ever being too friendly amongst the crowds.

Bo-T had grown a full beard and kept a hat pulled low over his head. Bo-T and Wizz told the twins to come up with a name for the club and with little thought, the name was created. Sweet & Spicy was now open for business and they planned on having their grand opening in two weeks on a Friday. Everything was running smoothly.

The floor to ceiling glass window Wizz was standing in front of gave him a view of the whole entire club and its foggy glass allowed him to clearly look out, but nobody could look in. He stepped away from the glass and said, "We bout to have this bitch jumping! I know everybody out there dying to get out the house and have some fun right now. We got a club in the perfect location too. You can see it from the interstate, and that's gonna attract a lot of people."

"I couldn't agree more, Skeecho," Bo-T spoke.

"Let's have some fun and get this money," Wizz concluded.

***

Tampa, FL

Four days later

Detective Jenkins had a pile of paper balls on his desk and one by one, he shot them across the room while leaning back in his office chair. His basket was a trash can in the corner of his office, and the large pile of paper balls growing on the floor around the trash can, said his skills were below average. Jenkins sighed deeply and took another shot, and his effort didn't even make contact with the trash bin.

He had been extremely frustrated over the last couple of months and he had many reasons why. The biggest reason being that right when he thought his many cases were getting hot, they quickly became cold and produced no further leads. This was the first time he had ever had so much trouble trying to find someone that lived so recklessly.

He had one last paper ball on his desk, and he was desperately craving a cigarette. He had quit smoking a few months ago, and his wife had given him some type of magical chewing gum that was supposed to help him when he got urges. He normally didn't need it but right now, it seemed like he needed a whole pack.

He opened the drawer under his desk and reached inside. He felt around for the pack of gum and when he found it, he noticed a piece of yellow sticky note paper stuck to the side. When he pulled the paper off, it had a phone number scribbled on the back.

He stared at the number and thought for a long moment about who's number he was reading. Eventually, he remembered the number belonged to the FBI agent that had called him months ago.

He decided to dial the number and began mumbling to himself, "I don't know what the hell this dude wanted, but he damn sure seemed interested in my business. . . and he was specifically interested in my untraceable fingerprints. I think this dude knows a little more than he led on. Either that, or some other sort of hidden agenda. At this point, I ain't got a damn thing to lose, so I might as well give him a call and see if he still has any interest. I can give him some new information and maybe he'll have more to say . . . Fuck it, why not?"

He restlessly tapped his fingers along his desk until he heard a voice in his ear say, "Hello?"

"Hey, how's it going, this is the homicide detective from Hillsborough County, Jeremy Jenkins. Remember me?"

"Yes, of course. How can I help you, Detective? I'm sorry I couldn't get back at you with that request you made. My apologies" Fisher spoke.

"Well, I'm sorry to bother you right now, but since you never called me back, I felt the need to take initiative and make the call myself. Long story short, I'd like to have a follow-up to our previous conversation."

"I see . . . Well, I'm not sure if I can be of any assistance to your cases, Detective. That's why I never called back."

"I'm aware of that, Agent, but at the same time I've stumbled upon a great deal of new information since our last conversation. And I feel like since you had interest in the first place, you may find some of my new insight very appealing. What do you say?"

"Well . . . alright, let's hear it, Detective. What do you have?"

"I believe the most important detail I have at this moment in relation to your original interest, is the fact that I have an identity now for the man once known as the mystery man."

Agent Fisher sat up in his bed with genuine interest and said, "Really? You know who he is?"

"Not exactly . . . I don't know who he is, but I do know what he looks like. I've got a clear picture of his face. Clear as day. Maybe you can take a look at him and see if he's any interest to your team."

Fisher thought about his own mystery men, and then thought about the photo he possessed form the prison. His curiosity to see if their men were one and the same was unimaginably high. He absolutely had to know, but he was suspicious of the fact that he was being monitored by his ex-bureau. He didn't want to expose his hand, so he offered Jenkins the opportunity of a private meeting.

He explained to Jenkins that he would come down to his office, and they would discuss further information in person. He told Jenkins the topic was too delicate to speak on at the moment but assured him that if his man was of any interest to his federal team, then he would assist him in his search. They scheduled a meeting for the following Saturday and concluded their call.

Detective Jenkins felt like this meeting could turn out to be very interesting in a way he was unsure of. You just never knew when it came to all the notoriously known secrecy that comes with the FBI.

His suspect was already wanted for multiple murders in multiple cities. What else could he be guilty of?

Jenkins picked up the last paper ball on his desk, leaned back in his chair, and took his final shot.

SWISH!

He finally made a shot, and he no longer had the urge to smoke.

Fly Rock

Chapter 26

Tallahassee, FL

One week later

Fisher packed a few clothes and hygiene supplies into a small rollable luggage bag and prepared himself for a short weekend away from home. It was Friday evening and his meeting with Detective Jenkins was scheduled for tomorrow afternoon. He was going to leave early tomorrow morning but decided that leaving tonight would benefit him better.

He could stay in a hotel overnight and be well rested and ready for the meeting. He made sure he had any papers he may possibly need to show and then he left the house. He wanted to stop somewhere and grab a bite to eat and gas up. After that, he'd be hitting the highway.

***

Ocala, FL

Three hours later

"She bustin it wide open and shaking it on the floor, I'm finna go to the bar and get some drank and hit the floor, I'm finna get on the floor, I'm finna get on the floor, I'm finna get on the floor, I'm finna get on the floor, she wanna drop and give me fifty, drop and give me fifty, drop and give me fifty, girl drop and give me fifty . . . ." Hurricane Chris and Mike Jones's club anthem blared through the speakers of the new strip club, Sweet & Spicy.

Tonight, was the grand opening, and to say the club was a huge success would be an understatement. Big-time ballers and high rollers came from all over the state to check out the club being promoted as the next big thing, with some of the finest and flyest women in the state.

The club was packed, and fully naked women were flooded throughout the building Music was blasting, lights were flashing, ass and titties were bouncing, and thousands of dollars were constantly soaring through the air.

Sugar and Spice were walking around the club looking fly in their matching black and gold Versace dresses. Bo-T and Wizz were posted up by the bar in their black and gold security shirts and Balmain jeans.

Everybody was enjoying themselves and the night was young. There was still a whole night of fun ahead of them.

***

Fisher cruised down I-75 with a clear mind. He honestly didn't expect much from the meeting he had scheduled for tomorrow, but his past experiences taught him to always expect the unexpected. So, with that, he kept his mind clear and open for possibilities.

While cruising silently through the dark night, it was impossible for him to not notice the extremely bright neon lighted sign, flashing in the middle of the night's sky ahead of him. The sign showed two erotic women hanging from a pole with enormous body parts.

The sign then changed and the words, "Sweet & Spicy" flashed across the sky. The sign then changed again and had the words, "Grand Opening" brightly on display. After that, the sign went back to the two curvy women and repeated the same process.

I can't even remember the last time I saw a nice ass and a pair of tits, Fisher thought. *And I sure as hell ain't been to no strip club in over ten years. I deserve a chance to relieve some stress and see some innocent entertainment.*

Without even thinking, he found himself merging into the far-right lane and about a mile later, he was turning off an exit ramp into the city of Ocala. He followed the bright sign until he found himself turning into a packed parking lot with a large dark warehouse to the side.

He struggled to find a parking spot, but eventually found one in the corner between a Honda and a Lexus.

"This shit might not even be worth my time or money, but then again, I doubt it would be this crowded out here if the place wasn't worth the trip," he spoke to himself.

He stared into his rearview mirror and inspected his appearance. His physical appearance was as good as it was going to get, so he focused on his attire and decided to change his shirt.

He reached into the backseat for his luggage and retrieved a while polo shirt. His plain black jeans and black boat shoes would have to do. Nobody would see his feet anyway he hoped. He popped a piece of Orbit gum into his mouth and exited the car.

He quickly crossed the parking lot and approached the roped-off double doors and was patted down by two burly bouncers.

"Twenty-five bucks," one of the bouncers stated.

"That's a little steep for an entrance fee," Fisher complained.

The bouncer stared at Fisher with a blank face and that let Fisher know the price was not negotiable. He reached into his wallet and paid for the admission.

A beautiful, short light-skinned woman placed a red band around his wrist and ushered him through the double doors. The moment the doors shut behind him, the loud music surged through his ears, and a series of bright white flashes blinded his vision.

He threw his hands over his eyes and when the flashes stopped, he realized he was on a red carpet and his picture had just been taken. A long-legged white woman with long blonde hair, and big peach-colored nipples protruding from her bare chest, approached him and asked if he wanted to purchase his entry photos.

Her accent quickly let him know she wasn't an average white woman. She sounded either Russian or French, either way she definitely wasn't a local.

"No, thank you," he said in amazement of the red-carpet entrance.

He continued forward and the music became clearer.

"Somebody, come get herrrr- she's dancing like a striiiiiper, somebody come get herrr- she's spilling all the liiiquor," echoed through the building.

As he approached the bar, he looked around and said to himself, "Wow! This place looks amazing."

The entire building was packed and there was money everywhere. He looked up at the VIP section and saw a naked brownskinned woman standing on the balcony shooting money over the crowd through a long plastic gun. Bills rapidly flew out of the long tube and rained over the stages on the main floor.

The floors were covered in money, and he couldn't believe how decked out the place looked. He found a seat at the bar and continued to survey the area.

An obviously drunk black man jumped on top of the marble counter with wads of money in his hands and started rocking back and forth to the beat of the music, while screaming, "Ayy! Ayyy! Ayyy-ayyy-ayyy!"

"Aye! Get yo black ass down before I kick yo drunk ass out!" a heavily jeweled bouncer with a large beard shouted and rushed towards the black man.

The drunk man quickly hopped off of the bar and vanished into the thick crowd. A black woman with long red dreads approached Fisher and said something he couldn't understand over the music.

Fisher leaned over the counter and said, "Excuse me?"

The naked red dreaded bartender leaned over and repeated, "I said, welcome to Sweet & Spicy . . . May I get you something to drink?"

Her accent was clearly Jamaican and her large breasts swung forward and nearly brushed Fisher's hands when she leaned forward to speak.

He tried not to awkwardly stare at her beautiful breasts and said, "Umm, yeah . . . I'll take some vodka."

The Jamaican beauty smiled and said, "What type of vodka would you like?" She pointed to a section of bottles and Fisher was shocked when he saw the many different bottles and flavors that were being presented.

This motherfucker got more liquor than a liquor store, he thought. "I'll take the Absolut, put me on the rocks, no chaser."

"Coming right up," she replied and turned to prepare his drink. Her round chocolate booty was shaped like an apple, and she skillfully made it jiggle while she fixed his cup.

Fisher quickly removed all of his cash from his wallet and counted it under the table. He had three hundred and forty-six dollars.

Not bad. I can make this work, he thought. He paid for his drink and then asked his chocolate host if she could give him all ones for his billed money.

She happily attended to his request, and he tipped her twenty. He watched three gorgeous women make their asses jump and jiggle to a new song, while money showered them on the stage inside the bar. He quickly downed his first drink and quickly purchased another one.

Once he grabbed his second drink, he left the bar and decided to check out the women on the main floor. A petite Asian woman with a bubble butt and cantaloupe breasts caught his attention first, so he approached her stage.

He joined the gathering the Asian woman created and pulled out a hundred-dollar stack of one-dollar bills. He started feeling the effects of the alcohol and knew he would be wasted before the night was over. He hadn't been drunk since he was in college and Lord knows how long ago that was.

He was feeling loose and relaxed. He started awkwardly nodding his head to the music, trying to find some rhythm, while tossing dollars onto the Asian woman. After throwing the hundred and finishing his second cup, he wobbled away from the stage and began browsing for a new piece of eye candy to throw his money at. He staggered through the crowd while waving his arms and bumped into another heavily jeweled bouncer.

"Watch where the fuck you going! Drunk mothafucka!" the bouncer growled.

"Sorry dude," Fisher spoke and looked him up and down.

The bouncer walked away, and Fisher thought for a quick second that he had seen the man before, but he quickly disregarded the thought and kept moving through the crowd. He found a stage with a Spanish woman that had long, jet-black hair and watermelon titties. It didn't take him long to realize he was in love.

He pulled out another hundred-dollar stack and slowly showered the woman, while never taking his eyes off of her juicy breasts. When she got down on all fours and gave him a view of her backside, he pulled out his final hundred-dollar stack and threw it all in one motion.

He only had a few dollars left now and decided it would be best spent on another drink. He slowly slugged his legs back to the bar and found a new seat. He was quickly attended to by his Jamaican queen and ordered another round.

He swayed in his seat while gulping his cup and when the last drop hit his tongue, he slammed the cup down and shook his head. The constantly flashing lights began to get darker and darker, and before he knew it everything went black, and he could no longer see.

"Aye! Aye! Get yo lazy ass up!" a voice echoed in Fisher's ear.

He felt a hand roughly shaking against his shoulder and he opened his eyes. The familiar bright flashing lights swarmed into his vision, and he found himself face to face with the bars marble countertop.

The anonymous hand roughly shook him again and the echoing voice shouted, "Are you stupid, or dumb? I said get yo lazy ass up! Yo drunk ass taking up space in a very lucrative seat. You need to move ya cheeks before I move 'em for you!"

Fisher lifted his throbbing head off of the counter and realized he must have passed out. He was extremely drunk and slightly incoherent. He looked into the angry face of the bouncer that was shaking him back to life and mumbled, "Hey . . . Don't I know you from somewhere?"

"Yeah, duhh! You bumped into me on the other side of the club, you dumb fuck! I should've followed my first mind and kicked yo dumb ass out then! Get yo clumsy ass up! Dip shit!"

Fisher braced his hands against the stool he was porched on and attempted to rise. The moment one of his feet connected with the floor, he lost all control of his balance and fell flat on his back. He stared up into a group of laughing faces, flashing lights and couldn't move.

"I see you gone make me do this the hard way," The bouncer huffed. "Aye, Bo-T! Aye help me toss this trash out real quick!" Wizz yelled over his shoulder and over the music.

Bo-T quickly approached the scene and helped Wizz lift Fisher's body into the air. Fisher felt like he was either floating on a cloud, or crowd surfing at a Beetles concert as he passed through a sea of spectators. He threw his arms up and began to embrace the thought of crowd surfing at a Beetles concert, then suddenly he no longer felt his holders and a sharp pain thundered through his spine.

Everything was dark again, but once he heard a door slam, he realized he was laying on the ground outside and staring up into the night sky. He staggered to his feet and braced himself against the building. He felt a sickness rising in his throat and leaned forward.

A waterfall of vomit poured from his mouth, and he began heaving. He looked around and noticed he was alone. He wiped his mouth with the back of his hand and gasped for air. Eventually, he built up enough energy to stumble forward through the parking lot.

At some point, he managed to find his car and crashed into the driver's seat. He slammed his door and eventually found a way to stick his key into one of the three ignitions he was faced with. He started up the car and leaned back into his seat.

He took a deep breath and strapped on his seat belt. When he placed his hands on the steering wheel, he was suddenly overwhelmed by an uncontrollable force that caused him to lean forward and throw up all over the dashboard.

He relaxed his head against the top of the steering wheel and tried his best to catch his breath. Whether or not he ever caught his breath became unknown, because his world slowly went black again and he passed back out.

***

The club had ended about two hours ago and in the last hour, all of the staff had collected their nightly earnings and gone home. Bo-T and Wizz had left about thirty minutes ago, and only the twins now remained in the building. After placing the profit in a safe, they waited for the cleaning crew to arrive while lounging in their office.

Sugar scanned through many small screens on the large TV and noticed something unusual in the parking lot. The only car that should've been present at this time was their barney purple Porsche. Instead, she gazed through the parking lot and come across another car in the far corner.

"I'll handle it," Spice said over her shoulder. She quickly scurried out of the building and tiredly strutted across the parking lot.

When Spice approached the car and peeked inside the window on the driver's side, she witnessed a man slumped over his steering wheel with vomit everywhere. She tapped on the glass and noticed the man move. The man stirred awake and when she tapped the glass again, he sat straight up and looked directly at her.

She waved her hand at him, and he looked around with confusion on his face. Once he saw all the vomit everywhere, images of the night flashed through his mind and his face went from confused to embarrassed.

He rolled his window down and said, "I'm very sorry, ma'am, am I in your way?"

"No, not at all, I'm the owner of the club and I noticed your car parked way out here by itself, so I wanted to make sure you were okay."

"Oh, okay. Well, in that case, I'm very sorry for making a fool of myself then. You have an amazing club, and I had a wonderful time."

"Thank you, feel free to come back anytime." Spice stepped away from the car and gave the man a wave.

Fisher took that as his cue to leave and quickly placed the car in reverse. He backed out of his parking spot and switched the gears to drive. While zooming away he said to himself, "That was one hell of a night."

A couple of hours later, Fisher had taken his car to a car wash and paid to have it thoroughly cleaned, inside and out. He had changed his messy clothes and was now checking in to a hotel in Tampa. He showered himself and checked the time.

It was now 10:00 am and his meeting wasn't scheduled until 4:00 pm, so he decided to take a nap and rejuvenate his exhausted body. After his wild night, he definitely needed it.

Chapter 27

Tampa, FL

The alarm on Fisher's watch woke him up at 2:00 pm and after struggling from under the sheets, he made his way to the bathroom and took another shower. Once he got himself together, he slowly made his way to the hotel's lobby.

A sign by the front desk told him a discounted lunch was being served in the hotel's small cafeteria. Since all his cash was gone, he would have to use his credit card to eat, but not accepting the affordable offer wasn't an option.

In the cafeteria, he ordered some French fries and chicken tenders. He helped himself to the free coffee dispenser, and after eating his meal and drinking two cups, he was fully awake and ready to roll. He took another look at his watch and still had an hour to spare. He figured it would take him around thirty minutes to arrive at his meeting, so that left him with a thirty-minute window. The best place to be for those thirty minutes in his eyes, was at the office, waiting for the meeting.

Better to show up early and get this fiasco over with. He left the hotel and proceeded towards his meeting.

***

Detective Jenkins was in a good mood as he answered his office phone and blurted out, "Talk to me."

"Your 4:00 meeting is here," Joyce informed.

Jenkins checked his watch and noticed he still had twenty minutes before his meeting. "Send him in."

Fisher was quickly ushered through the door and into the office. Jenkins stepped around his desk and extended his hand for Fisher to shake.

"Pleasure to meet you," Fisher offered.

"The pleasure is all mine," Jenkins replied. "So, where should we begin?"

"Well . . . I believe the best place to start would be from the beginning. Just lay it out for me and we'll go from there," Fisher reasoned. There were two comfortable-looking chairs in front of Jenkins' desk and Fisher opted for the one on the left.

Jenkins took a seat behind his desk and gently brushed some lint off the top of a thick file resting on the desk. He leaned forward with his elbows on the desk and said "Alright, let's get to it. You're already fully aware of my cases, for the most part, but now I would like to take the time to actually walk you through my tangled web from the beginning. I'm hoping my added details and photos may trigger a better perspective and new insight."

Fisher casually leaned back to gain more comfort for the presentation, and replied, "Very well, Detective . . . proceed."

Detective Jenkins opened the file and started with the double homicide. He slowly explained everything in detail and showed evidence to reflect his thoughts and conclusions. He tried his best to put Fisher in a position that would make his views understandable.

So far, he had Fisher's undivided attention so that had to mean that so far, he was doing a fairly decent job. A little under half an hour later, Jenkins ended his carefully planned speech with the story, images and lab reports of an obviously wealthy dead black man and his wife. He then produced the photo of his suspect and slid it across the desk towards Fisher.

"This your man?" Fisher questioned while examining the photo.

"One and the same," Jenkins replied. "So, what do you think?"

"Well, it's definitely not the man I'm searching for. Nor is my agency, but he does seem awkwardly familiar."

"You may know him as the man wanted for multiple counts of homicide for his actions at a gas station in Orlando."

"You're absolutely right! That's definitely who this is… wow! Seems like your perp has had his hands full and a lot on his plate."

"His plate is full, and he's been leaving lots and lots of crumbs and leftovers. Unfortunately, his carelessness isn't getting me any closer to his whereabouts."

"I wouldn't say that. I understand the frustration that comes with the job, but when you consider the carelessness of this man's actions, it's those same actions and carelessness that has his picture in your desk right now."

Jenkins adjusted his tie and said, "Yeah, well, I guess you're right but you know what I mean."

Fisher allowed his mind to roam for a few minutes and then he took a second glance at the thick file opened up on Jenkin's desk. Jenkins had flipped through the entire file, page by page. He covered everything he could over the last half hour, but now that Fisher gave it another look, he realized there was still a few pages at the end of the file that the detective didn't speak on.

"What's on them last couple pages?" Fisher questioned. He figured since he sat there and heard everything else, he might as well hear it all.

Jenkins looked down at the remaining pages and said "Oh that's nothing really. Just a little information on a guy in Orlando. Some crack head called the tip line and claimed he knew my suspect on a somewhat personal level and knew exactly where he could be found. That turned out to be a completely dead-end road."

"Did you travel down that road personally?"

"Actually no, I didn't. a couple of detectives from Orange County took the call, since it was in relation to their own investigation. After following up on the lead they came to the conclusion that the tipper was full of shit. They filled me in because we have a mutual understanding as far as access to each other's notes and evidence."

"Alright, well just for shits and giggles, what happened?"

"Well, long story short, the junked-out tipper told the Orange County detectives that he knew our suspect and had personally been in multiple physical altercations with him. When they went to see him, he told them that our suspect is always over there, hanging out with his girlfriend's brother. So, of course, the detectives went over to the girlfriend's house and after brief questioning, they quickly realized they'd made a big mistake. They uncomfortably found out the girlfriend's brother is dead and has been that way for a while now."

"Interesting . . . how did the brother die?"

"Okay, this is actually crazy, because I remember hearing about it. Her brother was one of those prisoner dudes that got killed in the prison transport accident a year ago and—"

"What!" Fisher quickly interrupted and nearly fell out of his seat.

"Crazy, right? She—"

"Hold up, hold up, hold up . . . So, you're telling me the brother died in the prison bus bullshit, and this random junkie claims he isn't dead, and he knows him?"

"Uhh, I guess . . . That's not exactly how the conversation went, but that's pretty much the basics."

"I want to speak with this junkie immediately!" Fisher demanded.

"Calm down, Agent. The junkie is a lying piece of shit. Out of all the people I've mentioned, what the hell would you want to talk to him for?"

"Let me slow it down and lay it out for you. A junkie called the tip line and said he knew your suspect. Is that correct?"

"That's right."

"The junkie claims your suspect hangs out with his girlfriend's brother . . . right?"

"That's right."

"The junkie's girlfriend claims none of that is true, because her brother is deceased and lost his life in a so- called accident . . . right?"

"Right."

"And now, I'm telling you, that things may have certainly gotten very, very interesting. I must speak with this junkie . . . now!"

"Can you at least tell me what you expect to gain from speaking with him?"

"Let's just talk to him first. Show him a picture of my suspect and if he says he knows my suspect, which I'm assuming right now he does, he'll identify my guy as the girlfriend's brother. Then, I'll tell you a story that'll blow your mind."

"Can I see the photo first?"

Fisher produced the small black and white mug photo and handed it to Detective Jenkins.

"Never seen him in my life," Jenkins spoke. "And exactly what is the crime that you're pursuing on this man?"

"That will all be a part of the story if it comes together. Now, can we find this junkie or what?"

"That's easy, he's in the Orange County jail."

"We taking your car or mine?"

"This better be good. We'll take yours," Jenkins stated and rose from his desk. He checked his watch and said, "It's getting late and we're not exactly down the street. We better make this fast."

Fisher leaped out of his seat and quickly followed Jenkins out of the office. *This might be the jackpot*! Fisher thought.

Chapter 28

Orlando, FL

Two hours later

After using their credentials to gain access into the Orange County Jail, Fisher and Jenkins entered an interrogation room and impatiently waited for their requested inmate to appear. After a long, fifteen-minute wait, the door to their room was opened by a correctional officer, and then a ashy black man wearing a navy blue jumpsuit walked inside. The inmate looked like he had just participated in a food fight.

Mikey stepped into the center of the room and looked puzzled as he wondered what the two white men could possibly want.

Fisher and Jenkins stared at Mikey with serious faces and watched him uncomfortably fidget under their gaze.

Fisher broke the silence and said, "Take a seat."

Mikey did as he was instructed and sat down in one of the cold seats.

"Michael Black . . . right?" Fisher asked.

"Uhh, yes . . . yes, sir."

"Alright, I'm Federal Agent Fisher and this is Homicide Detective Jenkins. We're here about a homicide you—"

"Whoa! Whoa! Hold up, man, I don't know shit about no homicide! I ain't never killed nobody in my life! I ain't never even thought about killing somebody, I ain't—"

"Relax!" Fisher blurted. "This isn't about you killing anybody. It's about your knowledge of someone who has committed murder. Now tell me. . . do you know this man?" Fisher showed Mikey the notorious picture of Bo-T and watched Mikey's eyes light up like a lamp.

"Yeah! Yeah! I know him! I swear to God, I know him!" Mikey shouted.

"Okay, okay. . . calm down, Michael. Why are you so excited?"

"Because I tried to tell some detectives before that I knew him, and they didn't believe me. They called me a lying piece of shit and threatened to add more charges on me for bullshittin them, but I promise I'm not lying!"

"What you locked up for?" Fisher quizzed.

"I was buying some dope from this dude I usually do business with, and after copping a lil something to get the monkey off my back, the dude told me I could use his bathroom to handle my business if I was in a rush to get right. I was so eager to get a fix, I rushed into the bathroom and did what I had to do. Ten minutes later, I'm on the floor floating on clouds and the door burst open. The fucking DEA rushed the trap and I got caught up in the sweep. They charged me with possession and violation of probation."

"I see . . . So, tell me, how do you know this man?"

"Like I told the other guys, he hangs out with my girlfriend's brother. They're always doing crazy shit together and they hate me."

"What type of crazy shit?"

"Uhh, I've listened in on a few of their conversations and I always catch them talking about robberies, drugs, money and guns. The brother lives here and the other guy in your picture lives in Tampa, I believe."

Fisher gave Jenkins a quick glance and a smile. Jenkins began to gain more and more interest in the way things were starting to play out.

"Why do they hate you?" Fisher continued.

"Well, the very first time I met them, they jumped me. They showed up at the house one day out of the blue and my girls brother sucker-punched me. Before I could fuck him up, the other guy jumped in. I let the first incident go, but one day I was snooping through my girl's brother's shit in his room, and I found a box full of Molly and weed in his closet. I took the box out of spite and somehow, he found out it was me.

"I tried to avoid him, but he caught me slipping one day and they ambushed me at my sister's apartment. They beat the shit out of me! Broke my jaw, broke one of my ribs and even shot me in the hand . . . look," Mikey spoke and lifted his hand to show the bullet wound.

"Alright, listen, there's a really major problem we're having with your story. It's been brought to our attention that your girl-friend's brother isn't even alive. He's been dead for nearly a year, so how do you explain that?"

"Listen, I thought the same thing at first. She told me her brother was in prison when I met her, then she told me he died one day. She was all emotional for a while, but one day dude just popped up at the front door, like I told you. I answered the door and this dude I've never seen before introduces himself as my girl's brother . . . Since her brother was supposed to be dead, I didn't believe a word that came out of his mouth.

"I tried to question his story and that's when he sucker-punched me. I didn't even know the other guy was there until they started jumping me. Once I got myself back together and ran into the house behind them, I saw my girl and the dude together and the resem-blance was undeniable. They're twins! I still don't know the story, but that's what happened, and I swear I'm telling the truth!"

"Alright, well, I've got a picture right here of some other guy that may have been with your girlfriend's brother before, and I want to know if you've seen him around." Fisher held up the picture of the black and white mug photo and Mikey went ballistic.

"That's him! That's him! I swear to God, that's him!"

"This is who? You've seen him with your girlfriend's brother before?"

"No, man! That's him! That's my girlfriend's brother!"

"Really? Are you sure?"

"Hell yeah!"

"What's your girlfriend's address?"

"Give me a pen." Mikey quickly accepted a pen and paper from the agent and scribbled Ashley's address on it.

"This is barely legible," Fisher pointed out.

"Want me to rewrite it?"

"It's alright, this will work."

"So, what happens now?" Mikey questioned.

"Like the detectives before, we're going to check things out and if your help gets us anywhere, we'll gladly put a good word in with your attorney and your judge. How would you like to have your probation reinstated?"

"Hell, yeah! They tryna send me to prison for four years . . . I can't go to fucking prison! Please get me reinstated."

"Just keep doing what you're doing and you'll hear something in a week or so."

"Thank you, sir, thank you!"

"No need to thank me, it's all on you . . . you can leave now."

Mikey quickly bolted from the room and was escorted back to his dorm.

"What now?" Jenkins asked Fisher.

"Now we visit the sister / girlfriend."

"Alright, but you said that if your guy got identified as the girl's brother, then you'd tell me some story I'd never believe. This shit's already weird as fuck, so what's up?"

"Let's get in the car . . . you drive, and I'll explain."

***

"Alright, lay it on me," Jenkins spoke, while occasionally glancing at the GPS monitor and following the highlighted path to Ashley's house.

"Drive, listen, and do not ask questions until I'm finished," Fisher began. He took a moment to consider where he should begin. He took a deep breath and started speaking. "Alright. . . look, for starters, the whole prison bus incident was complete bullshit. That was a staged accident that never really happened, and—"

"What!" Jenkins blurted.

"I told you not to interrupt!" Fisher shouted. "Once you hear what I've got to say, you'll be a part of a conspiracy that's way bigger than the both of us and once you're in . . . you're in . . . no turning back!"

Jenkins kept his eyes on the road and sighed. "Alright, I'm listening."

"Like I was saying, this goes back a little bit before that. It all started with the president and—"

"The president of the United States!"

"Jenkins, please! Let me finish . . . but yes, the president of the United States." Fisher rubbed his hands together. "The president called us, him and the CIA . . . They informed us about these new mini nuclear warheads being made in China. The warheads were being manufactured into the tips of bullets made for assault rifles and other military weapons.

"The purpose of these new nuclear weapons was to increase the probability of a kill shot during war. A single bullet could make contact with something as simple as your pinky toe and the nuclear warhead would explode and the radiation would evaporate your whole body. Tricky head shots are no longer needed. Vests and other forms of armor would be useless and our soldiers would be nearly unstoppable.

"China decided to sell their invention to the U.S., so the president said he wanted a legitimate test run, before he made the deal. He called us up and gave us the rundown and we ended up finding a prison in Milton, Florida that would serve the experiment perfectly. Yes, a lot of innocent lives would be lost, but then again, we're talking about a bunch of lowlifes that threw their lives away anyway. They're really not that innocent when you think about it.

"I put a team together and we went in with the China-made weapons. One by one, we tested them out. They did exactly as they were promoted to do, and the experiment was on overall success. But then, somehow, two of the inmates escaped! How? Nobody knows. But I never believed it. I thought it was all a lie to get me fired so ever since then I've been searching for clues or evidence that would show proof of two men escaping. My search led me to your doorstep and now, here we are.

"Two indictable criminals and both have been identified as men from our experiment. I found this picture of my ghost man inside the prison under a bunk. Now that we've got a trail on the ghost, we have to apply pressure and guarantee we don't lose it. We've got to find these fuckers and haul them in. . . . dead or alive . . ."

221

The detective stared straight ahead and kept pushing forward. The GPS monitor announced that he had missed a turn, so he quickly maneuvered to make a U-turn.

"So, you don't even work for the FBI as of now?" Jenkins asked.

"They blamed the body count shortage on me and gave me the boot."

"If it weren't for the conversation we just had with that man in the county jail, I'd think that whole story you just gave me was bullshit. Really, it's still borderline bullshit, but at the same time, how else could I explain my unsolved mysteries?" Jenkins pulled into Ashley's driveway and turned off the car. "So, how do we play this?"

"Just follow my lead. Things might get a little out of hand but whatever you do, don't panic!"

They exited the vehicle in unison and approached the porch. Fisher lightly tapped on the door, and they rang the doorbell. They could hear the doorbell echoing through the silent house as Fisher pressed the bell again. Eventually, the silence gave way to footsteps and when the footsteps stopped in front of the door, the door opened.

"Ummm, hey," Ashley spoke in a suspicious voice.

Fisher looked down at a piece of paper and said, "Ashley Watson?"

"Yes, problem?" Ashley quizzed.

"Actually, yes. . . possibly. . . Can we come in and ask you a few questions?"

"Why come in when you can ask me right here?"

"Your answers might lead to more questions and this is very, very serious. I think it would be best if we all had a seat and discussed this matter privately."

"You haven't even identified yourselves, but you expect me to let you in my home?"

Fisher produced his ID and back-up badge, then stated, "Special Agent Fisher, FBI."

Jenkins quickly followed suit and showed his badge. "Homicide Detective Jenkins."

Ashley looked surprised, puzzled and scared, but she held her ground and asked, "What do y'all want with me?"

"Like I said, this would be better off discussed in private."

Ashley rolled her eyes and decided the easiest way out of whatever this was, would be to just get it over with. If she needed to lie, she would. And she would say whatever needed to be said to get these guys out of her house as quickly as possible.

They casually made their way to Ashley's living room, and all took seats on the couch. Jenkins and Fisher sat close together on one couch and Ashley sat across from them on another.

"Well?" Ashley spoke.

"Do you know this man?" Fisher asked while holding up a picture of Jenkin's suspect.

Ashley immediately recognized the popular picture of Bo-T, but kept a straight face while replying, "Never seen him in my life."

"What about this man?" Fisher asked and held up a picture of Mikey.

"That's my ex-boyfriend and if this conversation has anything to do with him, then I have no further answers. I already talked to some detectives about him. I do not talk to him anymore and I don't want anything to do with him."

"Fair enough, one more quick question though . . . where is this man?" Fisher asked and held up the picture of her brother.

A perfectly timed tear fell from Ashley's eye, and she shouted, "Get the fuck out my house! I'm tired of y'all disrespecting me in my home like this and—"

"Shut the fuck up and answer the question!" Fisher yelled and rose from the couch.

Ashley nervously stood up as well and said, "I keep telling y'all my brother died in a—"

"Accident?" Fisher interjected. "Let's skip the bullshit. I know all about the accident, and I know just like you know, it wasn't an accident. Where's your brother?"

"I have all the reports and all the—"

"Bitch, I made the reports! I created the whole accident and I know you know the truth! Last chance, where's your brother?"

"I-I-I don't know!" Ashley cried.

"When's the last time you saw him?"

"I don't talk to him, I—"

Fisher lunged across the living room and slapped Ashley clean across the face. When her head flew back, he grabbed her by the throat and slung her into a bookshelf against the wall. Her head snapped hard into the wood, and she collapsed to the floor.

"What the fuck, man!" Jenkins shouted and jumped from his seat.

"Shut the fuck up!" Fisher snapped. "I told you not to panic!"

"We're fucking law enforcement! You just physically assaulted this woman in her own home!"

"Says who?"

"She knows our fucking names!"

"What the fuck is she going to say? Two officers came into her house and assaulted her, because they were looking for her dead brother that's really alive and she's been hiding? Get a fucking grip!"

Jenkins shook his head and paced the floor. Fisher stood over Ashley's unconscious body and knelt down to examine her. He placed two fingers against her neck and checked her pulse.

"She'll be fine," Fisher stated. He stuck his hand inside her sweatpants and pulled out her cell phone.

He activated the screen and was delighted to see there wasn't a code. He could inspect its contents freely. The first thing he did was look through her picture gallery for evidence of them recently together. He also wanted to see if she may have any photos at all that would reveal her brother's current appearance. All he found was a large collage of nude selfies.

"Someone's a freak," Fisher mumbled.

He then scrolled through her contacts and when he saw the name Twin, something registered in his mind, and he stopped. He copied the number into his phone and the scrolled through her text messages. One of her last texts was to the same number labeled under Twin. He tapped the name and read the recent messages.

Twin: Everything was great! You would've had a good time if you came out.

Me: Yeah, I'm sorry I couldn't make it, but I promise to come when I get a chance. I really wanna see you, twin.

Twin: Yeah whatever, you need to get yo lame ass out the house. You missed the best day. Ain't nothing gone top the grand opening!

Me: I know I know. I'm sorry. I'll try to come next weekend. Ocala, right?

Twin: Yup

Me: I love you, twin

Twin: Love you too, mini-me.

Fisher closed his eyes and images of the amazing strip club he was in last night rushed his brain. He thought about the whole night and froze when he remembered being tossed out by the two iced-out bouncers. "Fuck!" he shouted and slammed the phone down. He sprung to his feet and rushed towards the door.

"What's up?" Jenkins blurted while quickly following behind.

"I know where they're at!" Fisher shouted.

"Where?"

"Get in the car! I'm driving!"

Fly Rock

Chapter 29

Ocala, FL

Sugar stood in their bird's-eye-view office and let her eyes roam around the club. It was their second night, and everything was going just as well as the first night. She looked down at one of the strippers making her ass cheeks pop while in a split and said to herself, "Damn, that's a good trick!"

"How's it looking out there?" Spice asked.

"Looking great!" Sugar replied.

"Where's Bo-T's big head ass?"

Sugar looked around again and said "Umm, I'm not sure . . . . I don't see him. I don't see him or Wizz, actually."

"It's alright, I'll check the cameras."

While Spice stepped over to the camera monitors, Sugar continued to search through the thick crowd with her eyes.

"What the fuck!" Spice shouted and leaped towards the door.

Spice's sudden outburst and movements made Sugar flinch and shout, "What happened bitch?"

"This nigga got me all the way fucked up!"

Before Sugar could ask another question, Spice went flying out the door and running down the stairs. Sugar quickly ran behind her and tried her best to mimic Spice's movements as she elbowed her way through the crowds. Sugar could see Spice's mouth moving, but her words weren't audible over the screaming music. Her facial expressions said a mouthful though. Something wasn't right and whatever it was, it had Spice furious.

"Mmmm . . . you taste soooo good, daddy," the brown-skinned beauty moaned, while sliding Wizz's dick into her throat. The stripper's name was Pleasure and Wizz was beginning to see why.

Wizz and Bo-T were doing their usual rounds around the club, making sure the strippers weren't being harassed or bothered.

During their rounds, two gorgeous women named Pleasure and Pain approached them with a problem they needed assistance with.

The women led Bo-T and Wizz into the locker room and began to explain their problem. Pain told Bo-T she needed help applying oil to her back, and explained that Pleasure wouldn't do it, because she was uncomfortable rubbing on women.

Bo-T initially laughed at the request but went along with it. What started out as oil being applied to Pain's back turned into a full body massage and when Pain bent over and spread her luscious cheeks, her deliciously pouty pussy became suddenly irresistible, and Bo-T had to taste it.

Now Wizz was getting his dick swallowed, and Bo-T was leaning back in a chair, enjoying a mind-blowing rodeo ride.

"Ooooooh, shit! I'm bout to cum!" Pain shouted while bouncing on top of Bo-T's lap.

The door suddenly flew open, and Spice ran into the room full speed and charged at the woman bouncing on top of her man. When Wizz saw the door fly open, he immediately pulled his dick out of the stripper's mouth and pulled his pants up.

"Nasty bitch!" Spice shouted and grabbed a handful of Pain's hair. She viciously punched her on the side of her face and slung her to the ground.

"Owww! What the fuck!" Pain screamed while trying to brace her fall.

"Oh, shit! Chill out, Spice!" Bo-T blurted in shock.

"I'll kill you, bitch!" Spice yelled and quickly removed one of her six-inch heels. Tears flooded her eyes and she screamed again. "I'll fucking kill you!"

WHAM! WHAM! WHAM!

Spice began to ruthlessly beat Pain in the head with her shoe.

Sugar bolted through the door and looked at Wizz.

"I wasn't doing nothing!" Wizz blurted with a straight face.

Sugar turned her attention to Spice and shouted, "Ohh, my goodness! Spice, stop!"

Bo-T quickly fixed his attire and snatched Spice up by her waist. Blood was all over Spice's legs and a large pool of red liquid began flooding around Pain's lifeless face.

Bo-T slung Spice to the side and shouted, "What the fuck! Are you fucking stupid! What the fuck!"

"Fuck you!" Spice cried.

"Oh, my God, she's dead!" Sugar shouted.

A loud screech suddenly erupted from the doorway and when everybody looked back, one of the white dancers had her hands over her mouth and then shouted, "Somebody get some help! Somebody, help!"

Another stripper quickly appeared and shouted, "Oh, my God, she's dead! Call 9-1-1!"

Bo-T looked at Wizz and shouted "Fuck! This is bad, Skee! We gotta go!"

"Ain't no way in hell I'd be here when the police show up! Skram, Skee, skram!" Wizz blurted while bolting for the door.

A large crowd was quickly forming around the door, but Bo-T bulldozed through them and quickly evacuated the club. They jumped inside their black and red Bentley and burned rubber before the blue and red circus appeared.

***

Fisher swerved into the Sweet & Spicy parking lot and was forced to come to a complete stop by the barricade of law enforcement. Jenkins took in the scenery and wondered what the reason was behind the ambulance and swarm of police cars. Yellow caution tape had been plastered over all the entrances to the building and officers were scattered around, asking beautiful half-naked women questions.

"What the fuck is all of this about?" Fisher blurted to himself.

"Whatever it is, if our guys are really here, then it can't be pretty," Jenkins stated.

"Let's continue on foot," Fisher recommended.

They exited the car together and approached the biggest cluster of officers.

"Whoa-whoa-whoa! This is a crime scene!" one of the officers blurted with his hand out to stop them from walking any further. "The group of police and the yellow tape should be a clear sign to get lost."

Fisher held up his back-up badge and said, "I'm Federal Agent Fisher and this is my partner, Jenkins. We've got questions in regards to this establishment, and possibly your crime scene. We expect our questions to be thoroughly answered. We want to speak with whoever's leading the crime scene and we need to speak with the woman that owns this club."

The officer leaned in for a closer looked at Fisher's badge and said, "My apologies, Agent. The lead officer is that sergeant over there and he will inform you about the owners."

Fisher followed the officer's point and rested his eyes on a middle-aged white man, conversating with the woman he had seen the previous night when he regained his consciousness and left the club. "Thank you." He concluded with the officer and walked away.

Jenkins followed behind Fisher and kept his mouth closed. This new revelation was still shocking, unbelievable, and clearly much bigger than him, so he just kept his eyes and ears open, and his mouth closed.

"How's it going, Sergeant?" I'm Federal Agent Fisher and this is my partner." He flashed his badge long enough to be read and continued "I've been told you're running lead on this investigation, and I might have a few questions for you." He turned his attention towards the shockingly beautiful club owner and said, "But I'd most definitely like to speak with you first. I'm sure you've got a lot to deal with right now, but I have some very serious questions that must be answered. For starters, do you remember me from last night or rather early this morning?"

Sugar looked sad and exhausted, and her voice reflected the same emotions as she said, "No sir, I don't remember you."

"I was at your grand opening last night and got kicked out, or should I say thrown out, by two of your staff members. I passed out in my car, and you politely woke me up the next morning, which was this morning. You told me you owned the club and I apologized for my behavior and left."

"Umm. . . okay, I remember the scenario, but that wasn't me you talked to. That was my sister . . . we're twins."

"Seriously?"

"Yes, sir."

"So, she's the owner?"

"We both own the club. That's why it's called Sweet & Spicy."

"Oh, okay. Well, uhh, where is your sister? It might be better if I talked to the both of you."

"My sister isn't available at this time." A lone tear fell down Sugar's cheek. "She just got arrested for first-degree murder."

"Damn! Is that what all of this about?" Fisher asked while waving his arm around the cop-filled area.

"Yup."

"What happened?"

"I'd rather not talk about it right now, and I'm honestly too tired and emotionally drained to answer any more questions. I just spent the last hour answering questions. Can this at least wait until tomorrow?"

Fisher felt sorry for the woman, but his trail was far too hot to let go. "Answer one more question please . . . where are these two men?" He held up the photo of Wizz in one hand and the photo of Bo-T in the other.

Sugar's eyes revealed a quick hint of fear and confusion as she replied, "I don't even know who those men are, so I don't believe I can tell you where they are."

"How could you not know them, and they work for you?"

"I know all of my workers and neither of them work for me."

"Well, I may have been slightly drunk last night, maybe even very drunk, but I have a vivid memory of these two men throwing me out of your club last night. And since their shirts said Security like all the other bouncers, I have a very strong reason to believe these two men worked here. Maybe your cameras can reflect my opinions?"

Sugar felt herself getting nervous and started to say something, but the officer cut into the conversation and asked, "Can I take a look at those photos?"

Fisher handed him the photos and the sergeant said, "There's a few differences in appearance as far as facial hair and weight, but I'd definitely say these are the same two men we're looking for right now."

"Looking for them for what?" Fisher questioned.

"From the evidence and information, we've gathered so far tonight, these two men are definitely a part of the security detail. And they were both in the back of the club engaging in sexual acts with two dancers. The other club owner is very fond of this guy right here and when she saw him on camera having sex, she went into a rage. We both know the term 'hell has no fury like a woman scorned.' She took one of her heels off and literally beat the dancer to death. The entire incident is on camera. Once everything hit the fan, these two guys ran out of the building and drove away in a black truck."

Fisher looked at Sugar and said, "So, you lied, and you do know these men?"

"They looked different in these pictures you have, and my mind is so burnt right now, I didn't recognize them."

"So, they're not here?"

"No," the sergeant and Sugar answered together.

"Can I please go home now? I need to sleep. I don't think I can take much more of all of this," Sugar whined.

"I would say yes . . . Agent?" the sergeant spoke.

"Uhh, alright, but I'm going to need to really speak with you tomorrow," Fisher stated to Sugar. "I need a number and address I can reach you at."

Sugar got a piece of paper and a pen from the sergeant and scribbled down her information.

"Will noon be a good time for you?" Fisher asked.

"Noon? That's too soon. It's nearly one o'clock in the morning right now. I need rest."

"Alright, 2:00 p.m., that's the best I can do."

"Alright, just give me a call first," Sugar stated. She then defeatedly turned around and walked away.

Fly Rock

Chapter 30

After leaving the club, Bo-T and Wizz rushed back to the house and considered their options. They quickly came to the conclusion that the police would eventually come there next if things fell apart, so they loaded up their truck with duffle bags full of money, pounds, bricks, jewelry, guns and about three weeks' worth of clothes. They then fled the house and found a local hotel not far from the inter-state, and paid a hefty amount of cash for a nice suite with no ID.

They showered up and decided that sleeping was their best op-tion at that point. Sometimes sleeping was a privilege in the fast life, so they decided to take advantage of the moment. In the morning, Wizz would take Sugar some money for Spice so she could supply her with all her needs and afford a good lawyer. Bonding out was probably out of the question and with the way things played out, she was probably about to be out of sight for a very long time.

***

Sugar woke up later in the morning a little before 8:00 am. Her body still felt tired, but her mind wouldn't allow her to sleep any longer. She had a lot to think about, a lot to deal with, and not enough time to make sense of it all.

She slipped out of her bed and slowly guided her naked body towards the bathroom. She looked into the mirror and frowned at her red puffy eyes and worried face. She thought Wizz and Bo-T would be in the house when she got back last night, but she thought wrong. She was forced to go to bed lonely and scared, and now she wasn't sure what to do.

Now that she was wide awake, she was being drowned with problems sleeping didn't solve. She stepped into the shower and let the steaming hot water soak her body. She stood in the shower for half an hour before eventually deciding to turn off the water and step out.

When she pulled the shower curtain back, she shouted, "Oh my God!" She took a deep breath and said, "Oh my God! You scared me, papi!"

Wizz lit up the blunt he had just finished rolling and deeply inhaled the smoke. He dropped a bag on the floor and said, "That's for Spice. Whatever she needs, get it. This should cover everything her heart will desire under her circumstances. I'm real sorry bout what happened, and I understand we're partially at fault. I accept that and I hope the two of you can forgive us one day. I'm not sure how this may play out, but it might not be good for Spice. Let her know to stay strong and keep her head up. So, where does that leave you?"

"What do you mean, where does that leave me?"

"For obvious reasons, me and Bo-T ain't about to be hanging out around here. The police might wanna ask you questions and I'm sure they'll wanna ask us some too, so we ain't tryna be hanging around until this shit blows over."

"Bae, the police are looking to question y'all, but I think there might be something else going on as well. After I talked with the police last night, the FBI showed up with a picture of you and Bo-T and had a lot of questions. I avoided the questions last night, but they scheduled a meeting with me today at two o'clock."

"The FBI?"

"Yes, papi."

"Did you see the picture of me?"

"Yeah, it looked like a mugshot. It was in black and white. You looked younger and you had an afro."

"Did they say what they wanted?"

"They just asked me where you were, because they knew you worked as a bouncer in my club. I told them I didn't know."

"Damn! I gotta go, bae, this ain't good," Wizz nervously stated while heading towards the door.

"Wait, papi! Wait," Sugar shouted and wrapped her arms around him. She tilted her head up and kissed him passionately like it could possibly be their last kiss. When they pulled away from each other, she said, "I love you, papi."

Wizz started backing away and whispered, "I usually don't say this too often . . . but I love you too, Sugar." He then turned around and bolted from the house.

Sugar stood in the bathroom and felt even more lonely than she did an hour ago.

***

Fisher and Jenkins didn't have many options when they left the club, so they decided to follow Sugar home and wait in the shadows, until they could meet with her in the afternoon. They didn't want to seem suspicious, so instead of parking in front of her gate, they trespassed into an empty house across the street. They backed up deep into the shadows of the large home and watched Sugar's house from the distance.

Hours had passed and they took turns dosing off until the sun rose and something amazing happened. A big black Bentley truck approached the gate and slowly entered the premises.

The early morning sun beamed off of the shiny truck and they both perked up. They watched closely as the young man they both knew as Ashley's dead brother casually eased out of the truck and used a key to enter the house.

"Holy shit! Sweet mother of Jesus! Let's get this bastard!" Jenkins shouted and reached for the door handle.

"Whoa-whoa-whoa! Calm down, Detective! We didn't come all this way for a damn cheeseburger . . . we need the whole meal, burger and the fries! They're obviously together If we lay on him, I'm a hundred percent positive we'll eventually find them both," Fisher reasoned.

"Damn it, you're right . . . let's see what this piece of shit is up to."

They waited less than an hour and their suspect suddenly flew out of the house looking around nervously. He jumped inside the truck and quickly sped away. Fisher gave him a little distance and then quickly trailed behind him. They followed Wizz at a distance for almost twenty minutes as he led him into the parking lot of a nice hotel. While they were parking, their suspect was walking through the hotel's glass doors.

"What now? Do we follow him in?" Jenkins asked.

"He ran out of the house so fast, I'd say he's in a hurry. I think the woman told him about us and now he's in a panic. I can almost guarantee our other man is inside this hotel right now. So, we can either go in and trap them, or wait until they come out."

"Well, I ain't gone lie . . . I've got to take a very serious shit right now. So, let's go inside and while you're working your FBI Special Agent magic on the desk clerk, I'll be in the bathroom taking the browns to the Super Bowl."

"You got the bubble guts? You scared?"

"Of course not. I just had too much damn coffee and that omelet I had yesterday picked a bad time to come out."

"Yeah, whatever. We're going in . . . be ready for whatever and if you have to, shoot to kill!"

"Should we alert the local authorities and ask for back up?"

"Fuck no! This is an A-B operation . . . no outsiders! We're going to take these fuckers down and we're going to do it alone!"

"Well, here goes nothing, I guess . . . let's get her done!"

Chapter 31

"I'm telling you, Skee, something ain't right! We need to slide ASAP!" Wizz stated after explaining his encounter with Sugar.

"Alright, fuck it. We got enough money to go anywhere in the world right now. Let's just hop in the car and just ride till the wheels fall off," Bo-T spoke.

They left all the small items they had in the room and stepped out the door. They quickly walked down the hall and waited for an elevator. When the elevator came, they stepped inside and pressed the button that would take them to the ground floor.

***

Jenkins stepped out of the restroom sweating. He adjusted his pants and met Fisher in the lobby. "Did you come up with anything?"

"Desk clerk recognized their photos and said they checked in last night under unknown. Apparently, they paid in nice amount of cash to sign in without identification. They're on the fifth floor in Suite 505."

"Alright, let's do this. How should we approach?"

"We're going to go straight up there and kick the door in! Guns blazing! Why waste time with a soft approach? We know these guys ain't going for that. . . we're going to go up there and either lay them down or gun them down! Once we kick the door down, the choice will be theirs."

"Well, it's showtime!"

They headed down a hallway that led to another hallway, with rooms going down both sides. They then approached an elevator and waited, after Fisher pressed the "UP" button. Both Fisher and Jenkins began to feel their adrenaline start to pump and they both knew this could possibly be their only chance to finally capture the most elusive criminals either of them had ever met. This was the moment of truth.

***

When the elevator doors slid open, Bo-T and Wizz made a move to step out and found their path blocked by two white men. Bo-T was already on edge and the look in one of the white men's eyes didn't sit well with him. When Bo-T looked down and saw the black and gold badge hanging off the white man's hip, his natural reflexes kicked in and he threw a quick left jab, followed up by a powerful right hook.

The left jab hit Fisher square in the nose and the right hook connected with Fisher's temple. The force caused his whole body to shift sideways and collapse.

Jenkins attempted to quickly unholster his weapon, but a swift kick to the groin from Wizz caused him to cease all actions and fold over.

Wizz attempted another kick that Jenkins managed to barely dodge. He quickly drew his own pistol and fired three loud shots into the center of Jenkin's chest. Jenkins collapsed to the floor, while the loud shots continued to echo down the quiet hallway.

An alarm suddenly began wailing throughout the building and Bo-T and Wizz bolted around a corner and down another long hallway.

Fisher dizzily sprang back to his feet and looked down at Jenkins.

"Go get 'em! Don't let them get away! I'll be fine," Jenkins groaned as blood began to soak through his shirt and onto the carpet.

Fisher quickly drew his weapon and bolted around the corner for their suspects. As soon as he turned the corner, a gun went off and bullets began raining in his direction. He dove to the side behind a laundry cart, while chunks of wall broke over his head.

Bo-T and Wizz turned down another long hall and realized they were heading down a dead-end hall. They needed to go back the way they came. As soon as they turned around, bullets began screaming down the hall in their direction. They were forced to run deeper down the hall.

There was an open room door at the very end of the hall next to a window, and they ran directly towards it, while blindly shooting over their shoulders and dodging bullets. The moment they approached the end of the hall, an extremely hot and sharp pain surged through Wizz's shoulder, and then a second hot bullet ripped through his left leg and sent him flying into Bo-T.

The force of the impact and Wizz's weight knocked Bo-T off balance and together, their tangled bodies crashed into the hallway window, and they flew through it. Glass shattered and put a deep gash across Bo-T's forehead, and he cut his hands as he sprang to his feet.

"Get up, Skee! We can make it to the car!" Bo-T shouted.

"I'm hit, Skee! I'm hit!" Wizz painfully shouted.

"Fuck that! Get yo soft ass up! Come on, nigga!" Bo-T yelled and pulled him up. He helped Wizz wobble as fast as he could towards the car, while keeping a tight grip on his pistol.

Fisher appeared in the broken window and sent two shots in their direction.

Glass shattered through a window in a nearby car, but Bo-T and Wizz kept wobbling forward. Bo-T let off a couple shots behind him and Fisher ducked behind the wall. Bo-T squeezed his trigger one more time and when it clicked, he threw the gun to the ground.

Bo-T lifted Wizz completely over his shoulder and used every muscle he had to run as fast as he could. And when he made it to the car, he quickly hit the button on his key to unlock it and tossed Wizz into the passenger seat.

Bo-T had Wizz's blood all over him as he jumped into the driver's seat and mashed the gas. The truck jumped forward and they screeched away.

***

Fisher rose from the ground and looked down at his blood-dripping arm. One of Bo-T's wild shots had grazed his right bicep. "These motherfuckers will not get away!" he shouted. He carefully stepped through the shattered window and then sprinted across the lot towards his car.

When he swerved away from the hotel, it wasn't hard for him to see which way they had went. Cars were swerving left and right trying to avoid being hit by the speeding truck. He followed the forcefully created path and increased his speed. Since he was going down a path already created, he was able to bring his car to a speed much faster than the truck's speed and it wasn't long before he had them in sight.

Fisher mimicked their stunt double moves and watched them as they dangerously cut across two lanes and merged onto the highway ramp. He followed them onto the interstate and the field became suddenly much bigger. The Bentley truck had speed, but nowhere near enough speed to outrun the Jaguar.

Fisher quickly closed the distance between them. He used his knees to control the steering wheel and keep the car going straight, while using his only good arm to remove his nearly empty clip and submit a new one.

He crept along the side of the Bentley and unloaded his pistol through his open driver's window. His bullets rained into the side of the truck and sent shattered glass everywhere. The truck then suddenly swerved over in a way that made Fisher believe the driver nearly lost control. He quickly maneuvered his way back along the side of the Bentley, and fired the rest of his clip into the front passenger tire.

The tire burst and caused the truck to lean over at an odd angle. The rubber from the tire flew off and the metal rim began sending sparks into the air.

Fisher positioned his knees under the steering wheel and repeated his movements to secure his last magazine into his gun. This would be his last chance to bring the vehicle to a halt. He had to make it count.

Bo-T struggled to keep the truck straight and the truck started decreasing in speed. He looked over at Wizz and shouted "Stay with me, Skee! I'ma get us out this shit! Just don't fall asleep on me, nigga!"

Wizz was losing a lot of blood and in a voice barely audible, he whispered, "I'm good, Skee . . . where we going?"

"I'ma shake this crazy ass cop first, then I'ma get you to a hospital!"

"Fuck the hospital! They gone book me, Skee!"

"I'ma take you to a hospital in another state! As soon as we—"

SKUUUUUUURRTT!

Bo-T swerved to the side as another storm of bullets rained in their direction. "Fuck!" he shouted. He tried to think of something to do, but couldn't concentrate. Between dodging bullets, trying to keep the car afloat and trying to get away, his mind was in a million places.

"I need your help, Skeecho!" Bo-T shouted.

Wizz had one hand over his bloody shoulder and his head was hanging down with his eyes closed.

"Wake up!" Bo-T shouted and shoved him.

Wizz opened his eyes and slowly lifted his head. "What's up, Skee, we made it?" he slurred.

Bo-T reached into the back seat and felt around for one of their weapons that had been loaded into the truck the night before. He felt his fingertips make contact with cold steel and he nearly lost control of the car as he grabbed for the weapon. He ended up with the MAC-90 in his hand and he tossed it on Wizz's lap.

"Get yo ass up, Skee! It's all on you! Get that cracka off our backs!" Bo-T shouted.

Wizz turned his head to look out of the window right when a final shower of bullets crashed into the truck. The back tire popped, and Bo-T finally lost control. The truck spun out and tumbled like a toy that just got thrown by a child.

Bo-T was thrown through the windshield of the truck and landed on a patch of grass against a large tree in the median of the interstate. He cried in pain and looked down at his broken arm. Blood poured over his face and began to blur his vision. He tried to move his legs but couldn't. He felt himself slowly losing consciousness and tried his best to fight it.

Fisher slammed his fist against the steering wheel with excitement and pride and shouted "Shit, yeah! I got you fuckers now! I got you!" He slammed on the brakes and pulled the Jaguar to the side of the road.

The truck looked like it had gotten hit by an eighteen-wheeler, and there was a body twitching in the tree-filled land on the other side of the guard rail. Fisher jumped over the rail like a maniac on a mission and rushed up to Bo-T.

There was blood leaking from Bo-T's face and his arm looked bent in a way it should never be bent. Fisher kneeled in front of him and punched him in the face. Bo-T's head jerked from the punch, and he coughed up blood.

"Still alive, huh? I gotta give it to you . . . you're a tough motherfucker! But I've got you now, don't I? Do you know who the fuck I am?" Fisher asked.

Bo-T continued to cough, and Fisher slapped him.

"Motherfucker, I asked you a question! Do you know who the fuck I am?"

Bo-T stared at Fisher with one of the most intense stares he'd ever seen. Fisher cocked his hand back to slap him again and received a thick wad of blood-filled spit to the face.

Fisher wiped the spit off of his forehead and looked disgusted. "Oh, yeah? Well, fuck you too!" he shouted and slapped Bo-T again. He then proceeded to tell Bo-T who he was and why he was there.

Fisher explained everything that Bo-T had no knowledge of but had been curious about over the past year. Bo-T simply stared at the rogue cop in disbelief while taking deep breaths.

"Now, I'm about to drag yo broken ass to my car and serve you on a platter to the round table," Fisher stated and stood to his feet.

Tat-Tat-Tat-Tat-Tat-Tat-Tat-Tat-Tat-Tat-Tat-Tat!

Fisher's body was suddenly ripped in half and thrown against the tree Bo-T was laying against. As the loud shots continued to thunder and pin Fisher's body against the tree, blood splattered all over Bo-T's body.

When the shots finally stopped, Bo-T was covered in blood, dirt and wood. Bo-T tilted his head up and saw Wizz leaning over the guard rail with the life-saving MAC-90. A smile spread across Bo-T's face as he watched Wizz use all the strength he had in his battered body to roll over the rail and limp to his rescue.

Wizz dropped the MAC-90 and took a deep breath. His body was in an unexplainable amount of pain and soaked in blood. He limped over to Bo-T and barely recognized him his blood-filled face. He noticed Bo-T's arm was broken at the elbow and frowned. He leaned over and cried through the pain as he pulled Bo-T onto his feet.

They used each other for support and limped back to the truck. The truck was upside down and of no use. They popped open the doors and slowly removed all of their tossed-up bags. One by one, they carried each duffle bag to the Jaguar the cop had been driving and loaded it up.

Once all of their money, guns and drugs had been loaded, they didn't care about anything else. Wizz got in the passenger seat and Bo-T took up the driver's seat. Bo-T eased the car back onto the interstate and merged back into the early traffic. He drove with one hand and tried his best to think about something other than the pain screaming from his broken body.

"You did it, Skee!" Bo-T spoke to Wizz. "That was all on you back there! You came through!"

"I think I'm losing too much blood," Wizz whispered. His face was getting pale, and his voice was low.

"Don't even worry bout it, Skeecho! We're unstoppable! Just lay back and think about the bitch you gone be fucking in Barbados!"

"Barbados sounds good, Skeeman."

"Damn right it do, and after we get you patched up, that's exactly where we're going!"

Wizz dropped his head and didn't respond.

"Get the fuck up, Skee!" Bo-T shouted.

Wizz opened his eyes and said, "I'm here, I'm here."

"Talk to me, Skeecho!"

"You talk to me, nigga," Wizz whispered.

"Alright, listen . . . I'ma tell you some crazy ass shit that's gone blow yo mind! That crooked ass cop told me why he was on us and you ain't gone believe what this cracka told me!"

"What he say?"

"Stay with me, Skee, and keep your eyes open. When I finish the story, you'll understand exactly what it means to be here today and gone tomorrow!"

Chapter 32

Bo-T pulled up to the front of the first hospital he could find. He wasn't sure what city he was in, but he knew he was in Georgia. He had entered the state almost an hour ago and had been struggling to find the nearest hospital, but he finally found one.

Bo-T had been driving non-stop other than his one pit stop to get gas. Darkness had eventually overcome the daylight during his travel, but he continued to push through the night. Now that he was parked in front of the hospital, he was having mixed emotions.

Wizz was slumped over in the passenger seat and hadn't spoken in hours. He was still breathing though, so Bo-T figured his body had simply shut down from the pain he was enduring.

Tears began to slide down Bo-T's dirty face. "You a soulja, Skeecho! You one of the realest niggas I done ever met and I love you, my nigga!" He stepped out of the car and went into the backseat.

Bo-T split all of the money and drugs down the middle and separated them in the duffle bags. Wizz's half filled up three duffles, and he knew it would be too much for him to carry, so he took most of the kilos and gave him most of the money. He squeezed a decent amount of drugs and as much money as he could into two duffles, and pulled them out of the car.

Bo-T walked around to the passenger seat and opened the door. He shook Wizz, but Wizz didn't move. He shook him harder and Wizz slowly opened his bloodshot eyes.

"We made it, Skeecho," Bo-T spoke.

"Where we at?" Wizz whispered.

"Right now, for you, we gone call this heaven. Get out the car."

Bo-T helped him step out and leaned him against the car. He lifted each duffle bag, one at a time, and hung them around Wizz's neck. He then placed a single pistol in his waistband.

"I love you, my nigga! Remember that!" Bo-T stated through his brotherly tears.

"I love you too, my brother! What you think gone happen when I go in?"

"I don't know, Skee. I don't know, but whatever happens, you can handle it. Remember, you can't be traced through any records, but yo prints will eventually register if you sit in there for too long. So, get patched up and run!"

"What about you? Look at yo arm, my nigga. Let's go in together."

"I don't want us to get caught up in the same spot, so I'ma keep moving and find another hospital somewhere else. I might keep going north, I don't know yet."

Wizz stumbled forward and nearly fell to the floor.

"Man, get yo ass in there before you pass back out!" Bo-T ordered. "We'll meet again. Believe that! Souljas together only need each other. I love ya!"

Bo-T then left Wizz standing alone and jumped back into the car. He slowly pulled away without looking back and left Wizz wobbling nervously in front of the ER building.

Wizz took a deep breath and felt himself slowly losing consciousness again. He was scared to go inside, but he knew if he didn't, he would probably die. When he took his first step towards the entrance, the doors opened up and a black woman wearing a long white doctor's coat walked out.

The woman took one look at Wizz and screamed, "Oh, my goodness! What happened to you? You need to get inside immediately!"

"I need a doctor. I got shot and then I was in a bad car accident," Wizz explained.

"Well, if you hurry up and get inside, you'll be a lucky man, because I'm the doctor and I'm also the best surgeon we have. Let's hurry up and get you inside!" she screeched and reached for his hand.

Wizz shouted, "Ouch! My shoulder!"

"I'm sorry, I'm so sorry! Please just follow me."

When she turned around, Wizz grabbed her by the waist and stuck his pistol in her back.

"Oh my G—"

"Shut the fuck up! Please, don't yell . . . if you scream, you gone make me do some shit I ain't tryna do. Please." Wizz took a deep breath. "Now listen, I need your help, but not in there! I ain't going in there! Take me somewhere safe and patch me up . . . please. I'll pay you more money than you make in a year!"

"You need to go inside, sir! You nee—"

"I ain't going in! Where's yo car?"

"Please don't do this."

"I'm sorry, but I have to . . . Just help me out and I promise, I won't hurt you. Let's go to your car."

The woman nervously led Wizz across the parking lot, into a parking garage and eventually to her car. She had a new model Benz and slowly unlocked the doors.

Wizz pushed her into the car through the passenger's seat and made her climb over the middle into the driver's seat while he took the passenger seat.

He kept his bags around his neck and told her, "Now take me somewhere safe and patch me up . . . please."

"I don't understand. You need specific medical attention. I'll need specific equipment and medication that only the hospital can immediately provide. Your wounds need to be cleaned and—"

"Fuck that! I'll be fine with whatever you can come up with! Stitch me up, give me a Band-Aid, some Tylenol, I'll be fine. Now drive!"

The woman slowly pulled away from the hospital and thought about what she should do. Whatever trouble this man was obviously in didn't concern her. She only cared about his well-being as a person. She had been kindhearted all her life and chose to become a doctor, because she took pride in saving lives.

However, this stranger had just forced her into a situation at gunpoint and threatened her safety. This frightened her and made her current situation confusing. She tried to keep her eyes on the road as she drove to avoid looking at the man with the gun, but after nearly ten minutes of silence, she couldn't help it.

When she looked over at the blood-covered man in her passenger seat, with two large duffle bags hanging around his neck, she instantly realized he had been quiet because he was either dead or unconscious.

The gun he had pressured her with was now laying on the floor of her car as it fell from the man's hand. She stopped at a red light and leaned over to retrieve the gun. Now she had a bloody gun in her hand, a possibly dead man in her passenger seat and a decision to make. She grabbed his wrist and checked his pulse. It was very light, but it was there.

When the light turned green, she decided to take this complete stranger to her own home and tend to his unknown injuries. Something about his energy and spirit told her he had just been through a lot, and he really needed help. She quickly decided she would do her best to save him, and if he became well, she would be curious to know his story.

To Be Continued...
Here Today Gone Tomorrow 2
Coming Soon

Lock Down Publications and Ca$h Presents assisted
publishing packages.

BASIC PACKAGE $499
Editing
Cover Design
Formatting

UPGRADED PACKAGE $800
Typing
Editing
Cover Design
Formatting

ADVANCE PACKAGE $1,200
Typing
Editing
Cover Design
Formatting
Copyright registration
Proofreading
Upload book to Amazon

LDP SUPREME PACKAGE $1,500
Typing
Editing
Cover Design
Formatting
Copyright registration
Proofreading
Set up Amazon account
Upload book to Amazon
Advertise on LDP Amazon and Facebook page

***Other services available upon request. Additional charges may apply
Lock Down Publications
P.O. Box 944
Stockbridge, GA 30281-9998
Phone # 470 303-9761

Submission Guideline

Submit the first three chapters of your completed manuscript to ldpsubmissions@gmail.com, subject line: Your book's title. The manuscript must be in a .doc file and sent as an attachment. Document should be in Times New Roman, double spaced and in size 12 font. Also, provide your synopsis and full contact information. If sending multiple submissions, they must each be in a separate email.

Have a story but no way to send it electronically? You can still submit to LDP/Ca$h Presents. Send in the first three chapters, written or typed, of your completed manuscript to:

LDP: Submissions Dept
Po Box 944
Stockbridge, Ga 30281

DO NOT send original manuscript. Must be a duplicate.

Provide your synopsis and a cover letter containing your full contact information.

Thanks for considering LDP and Ca$h Presents.

<u>NEW RELEASES</u>

FOR THE LOVE OF BLOOD 2 by JAMEL MITCHELL

RICH $AVAGE 3 by MARTELL "TROUBLESOME"
BOLDEN

CRIME BOSS by PLAYA RAY

LOYALTY IS EVERYTHING by MOLOTTI

HERE TODAY GONE TOMORROW by FLY ROCK

Coming Soon from Lock Down Publications/Ca$h Presents

BLOOD OF A BOSS **VI**

SHADOWS OF THE GAME II

TRAP BASTARD II

By **Askari**

LOYAL TO THE GAME **IV**

By **T.J. & Jelissa**

TRUE SAVAGE **VIII**

MIDNIGHT CARTEL IV

DOPE BOY MAGIC IV

CITY OF KINGZ III

NIGHTMARE ON SILENT AVE II

THE PLUG OF LIL MEXICO II

CLASSIC CITY II

By **Chris Green**

BLAST FOR ME **III**

A SAVAGE DOPEBOY III

CUTTHROAT MAFIA III

DUFFLE BAG CARTEL VII

HEARTLESS GOON VI

By **Ghost**

A HUSTLER'S DECEIT III

KILL ZONE II

BAE BELONGS TO ME III

TIL DEATH II

By **Aryanna**

KING OF THE TRAP III

By **T.J. Edwards**

GORILLAZ IN THE BAY V

3X KRAZY III

STRAIGHT BEAST MODE III

De'Kari

KINGPIN KILLAZ IV

STREET KINGS III

PAID IN BLOOD III

CARTEL KILLAZ IV

DOPE GODS III

Hood Rich

SINS OF A HUSTLA II

ASAD

YAYO V

Bred In The Game 2

S. Allen

THE STREETS WILL TALK II

By Yolanda Moore

SON OF A DOPE FIEND III

HEAVEN GOT A GHETTO II

SKI MASK MONEY II

By Renta

LOYALTY AIN'T PROMISED III

By Keith Williams

I'M NOTHING WITHOUT HIS LOVE II

SINS OF A THUG II

TO THE THUG I LOVED BEFORE II

IN A HUSTLER I TRUST II

By Monet Dragun

QUIET MONEY IV

EXTENDED CLIP III

THUG LIFE IV

By **Trai'Quan**

Here Today Gone Tomorrow

THE STREETS MADE ME IV

By **Larry D. Wright**

IF YOU CROSS ME ONCE II

ANGEL V

By **Anthony Fields**

THE STREETS WILL NEVER CLOSE IV

By K'ajji

HARD AND RUTHLESS III

KILLA KOUNTY IV

By Khufu

MONEY GAME III

By Smoove Dolla

JACK BOYS VS DOPE BOYS IV

A GANGSTA'S QUR'AN V

COKE GIRLZ II

COKE BOYS II

LIFE OF A SAVAGE V

CHI'RAQ GANGSTAS V

By Romell Tukes

MURDA WAS THE CASE III

Elijah R. Freeman

THE STREETS NEVER LET GO III

By Robert Baptiste

AN UNFORESEEN LOVE IV

BABY, I'M WINTERTIME COLD II

By **Meesha**

MONEY MAFIA II

By **Jibril Williams**

QUEEN OF THE ZOO III

By **Black Migo**
VICIOUS LOYALTY III
By Kingpen
A GANGSTA'S PAIN III
By J-Blunt
CONFESSIONS OF A JACKBOY III
By Nicholas Lock
GRIMEY WAYS III
By Ray Vinci
KING KILLA II
By Vincent "Vitto" Holloway
BETRAYAL OF A THUG III
By Fre$h
THE MURDER QUEENS III
By Michael Gallon
THE BIRTH OF A GANGSTER III
By Delmont Player
TREAL LOVE II
By Le'Monica Jackson
FOR THE LOVE OF BLOOD III
By Jamel Mitchell
RAN OFF ON DA PLUG II
By Paper Boi Rari
HOOD CONSIGLIERE III
By Keese
PRETTY GIRLS DO NASTY THINGS II
By Nicole Goosby
PROTÉGÉ OF A LEGEND II
By Corey Robinson
IT'S JUST ME AND YOU II

Here Today Gone Tomorrow

By Ah'Million
BORN IN THE GRAVE II
By Self Made Tay
FOREVER GANGSTA III
By Adrian Dulan
GORILLAZ IN THE TRENCHES II
By SayNoMore
THE COCAINE PRINCESS VI
By King Rio
CRIME BOSS II
Playa Ray
LOYALTY IS EVERYTHING II
Molotti
HERE TODAY GONE TOMORROW II
By Fly Rock

Available Now

RESTRAINING ORDER **I & II**
By **CA$H & Coffee**
LOVE KNOWS NO BOUNDARIES **I II & III**
By **Coffee**
RAISED AS A GOON I, II, III & IV
BRED BY THE SLUMS I, II, III
BLAST FOR ME I & II
ROTTEN TO THE CORE I II III
A BRONX TALE I, II, III

DUFFLE BAG CARTEL I II III IV V VI

HEARTLESS GOON I II III IV V

A SAVAGE DOPEBOY I II

DRUG LORDS I II III

CUTTHROAT MAFIA I II

KING OF THE TRENCHES

By **Ghost**

LAY IT DOWN **I & II**

LAST OF A DYING BREED I II

BLOOD STAINS OF A SHOTTA I & II III

By **Jamaica**

LOYAL TO THE GAME I II III

LIFE OF SIN I, II III

By **TJ & Jelissa**

BLOODY COMMAS I & II

SKI MASK CARTEL I II & III

KING OF NEW YORK I II,III IV V

RISE TO POWER I II III

COKE KINGS I II III IV V

BORN HEARTLESS I II III IV

KING OF THE TRAP I II

By **T.J. Edwards**

IF LOVING HIM IS WRONG…I & II

LOVE ME EVEN WHEN IT HURTS I II III

By **Jelissa**

WHEN THE STREETS CLAP BACK I & II III

THE HEART OF A SAVAGE I II III IV

MONEY MAFIA

LOYAL TO THE SOIL I II III

By **Jibril Williams**

Here Today Gone Tomorrow

A DISTINGUISHED THUG STOLE MY HEART I II & III

LOVE SHOULDN'T HURT I II III IV

RENEGADE BOYS I II III IV

PAID IN KARMA I II III

SAVAGE STORMS I II III

AN UNFORESEEN LOVE I II III

BABY, I'M WINTERTIME COLD

By **Meesha**

A GANGSTER'S CODE I &, II III

A GANGSTER'S SYN I II III

THE SAVAGE LIFE I II III

CHAINED TO THE STREETS I II III

BLOOD ON THE MONEY I II III

A GANGSTA'S PAIN I II

By J-Blunt

PUSH IT TO THE LIMIT

By **Bre' Hayes**

BLOOD OF A BOSS **I, II, III, IV, V**

SHADOWS OF THE GAME

TRAP BASTARD

By **Askari**

THE STREETS BLEED MURDER **I, II & III**

THE HEART OF A GANGSTA I II& III

By **Jerry Jackson**

CUM FOR ME I II III IV V VI VII VIII

An **LDP Erotica Collaboration**

BRIDE OF A HUSTLA **I II & II**

THE FETTI GIRLS **I, II& III**

CORRUPTED BY A GANGSTA I, II III, IV

BLINDED BY HIS LOVE

Fly Rock

THE PRICE YOU PAY FOR LOVE I, II ,III
DOPE GIRL MAGIC I II III
By **Destiny Skai**
WHEN A GOOD GIRL GOES BAD
By **Adrienne**
THE COST OF LOYALTY I II III
By Kweli
A GANGSTER'S REVENGE **I II III & IV**
THE BOSS MAN'S DAUGHTERS I II III IV V
A SAVAGE LOVE **I & II**
BAE BELONGS TO ME I II
A HUSTLER'S DECEIT I, II, III
WHAT BAD BITCHES DO I, II, III
SOUL OF A MONSTER I II III
KILL ZONE
A DOPE BOY'S QUEEN I II III
TIL DEATH
By **Aryanna**
A KINGPIN'S AMBITON
A KINGPIN'S AMBITION **II**
I MURDER FOR THE DOUGH
By **Ambitious**
TRUE SAVAGE I II III IV V VI VII
DOPE BOY MAGIC I, II, III
MIDNIGHT CARTEL I II III
CITY OF KINGZ I II
NIGHTMARE ON SILENT AVE
THE PLUG OF LIL MEXICO II
CLASSIC CITY
By **Chris Green**

Here Today Gone Tomorrow

A DOPEBOY'S PRAYER

By **Eddie "Wolf" Lee**

THE KING CARTEL **I, II & III**

By **Frank Gresham**

THESE NIGGAS AIN'T LOYAL **I, II & III**

By **Nikki Tee**

GANGSTA SHYT **I II &III**

By **CATO**

THE ULTIMATE BETRAYAL

By **Phoenix**

BOSS'N UP **I , II & III**

By **Royal Nicole**

I LOVE YOU TO DEATH

By **Destiny J**

I RIDE FOR MY HITTA

I STILL RIDE FOR MY HITTA

By **Misty Holt**

LOVE & CHASIN' PAPER

By **Qay Crockett**

TO DIE IN VAIN

SINS OF A HUSTLA

By **ASAD**

BROOKLYN HUSTLAZ

By **Boogsy Morina**

BROOKLYN ON LOCK I & II

By **Sonovia**

GANGSTA CITY

By **Teddy Duke**

A DRUG KING AND HIS DIAMOND I & II III

A DOPEMAN'S RICHES

HER MAN, MINE'S TOO I, II

CASH MONEY HO'S

THE WIFEY I USED TO BE I II

PRETTY GIRLS DO NASTY THINGS

By Nicole Goosby

TRAPHOUSE KING **I II & III**

KINGPIN KILLAZ I II III

STREET KINGS I II

PAID IN BLOOD **I II**

CARTEL KILLAZ I II III

DOPE GODS I II

By **Hood Rich**

LIPSTICK KILLAH **I, II, III**

CRIME OF PASSION I II & III

FRIEND OR FOE I II III

By **Mimi**

STEADY MOBBN' **I, II, III**

THE STREETS STAINED MY SOUL I II III

By **Marcellus Allen**

WHO SHOT YA **I, II, III**

SON OF A DOPE FIEND I II

HEAVEN GOT A GHETTO

SKI MASK MONEY

Renta

GORILLAZ IN THE BAY **I II III IV**

TEARS OF A GANGSTA I II

3X KRAZY I II

STRAIGHT BEAST MODE I II

DE'KARI

TRIGGADALE I II III

Here Today Gone Tomorrow

MURDAROBER WAS THE CASE I II

Elijah R. Freeman

GOD BLESS THE TRAPPERS I, II, III

THESE SCANDALOUS STREETS I, II, III

FEAR MY GANGSTA I, II, III IV, V

THESE STREETS DON'T LOVE NOBODY I, II

BURY ME A G I, II, III, IV, V

A GANGSTA'S EMPIRE I, II, III, IV

THE DOPEMAN'S BODYGAURD I II

THE REALEST KILLAZ I II III

THE LAST OF THE OGS I II III

Tranay Adams

THE STREETS ARE CALLING

Duquie Wilson

MARRIED TO A BOSS I II III

By Destiny Skai & Chris Green

KINGZ OF THE GAME I II III IV V VI

CRIME BOSS

Playa Ray

SLAUGHTER GANG I II III

RUTHLESS HEART I II III

By Willie Slaughter

FUK SHYT

By Blakk Diamond

DON'T F#CK WITH MY HEART I II

By Linnea

ADDICTED TO THE DRAMA I II III

IN THE ARM OF HIS BOSS II

By Jamila

YAYO I II III IV

A SHOOTER'S AMBITION I II

BRED IN THE GAME

By S. Allen

TRAP GOD I II III

RICH $AVAGE I II III

MONEY IN THE GRAVE I II III

By Martell Troublesome Bolden

FOREVER GANGSTA I II

GLOCKS ON SATIN SHEETS I II

By Adrian Dulan

TOE TAGZ I II III IV

LEVELS TO THIS SHYT I II

IT'S JUST ME AND YOU

By Ah'Million

KINGPIN DREAMS I II III

RAN OFF ON DA PLUG

By Paper Boi Rari

CONFESSIONS OF A GANGSTA I II III IV

CONFESSIONS OF A JACKBOY I II

By Nicholas Lock

I'M NOTHING WITHOUT HIS LOVE

SINS OF A THUG

TO THE THUG I LOVED BEFORE

A GANGSTA SAVED XMAS

IN A HUSTLER I TRUST

By Monet Dragun

CAUGHT UP IN THE LIFE I II III

THE STREETS NEVER LET GO I II

By Robert Baptiste

NEW TO THE GAME I II III

Here Today Gone Tomorrow

MONEY, MURDER & MEMORIES I II III

By **Malik D. Rice**

LIFE OF A SAVAGE I II III IV

A GANGSTA'S QUR'AN I II III IV

MURDA SEASON I II III

GANGLAND CARTEL I II III

CHI'RAQ GANGSTAS I II III IV

KILLERS ON ELM STREET I II III

JACK BOYZ N DA BRONX I II III

A DOPEBOY'S DREAM I II III

JACK BOYS VS DOPE BOYS I II III

COKE GIRLZ

COKE BOYS

By Romell Tukes

LOYALTY AIN'T PROMISED I II

By Keith Williams

QUIET MONEY I II III

THUG LIFE I II III

EXTENDED CLIP I II

A GANGSTA'S PARADISE

By **Trai'Quan**

THE STREETS MADE ME I II III

By **Larry D. Wright**

THE ULTIMATE SACRIFICE I, II, III, IV, V, VI

KHADIFI

IF YOU CROSS ME ONCE

ANGEL I II III IV

IN THE BLINK OF AN EYE

By **Anthony Fields**

THE LIFE OF A HOOD STAR

By Ca$h & Rashia Wilson

THE STREETS WILL NEVER CLOSE I II III

By K'ajji

CREAM I II III

THE STREETS WILL TALK

By Yolanda Moore

NIGHTMARES OF A HUSTLA I II III

By King Dream

CONCRETE KILLA I II III

VICIOUS LOYALTY I II

By Kingpen

HARD AND RUTHLESS I II

MOB TOWN 251

THE BILLIONAIRE BENTLEYS I II III

By Von Diesel

GHOST MOB

Stilloan Robinson

MOB TIES I II III IV V VI

SOUL OF A HUSTLER, HEART OF A KILLER

GORILLAZ IN THE TRENCHES

By SayNoMore

BODYMORE MURDERLAND I II III

THE BIRTH OF A GANGSTER I II

By Delmont Player

FOR THE LOVE OF A BOSS

By C. D. Blue

MOBBED UP I II III IV

THE BRICK MAN I II III IV

THE COCAINE PRINCESS I II III IV V

By King Rio

Here Today Gone Tomorrow

KILLA KOUNTY I II III IV

By Khufu

MONEY GAME I II

By Smoove Dolla

A GANGSTA'S KARMA I II

By FLAME

KING OF THE TRENCHES I II III

by **GHOST & TRANAY ADAMS**

QUEEN OF THE ZOO I II

By **Black Migo**

GRIMEY WAYS I II

By Ray Vinci

XMAS WITH AN ATL SHOOTER

By Ca$h & Destiny Skai

KING KILLA

By Vincent "Vitto" Holloway

BETRAYAL OF A THUG I II

By Fre$h

THE MURDER QUEENS I II

By Michael Gallon

TREAL LOVE

By Le'Monica Jackson

FOR THE LOVE OF BLOOD I II

By Jamel Mitchell

HOOD CONSIGLIERE I II

By Keese

PROTÉGÉ OF A LEGEND

By Corey Robinson

BORN IN THE GRAVE

By Self Made Tay

MOAN IN MY MOUTH

By XTASY

TORN BETWEEN A GANGSTER AND A GENTLEMAN

By J-BLUNT & Miss Kim

LOYALTY IS EVERYTHING

Molotti

HERE TODAY GONE TOMORROW

By Fly Rock

<u>BOOKS BY LDP'S CEO, CA$H</u>

TRUST IN NO MAN

TRUST IN NO MAN 2

TRUST IN NO MAN 3

BONDED BY BLOOD

SHORTY GOT A THUG

THUGS CRY

THUGS CRY 2

THUGS CRY 3

TRUST NO BITCH

TRUST NO BITCH 2

TRUST NO BITCH 3

TIL MY CASKET DROPS

RESTRAINING ORDER

RESTRAINING ORDER 2

IN LOVE WITH A CONVICT

LIFE OF A HOOD STAR

XMAS WITH AN ATL SHOOTER

Fly Rock

CPSIA information can be obtained
at www.ICGtesting.com
Printed in the USA
LVHW041223140123
737130LV00012B/364

9 781958 111659